Other Books by Sarah Robinson

Dreaming of a Heart Lake Christmas

"Are you sure you don't need help?" he said,
less than an inch away from her now.

When the heck had he gotten so close?

She startled at the sudden proximity, and suddenly her balance was desperately in question. The stool was no longer firm beneath her feet, and she felt herself tipping closer to the ground. "Ah!"

Strong arms immediately steadied her, however, as she came face-to-face with a chest made out of brick.

"Whoa...are you okay?" Evan's arms were anchoring her to his chest, preventing her from hitting the floor, but also from...breathing. Not because he was holding her too tight, but...jeez, what cologne was he wearing? The musky sandalwood scent she was suddenly enveloped in had her picturing things out of the romance novel she'd finished reading last night, and now was not the time or the place.

"Uh, yeah. I'm fine." She pushed away from him, but he kept his large hands on her forearms. "You can let go now."

The
Little Bookstore
on Heart Lake
Lane

The
Little Bookstore
on Heart Lake
Lane

SARAH ROBINSON

FOREVER

NEW YORK   BOSTON

Copyright © 2023 by Grand Central Publishing
Kiss Me in Sweetwater Springs copyright © 2022 by Annie Rains

Cover art and design by Elizabeth Turner Stokes
Cover photos © Shutterstock
Cover copyright © 2023 by Hachette Book Group, Inc.

Forever
Hachette Book Group
1290 Avenue of the Americas, New York, NY 10104
read-forever.com
twitter.com/readforeverpub

First edition: May 2023

Forever is an imprint of Grand Central Publishing. The Forever name and logo are trademarks of Hachette Book Group, Inc.

The publisher is not responsible for websites (or their content) that are not owned by the publisher.

The Hachette Speakers Bureau provides a wide range of authors for speaking events. To find out more, go to hachettespeakersbureau.com or email HachetteSpeakers@hbgusa.com.

Forever books may be purchased in bulk for business, educational, or promotional use. For information, please contact your local bookseller or the Hachette Book Group Special Markets Department at special.markets@hbgusa.com.

ISBNs: 9781538755129 (mass market), 9781538755105 (ebook)

Printed in the United States of America

OPM

10 9 8 7 6 5 4 3 2 1

The
Little Bookstore
on Heart Lake
Lane

Chapter One

The recipe had said five cups of flour, but that was clearly a typo—unless these crisp sugar cookies were really supposed to be soggy dough blobs. Rosie Dean let out a low groan as she dumped her second batch of failed experiments into the garbage bin. She wasn't generally a bad baker, but these instructions from the PTA moms—or as Rosie referred to them, the pain-in-the-ass moms—had been incredibly specific. They had directed her to contribute wafer-thin sugar cookies in the shape of canoes to match the "summer fun" theme for the end-of-the-year picnic at the twins' school tomorrow.

Rosie picked up the recipe again and looked over the ingredients, retracing her steps. She'd gone to college. She was a capable woman who ran a business and raised twins on her own. She could make a dang cookie canoe, right?

Right.

"Mom!" her eight-year-old daughter, Becca, shouted from the living room. "Zander won't give me back my special Lego guy!"

She furrowed her brow, glancing up from the sheet she was holding, and tried to refocus. Her twins were always either engrossed in their iPads and pretending the other didn't exist or arguing with each other over the smallest thing—there was no in-between. "Special? Guy? Huh?"

A loud thud sounded and Rosie tensed for a moment, waiting to hear a scream or a cry or something she'd need to attend to. A high-pitched wail cracked through the air seconds later.

Yup. There it was.

Rosie made it to the living room in less than two seconds, but Becca was already trying to quiet her crying twin brother.

"Zander, shhh. It doesn't hurt that bad! I barely touched you," she insisted, trying to push a small Lego character into his hands. "Here, you can have it! Here!"

"Mom!" Zander continued wailing, giant crocodile tears pouring down his cheeks. He was holding his arm close to his chest, as if protecting it. "Mom, Becca pinched me."

"If you two aren't able to play nicely with these toys, then I'm going to take them away," Rosie threatened, giving Becca a stern look and checking Zander's arm. There was a tiny red mark where he'd been rubbing it, but he otherwise seemed unharmed. "This room needs to be cleaned up anyway. Let's get a move on. We've got to go to the store."

Becca immediately groaned. "Why do *I* have to go? I can stay home alone 'cause I'm the responsible twin. Just take Zander."

Rosie wasn't having this discussion again, especially when she needed to hurry up and get to Hobbes Grocery Store before closing to get more flour for her third—and please God, final—attempt at those cookie canoes. "Shoes on! In the car in five."

They bickered behind her as she headed back into the kitchen to grab the list of ingredients, which took a minute to find underneath the mess of flour, empty wrappers, scattered sugar, and God knows what else completely covering her kitchen countertops. Her kitchen was small and quaint, almost like the inside of a cabin with how much wood was everywhere. Wooden walls, counters, floors—the entire thing. She was proud of it, though. Her father and brother had a construction company, so they had helped with a lot of the supplies and the labor in putting this house together many years ago, but she'd been involved every step of the way. She'd paid for the land all on her own after working three jobs to save up her nest egg up until the day she gave birth.

After the kids had gotten old enough for a babysitter, she'd put her efforts into opening her bookstore on Heart Lake Lane—Fact or Fiction. Of course, her grand opening was a year before e-books truly eclipsed the market and became the newest trend while brick-and-mortar bookstores began to take a back seat. She hadn't been fazed, though. It was a setback, sure, but she knew people still loved the feel and smell of a paperback, and the close-knit community feeling of being in your hometown bookstore.

She finally found the recipe and folded it in half, sliding it into her back pocket. "Everyone better have their shoes on," she called out in her mom voice that she only used when she was absolutely not playing around.

"I can't find my flip-flops," Zander shouted back.

Rosie walked into the main room and surveyed the stack of shoes in a pile by the front door. "Your sneakers are right there. Wear those."

Zander began to whine. "But I want to wear my flip-flops!"

"It would be better to wear the sneakers, Z," Becca said to her twin. "You don't want people seeing your ugly toes."

"Mom!" Zander immediately turned to her, but Rosie was already walking out the door.

"Car. Now." She slid into the driver's seat and pulled down the mirror, checking her reflection. There was a smudge of flour on her cheek and she wiped it off as she watched the twins jostle their way into the car, still somehow arguing the entire time as they battled over putting on their seat belts.

Being a single mother had not been in Rosie's plans. Heck, raising twins had definitely not been in her plans. But here she was. Single with two kids and absolutely no interest in dating anyone anytime soon. She didn't need or want a man in her life—she'd proved that by how she'd taken care of her family over the years. Not that she'd had any other option. But, whatever. She'd risen to the challenge. Scratch that. She'd thrived. She'd raised two great kids—most of the time—and had a business, and she owned her own home.

Queen of the castle. Master of the house.

Yet, sometimes, it still felt like her crown was mere centimeters from sliding off her head. And, admittedly, sometimes late at night she thought it might be nice to have someone touch her... crown.

She'd tried dating once when the kids first started school, but that had been an immediate disaster. Dating apps in small towns were truly a nightmare—she'd matched with the stoner from high school that still lived in his mom's basement, and the owner of the exotic pet store two towns over. When he had promised her a "slithering good time" in a DM, she'd just deleted the entire app from her phone and given up.

There had been one weekend in Chicago a few years ago when she'd gone to visit her best friend, Nola, for a girls-only vacation before her bestie moved back to Heart Lake. That had resulted in way too much alcohol and making out with a stranger in the back of a dark bar—which was probably the last time she'd been with a guy, now that she thought about it. But then again, a battery-operated boyfriend never left socks on the floor or the toilet seat up.

Rosie put the key in the ignition once the kids were both buckled in and started the car. The lights all flashed on and it roared to life for a moment before an alert went off on the dashboard.

Low gas.

Of course. She'd meant to fill up on the way home from work the other day, but it had completely slipped her mind. It seemed she had enough to make it to the Gas and Pass station at the corner of Main and West Street, but she'd be cutting it close to Hobbes Grocery's closing time.

Her phone rang in its holder and she clicked the answer button before reversing the car out of her driveway.

"Hello?" she answered as she let the call go to speakerphone.

"Rosie?" Davon's voice blasted through the car and she reached forward to turn the volume down a bit. "It's completely dead here. No one has come in for hours."

"Are you serious?" Rosie frowned. Davon was her only employee. He worked part time at Fact or Fiction so that she could make sure she had time with the kids. "How many customers have we had today?"

"One since lunch. Two since opening." Davon sighed and she could hear him jiggling keys or something like that in the background. "All we sold was a graphic novel to some kid and her grandfather. The earlier customer placed a pre-order for that new Colleen Hoover book coming out next month. This is bad."

"Yeah. Shoot. Yeah, it is really bad." Her heart sunk as

she thought about the rent due at the end of the month to the storefront's landlord. They'd barely been making enough sales to cover expenses, and the café addition that she'd planned to revitalize business had been put on indefinite hold. Turns out, she needed a costly permit for that, and construction prices had gone through the roof.

So, for now, Rosie's dreams of expansion needed to remain just that... another sweet dream that hadn't managed to come to fruition.

"Anyway, so I was wondering," Davon continued. "I've got a date tonight with this really cute guy from Sweet Market. I'd love to close up an hour earlier so I can go get ready. I've got to wax—you don't even want to know the situation happening under these clothes right now. I'm practically a wolverine."

Her laugh felt hollow in her chest. While she was happy for his social plans, she couldn't help but worry that next month she'd have to cut his hours in half—or entirely— unless more sales started to come in. "Okay. Yeah, that's fine. Close up a bit early."

"You are the best boss *ever!*" Davon let out a loud whooping noise and then hung up the phone.

Rosie concentrated on the road as she pulled up to the Gas and Pass station, barely making it to the pump. "Kids, stay in the car. I'll be right here."

"Can I get a chocolate bar?" Zander asked, pointing at the convenience store attached to the gas station pumps.

"No," she replied firmly. If she gave in and bought treats at the gas station once, they would hound her forevermore.

"Look." Zander pointed. "I think Grandpa already got us one!"

She turned to see her father walking out of the store with

his cane in one hand and a giant Hershey bar in the other. *Ugh, this town is too small.* She gave him a lackluster wave as she put the pump in her gas tank and grabbed her card from her wallet.

"Hey, kiddo!" Her dad ambled over to their car. The twins had already rolled down the back windows and he was handing them both pieces of his chocolate bar. "How are you all doing?"

"Hey, Dad. We're great. But they are going to bed soon—that's too much sugar." She made no moves to stop him though as she slid her card into the pump. The light flashed and the machine let out a low beeping noise.

Declined.

Rosie groaned. "Shit."

"Mom said a bad word!" Zander caught her mistake immediately. That kid had selective hearing. Ask him to clean his room and he had no idea what you were saying, but mumble one little curse word and he had supersonic hearing.

"Here." Her dad waved her aside and put his card into the machine instead. "Let me get it."

"Stop, you don't have to do that," she insisted. "I'm fine. It's just a mix-up at the bank, I'm sure."

"Eh, let an old man feel like he can still contribute once in a while," he replied, shrugging it off.

The machine began pumping gas into her car and Rosie leaned against the side door. "Well, thanks. I appreciate it."

"How are things going at home?" he asked, sneaking another piece of chocolate to Zander.

"Mom burned all the cookies for the school picnic," her son revealed with no loyalty whatsoever. "We have to go buy more flour."

Her dad lifted one brow as he shifted his gaze from his

grandkids to his daughter. "You know, Marvel went crazy on baking yesterday and we have at least three dozen extra cookies at home. Why don't you come grab those?"

"I can't take your food, too," she insisted. "You know me, I'm allergic to getting help."

But he shook his head. "We can't eat all those cookies. Scratch that, we shouldn't eat all those cookies. We had a few cocktails yesterday and it seemed like a good idea at the time." Thomas grinned, and he looked youthful in that moment. Marvel brought that out in him, and she was so glad that the woman had come into her father's life. After Rosie's mother had died when she was a teenager, her dad hadn't been interested in moving on—ever. He still wore his wedding ring to this day.

But last year he'd begun spending more time with the owner of the local pottery studio, Dirty Birds Clay, and the two had been inseparable since. She'd brought a spark back to him that Rosie loved seeing again. "Come take them, because Lord knows my doctor would kill me if I ate that much sugar. He keeps trying to tell me I'm prediabetic, but I told him to come talk to me when I'm past the *pre* stage."

"Dad, you cannot blow off your doctor's advice," Rosie began, but then immediately stopped. Another argument she wasn't going to repeat today. As much as it scared her, she was trying to remind herself that her father was his own person and she couldn't make him do what she wanted. But, oh, how she had tried. "Okay, we'll take the cookies." God, she hated how relieved she felt saying the words, like she was a failure. They were just PTA cookies for god's sake, but the fact of the matter was, Rosie would bend over backward for anyone she cared about. She just didn't want anyone bending for her. It was just how she was wired.

"I'll just follow you back to the house."

"Great!" Her dad clapped his hands. "And while you're at it, call your brother and Nola. See if they'll come join us. We can all do dinner."

"We had dinner earlier—"

"Dessert then," he insisted. "You know, I think we got a new tub of Neapolitan ice cream that hasn't been opened. Becca loves the strawberry."

"Mom, please, can we go?" Becca called out from the back seat. "Zander got so much chocolate! I should get some ice cream."

She sighed. "Okay, we can go, but only for one hour. And baths and pajamas immediately when we get home—without fighting!"

"We promise!" Zander and Becca sang in unison.

"I'll see you back at the house," she said to her dad as he climbed into his old station wagon.

Once the gas pump finished, she replaced it back in the holder and closed up the tank. It was only a five-minute drive back to her father's house, and the kids barely waited for her to park before they barreled out of the car and ran across their grandfather's yard.

"Looky here, Thomas!" Marvel was standing on the front porch and gave her a big wave. She was wearing a hot-pink kaftan with some sort of design on it that Rosie couldn't decipher from the driveway. "You brought some treats home with you!"

Thomas chuckled in a low belly laugh as he climbed out of the station wagon slowly. It took him a few attempts to swing his weight forward to standing, but with the help of his cane and one hand on the doorframe, he pulled himself up. "They are on a cookie mission."

"Oh, well thank goodness we have some of those," she teased, ushering the kids inside. "And ice cream, too!"

Rosie approached her father, walking alongside him. She knew better than to offer him help—the man was more stubborn than anyone she'd ever met. Well, save for maybe her brother, Tanner. Still, she worried about him as he got older, and to have him helping her with things like gas at her age just felt like a new low in her life.

"How's the store going?" Thomas asked. He paused at the bottom of the steps up to the porch and switched his cane to his other hand while he gripped the railing. "Business doing good?"

"Uh," Rosie faltered, not sure how to answer that without either lying or making him take pity on her and her flailing business. Neither option sounded enjoyable at the moment. "It's . . . going."

He lifted one brow and shot her a look. "When are you going to expand with the café? Bring people in with food and they'll buy books."

"Soon." She suppressed an exhausted sigh. "The permit is basically already filed. Just waiting on admin stuff." That wasn't entirely true, but it wasn't really a lie either. "Maybe I'll start something before we finish the renovations—like a free snack on weekends or something, to bring people in and get them used to the idea."

"What about Marvel's cookies?" Her dad reached the top step and Rosie waited behind him as he switched his cane from one hand to the other again. "You know she loves to bake, and she uses all of Gigi's old recipes. No doubt people would come in to snag a few of those."

Gigi was Nola's grandmother; she'd passed a few years ago but still remained a huge presence in Heart Lake. Her cookies and tea were the stuff of legends, and, somehow, she'd become bosom buddies with Marvel in the later years of her life, despite how different their personalities were. Gigi was everything high society, buttoned up, and Marvel didn't believe in wearing underthings.

"Books and cookies…" Rosie mulled over the idea as they walked into the foyer. There was something to that. "I mean…it's not a terrible idea. People would come for her cookies."

Actually, it was a pretty damn good idea, and she decided to text Davon about it as soon as she got home. She felt an excitement stirring in her stomach, butterflies flickering around as she imagined the store full of people browsing the bookshelves while munching on a complimentary cookie. She wouldn't need the permit in place for that if the cookies were free. It could be like a test run. It was yet another item to add to her never-ending to-do list, but she'd just have to dig in and find the strength. And who needed sleep anyway?

Chapter Two

It's hard to make a body part insurance company sound sexy, but that's exactly what Evan Nowak was tasked with as he sat at the makeshift desk in his parents' guest cottage loft that he'd temporarily turned into an office for the summer. This was certainly one of his more unusual jobs, but the company that he contracted to create marketing resources for seemed to attract a unique clientele. Before this project, he'd never even known that you could get a specific body part insured, and the more research he'd done into it, the more he felt like he didn't understand this world one bit.

Evan pushed his straight hair out of his eyes, sliding his hands back across his head as he let out a slow breath. Something was off in his color scheme, and he couldn't seem to find the answer. He was more of a copy guy, but this gig involved some graphic design, and it was slow going. He scratched at the scruff on his jaw, still trying to get used to letting his beard grow out a bit this summer.

Suddenly, something grabbed his arm and pulled him backward away from the computer. "Dad!"

"What?" Evan jolted slightly in surprise and turned to see his nine-year-old daughter, Tess, standing behind him holding up a book. Even seated in the computer chair, he was still significantly taller than she was while standing. He owed a quietness to him that seemed deeper than just his intro-verted personality. Hell, the entire family was introverted, and they weren't big talkers. They communicated about the important things like scheduling and chores, but if he wanted to vent about work or talk about heartbreak, he had learned long ago to push those feelings down and just try to let it go. He was pretty sure his father had been doing the same his whole life. "Go on now. I'll hold the book for you while you go catch us dinner."

"Thanks, Grandpa!" Tess handed him her novel and prac-tically skipped down the hallway back to Evan. "Dad, I got a new lure I want to try."

"I remember," he replied, as he followed her out the back door to the shed. "I'm the one who got it for you."

"Oh, yeah!" She laughed as she pulled open the wooden shed doors and immediately got to work grabbing their fish-ing poles and a bucket of worms that were stored there.

He loaded his arms up, helping her carry everything while they walked to the edge of the lake at the very end of the property. His parents had purchased this lot almost thirty years ago and the value had since doubled, due to the waterfront view. Heart Lake was a lively bed of water for wildlife because they didn't allow motorized boats on it. Canoes and rowboats were fine, because they didn't disturb the fish much, but any sporting equipment had been banned. Thanks to that, the lake was teeming with fish of dozens of species, and it wasn't unusual for them to spend their eve-nings catching dinner out here. Western Michigan ended its days slowly, the sun gradually fading away over the horizon, which allowed for plenty of time outside.

The long wooden dock jutted out far enough into the to give them a deep spot to fish, and there were two

his height to his father, Antoni Nowak, who was standing behind her with a big grin on his face. "What's going on?"

"Do you need to get your hearing checked"? she joked as she shook her head. A necklace of various mismatch-ing beads made a clacking noise around her neck as she moved, and he wondered when she'd crafted that because he couldn't remember her wearing it before. "I've been calling your name for like eighty minutes."

He smiled sheepishly, knowing she was exaggerating but also feeling a pang of guilt at having not paid attention to her sooner. Being a single father had not been something he'd expected out of life, but when his wife passed away five years ago, he was suddenly thrust into the spotlight. "Sorry, kiddo. What did you want to tell me?"

She held up a graphic novel with a pinkish-orange cover and two animated characters standing close together. "Look what Grandpa got for me! There is a cool bookstore on Main Street that has literally everything—we have to go back. This one is *The Prince and the Dressmaker*—my friends at camp said this is one of their favorites!"

Evan frowned as he took the graphic novel from her and looked it over. He scanned the description on the back but wasn't blown away. Honestly, it looked like fluff, and he wanted to make sure that he was pushing Tess to reach her full potential. "What about the *real* books I got you? Are those still in your backpack?"

She scuffed the tip of her sneaker against the carpet as she looked down. "Yeah. I'm going to read them, but I want to read this, too."

He'd spent a lot of time preparing her summer curricu-lum, and he'd found an entire list of "100 Books Your Child Needs to Be Reading" on a teacher's website that had all the classics. He'd bought her *Charlotte's Web*, *Little Women*, and *Anne of Green Gables* to get started. Just because she was out of school for the summer didn't mean he was going to let her fall behind her peers. He had a responsibility to help her excel now that he was the only parent here to do so, and he did his best to take it seriously, even though sometimes it all felt so…empty. "Tess, you've got to read those first. Then maybe you can read the fluffy stuff like this."

Antoni cleared his throat. "She likes it. All her friends are reading it."

He shot his dad a long look. *Since when does that have anything to do with anything?*

Evan bit the inside of his cheek to hold back the retort. But seriously, it stung in a strange part of him, hearing his dad singing such a different tune now. When Evan was a kid and falling behind in grade-level reading, his father had gone so far as to ban reading material with pictures altogether. All his beloved Marvel and Garfield comics were put out with the trash.

But had it helped him?

Probably.

He might not read for fun these days, but he'd passed his English classes. And so would Tess.

"Yeah, probably because it's mostly pictures," Evan handed the graphic novel back to Tess. "I want to see at least five chapters of one of the real books finished by Friday."

"Dad, this *is* a real book," Tess protested, and the frown on her face seemed to get deeper by the second. "It's got pictures, but there's a lot of words and plot, too."

"Tess." Evan shot his daughter a serious look, his brows raised. "Five chapters by Friday."

She seemed to wilt in front of him, and his father put a hand on her shoulder.

"Come on, Tessy," he said to his granddaughter. "… pick out one of the other books and then we can get … on this one after."

She nodded and followed him out of the room while … felt like someone had just punched him square in the st… ach. The way her smile sank into a frown was almost id… tical to his late wife Layla's mannerisms sometimes. T… similarities between them had always been intense, but wit… Layla now gone, it was hard to see pieces of her on Tess's… face.

Even harder when it showed up in moments where he knew he'd let her down.

"Hey, Tess?" Evan called out, walking quickly to the doorway to catch her before she got too far away. She was at the end of the hallway and turned back to look at him. "What about some fishing this afternoon? Weather is good."

She shrugged, holding the book tighter to her chest. "Sure. Can we eat what we catch for dinner?"

Evan felt a surge of pride at what felt like her neverending talents. "Of course. Grandma loves to cook up som… fish."

"I'll tell Grandma," his dad said, seemingly grateful … things had smoothed over.

Evan tried not to notice that his father was movin… slower these days, his hair pure white at this point, b… thick as ever. He'd mellowed from the man who'… an outsize role in his childhood. The stern guy w… raised by Polish immigrants and had the drive t… Who believed that Evan needed to buckle dow… something of himself to honor the sacrifices o… come before.

Now his dad hunched slightly as he walke…

Adirondack chairs set up just for that purpose. Tess sat on the front edge of hers, rather than leaning back, because she was small for her age and needed the leverage to cast her line. Evan took a slightly more relaxed approach as he leaned back in his chair fully after casting his line in the water. They were quiet for a moment as they waited for fish to find them, but then Evan cleared his throat.

"How's French class going?" he asked, trying to find something to make conversation about. There wasn't a shred of doubt that he loved his daughter more than life itself, but learning how to relate and communicate with a nine-year-old girl all by himself was not an easy task. "Did you learn anything new today?"

"French class?" Tess frowned, but didn't look over at him. "Uh . . . yeah. French class. Good. *C'était bon.*"

The way she kept repeating herself struck Evan as odd. "Tess, you did go to French class this morning, right?"

"Dad," her voice immediately dipped into a long whine. "It's summer. I don't want to be in school."

"Tess, we've talked about this." Evan sat up and placed his fishing line in a holder so he could give her his full attention. "Your mother was French and she spoke the language beautifully. Don't you want to learn her language?"

"And keep Mom's memory alive," Tess recited, as if she'd already heard this speech a dozen times. And to be fair, she had. "Dad, I'm not going to forget Mom just because I don't want to take a class over the summer."

"Honey, I know that," he quickly assured her. "But we want to go into next year with as much ammo as possible to do well. Fourth grade is no joke, and once you hit middle school, languages will be a requirement. I just don't want you falling behind."

She glanced over at him, and her green eyes were heavy in reminders of Layla. They looked so much alike that it scared him sometimes—the thought of losing Layla twice was more than he could ever handle. And losing Tess once? He wouldn't survive.

But life was short, and he'd come to know that a lot more than he wanted to. Evan looked over his shoulder up toward the house and he could see his parents out on the deck. If he had to guess, his father was working on a crossword puzzle, but his mother was the one writing for him. A Parkinson's diagnosis several years back had left his dad with a much less steady hand than before, and Everly did everything she could to help accommodate him. He loved seeing how much they still cared for each other after almost fifty years of marriage, and he couldn't help but be envious that that wouldn't be him and Layla one day.

It had been awhile since he'd been back to Heart Lake— too long, he realized. He hadn't realized his father's condition had deteriorated as much as it had, since his mother often sugarcoated things in their weekly phone calls. Evan had moved down to Chicago after school and that was where he'd spent the last fifteen years or so. They came back to Heart Lake for holidays and such, but this was Tess's first summer staying here, while he was working remotely. He'd wanted to be around and help, make sure his parents were doing okay, and maybe try to convince them by the end of the summer to bring in home health care.

"I'm going to be okay," Tess assured him, pulling his attention back to their conversation. "You don't need to worry about me. Hey, did you ever take Mom fishing down here?"

A smile spread across his face as he thought back to the

summer before they got married when she had come to Heart Lake to meet his parents.

"I did," he confirmed, but his throat seemed to close up as his mind flooded with every memory and emotion from back then. He cleared it gently, trying to figure out which story to tell—the first time they'd gone fishing and Layla had cried because she felt sad for the fish, or the time he had proposed to her right on this very dock, or when she'd lost that same ring in the water when they were swimming.

Tess looked at him, waiting.

He wanted to tell her the story—all the stories—but his throat refused to open. His face felt warm and there was pressure below his eyes as he felt his tear ducts filling. He swallowed hard and tried to clear his throat again. He watched as her face grew stony with his silence.

"Fine. Don't tell me." Tess put her fishing line down. "I'm going to swim out to the floating dock."

Within seconds, she'd shed her clothes and uncovered the bright yellow one-piece bathing suit she'd been wearing underneath. She stepped to the edge of the dock farther away from where they were fishing and dove in as if she'd done it a hundred times.

Evan didn't get a chance to respond before he was watching her arms and legs cutting through the water as she swam in the direction of the large dock anchored in the middle of their inlet. He wanted to dive in after her and go sunbathing or look for snapping turtles, but every part of his body felt like it had locked up in that goddamn chair.

The fact was, he had no idea how to connect with his daughter, but that was all he wanted to do, more than anything in the world. He wanted to tell her how much he loved her and show her how he was trying to give her everything he could...because he couldn't give her the one thing she wanted—her mom back. Layla had been a presence to behold—stylish, full of life, and completely boisterous. She'd have known how to do all the motherly things, like braid Tess's long, mousy-brown hair, or teach her how to shut down the stupid boys in her grade who had already started teasing her for her beginning steps into puberty. Without her here to guide him, Evan felt paralyzed by the pressures of being a single parent and all the ways he knew he'd never live up to what his late wife could have given Tess.

He watched her pull herself up onto the floating dock and dance around in the sun before diving off the side again. The first year after losing Layla had been so dark and heavy that he wasn't sure either of them would be able to come up for air. But he'd put Tess in counseling at the strong recommendation of the school's guidance counselor and she'd improved little by little over the last few years.

There was light back in her eyes, and he wished he knew how to find that for himself. Because right now, everything felt so goddamn dark.

Chapter Three

"Pop the cookies in the trunk, please," Rosie instructed her son as she handed him the plastic bin of leftover cookies from the end-of-school picnic.

It had been an exhausting day, but they'd managed to make a lot of children happy and get some great pictures of the twins with their friends before they'd be heading to fourth grade in the fall. She couldn't believe that her kids were growing up so fast, as it had seemed like just yesterday when she'd been taking pictures of them in their first-day-of-school outfits on her front porch. Both kids had shot up several inches over the last school year, and she didn't want to think about how much they'd continue to grow over the summer.

"Can I eat one?" Zander asked as he tucked the bin under his arm and ran off in the direction of their car.

"You already ate four!" she reminded him. She pushed the folded-up tablecloth into her tote bag and swung it over her shoulder as she followed him to the car.

Becca was beside her carrying an empty watercooler that had been full of lemonade at one point. "Mooooooooom, can we go to Fact or Fiction and see Davon?"

Rosie smiled, loving how her kids had grown to adore her employee over the years. She suspected Becca might be developing a bit of a crush on the handsome clerk, but she'd find out soon enough that she was barking up the wrong tree on that one. "Sure. We got new shipments in this morning that I have to inventory anyway."

They loaded up the car and climbed inside, everyone fastening their seat belts. She turned on the radio to her favorite oldies station, and "Cats in the Cradle" came on.

Zander began singing along, already familiar with her song choices, but then he paused and looked at her in the rearview mirror. "Hey Mom? This song is about a dad, right?"

"Sorta, yeah," Rosie said absently.

"Why don't we ever see our daddy?"

Oh, shit. "Why do you ask, baby?" Rosie felt like a lightning strike just went through her body as her muscles locked up and her airway seemed to tighten.

"Zander!" Becca shouted at him and punched him in the arm. "Shut up. Can't you use your brain? Mom doesn't like talking about him."

"Ow!" Zander cried out. "Uh-uh. She didn't say that!"

"He's busy doing work and stuff," Becca continued, her eyes dull as she stared out the window at the passing landscape. "He doesn't care about us."

"Becca!" It was Rosie's turn to raise her voice now. She couldn't believe what she was hearing from her daughter, because she'd certainly never said anything like that about Billy. Sure, the man wasn't ever going to win an award for father of the year, but being immature and selfish wasn't criminal. He prioritized his music career and his chase for fame over being a father, but Rosie hadn't fought him hard on that over the years. "Don't say things like that about your father. Zander, that isn't true at all."

"Oh, come on," Becca replied, as if she didn't believe a word.

Rosie shook her head as she turned the car onto Main Street and could see the bookstore up ahead. She was not at all prepared for this conversation, but it wasn't like they never asked about their father. She brought him up on occasion when it seemed to fit the situation, but that wasn't too often. He had an open invitation to come see his children, but he never took Rosie up on that. He sent inconsistent and infrequent child support checks, but when it came to actually being involved physically, Billy had always been both feet out the door.

"Your father is a good guy, honey," Rosie tried to assure her, even though the words felt hollow in her mouth. "He just has a lot on his plate with his career. He wasn't ready to be a father."

"Why did he become a father then?" Zander asked. "Didn't he know he wasn't ready back then?"

Rosie squirmed in her seat, not fully ready to have the conversation with Zander about how children come into existence. Becca had already learned some bits and pieces of it from friends at school, and Rosie had filled her in about the rest. Zander, however, might be the same age as Becca but needed a little more time to mature before she tried to tackle that subject with him. "Uh, yes, honey. But it's more complicated than that."

Becca snickered. "Yeah, Zander. It's not like he knew beforehand."

"He didn't?" She could see Zander's brow furrowed in her rearview mirror and she knew she needed to change the topic fast before she'd be having a full-blown sex talk here and now.

"Hey, you know, Davon told me that we have copies of the latest Emily Windsnap novel in the store now." Rosie lifted one brow as she looked back at them in the rearview mirror, a hopeful smile on her face that this might be the distraction she needed to get off the topic of their father. "I would be willing to let you both get your own copy so you don't have to share."

"*The Tides of Edwandor*?" Zander practically leaned into the front seat with excitement, his seat belt stretching farther than it was supposed to. "It's out?"

Becca snickered in the back seat, even though Rosie knew she was just as big a fan of the adventuresome mermaid graphic novel series as her brother. "Wow, Zander. You're still into mermaids? We're almost nine years old now, you know."

"Hey, I'm thirty-four and I still love mermaids," Rosie stood up for her son, giving him a conspiratorial wink. "Mermaids are super cool."

"Okay, Mom." Becca rolled her eyes with all the sass of a preteen, and Rosie wasn't sure she was ready for that milestone yet.

They pulled into the small side lot where up to four cars could park for the bookstore—one taken up by Davon's Mini coupe and now her station wagon in the second. No signs of any customers in the parking lot, and even if there had been, they'd only be able to house two more cars comfortably. Rosie made a mental note to herself to talk to her brother about that for the expansion plans. If she was going to be bringing in more traffic, they'd need somewhere to park.

She waved through the storefront window to Davon who was seated at the counter inside Fact or Fiction as she pushed the kids toward the front door. The small bell above the hinge rang as the twins tumbled inside and raced for the new releases table display.

"One each!" Rosie reminded them, bracing herself to clean up scattered books as they attacked the table to try and grab the first copy of the new graphic novel. "Hey, don't knock those over!"

"Sorry, Mom!" Becca bent down and picked up a discarded book and replaced it on the table before following her brother over to the padded bench in the front window nook. They both settled in on opposite sides, their knees to their chests and their noses already in the first page of their new book.

"I don't know how you do it," Davon said as he leaned his elbows on the glass countertop and shook his head. "Your life is like a walking tornado."

Rosie laughed and picked up the stack of flyers next to him. "That's life with kids."

"No, thank you," Davon joked, though Rosie knew he adored her children almost as much as she did.

"I'm going to tornado into some paperwork in the office," she said. "Can you keep an eye on the twins?"

Davon nodded and Rosie headed through the aisles of filled bookshelves to a small door that led to a windowless back office. There was one wooden desk that had actually been a donation from the local high school—and by donation, she meant she found it by their garbage bins. Everything else in the office was basically ad hoc from various places—a lamp from her father's house, a swivel chair from Nola's old Chicago office, and a rug from Marvel that was far too orange for her liking and more of an obligation.

Rosie sat at the desk and shook the computer mouse, rousing the old machine to life. The operating system was from the Stone Age, but she didn't need it for much outside of writing, email, and accounting for taxes. She double clicked the file marked *Herald* on her desktop and pulled open her latest draft of this week's Miss Mommy column she was working on for the *Heart Lake Herald*. No one knew that she was the anonymous voice behind this popular parenting column in the local paper and Webzine, aside from Nola and Amanda—her two closest friends who it was literally impossible to keep a secret from.

She opened the letter she'd be responding to this week and reread the words with painful precision. Painful, because the topic made Rosie feel like an absolute hypocrite.

Dear Miss Mommy,

How do I know when to be honest with my children and when to shelter them from the truth? My husband and I are going through a separation, probably a divorce, and I want my children to be as unharmed by this process as possible…but, how? I feel like I need to tell them the truth about some of the things their father has done—they deserve to know—but also, I want them to still see him as their loving daddy and not hurt that relationship. I don't know what to do, but I feel like I'm always going to be the bad guy and that's hard. Signed,

Sad Mommy

When she first agreed to write behind-the-scenes on this column, the stories and letters had been more lighthearted, and it had been like a fun, secret side job. The popularity of the column led to increased traffic on the site, and the ad dollars were being raked in, which meant they were offering her more money to keep going. Literally. She'd tried to quit three times but the paper kept proposing new payouts per column that just felt impossible to turn down when she had so much at stake financially. But it felt fraudulent in many ways—or maybe that was just imposter syndrome rearing its ugly head. Miss Mommy had taken on a life of its own and become the aspirational mother Rosie wished she could be...and certainly failed to live up to daily.

Rosie took a restorative breath and tried to center herself, reflecting on her earlier conversation in the car with the twins as she began typing out a response. A half hour passed before Rosie felt like she had a satisfactory first paragraph that attended to the reader's emotional request but had not yet dived into the practical advice portion.

"Mom!" The loud call from her daughter jolted her away from her words as the office door swung open and Becca appeared. "Guess what, Mom?"

She quickly saved her document and minimized it. "What's going on, Becs?"

"I made a new friend," her daughter announced, tossing her novel onto Rosie's desk. "And she loves Emily Windsnap, too! She owns the entire collection now—except *The Tides of Time*. But she said her grandpa is going to buy it for her next week at Books and Cookies."

Rosie's attention was piqued. "They are coming to Books and Cookies?"

Becca nodded excitedly. "Yeah, she said that a lot of people are coming and she hopes that we can save a book for her! Can we, Mom? She can have mine if we can't."

She smiled at her daughter's kindness and loved that she was excited about a new friend. Becca wasn't the most sociable kid in her grade, which often caused issues since Zander made friends everywhere he went. It was just easy for him, and Rosie didn't like to admit it but his father had that same charisma. That wasn't the case with more-shy Becca, who tended to take more time to open up to new people. "We can definitely save her a copy, Becs. I'm sure there won't be that many people, so, it should be fine. I don't know how she even knew about the event already."

Her daughter shook her head and rolled her eyes. "Mom, seriously? Have you even looked at the shop's Instagram?"

"Our Instagram?" Rosie repeated, shaking her head. "What? No...we just had the idea. We are still planning it. How can there already be a graphic? And speaking of which, how can you even see Instagram?"

"Davon did it, and then he showed me." Becca grabbed her cell phone off the desk and logged in to the shop's Instagram as if she'd done it a thousand times before. She pulled up the feed for the bookstore and pointed at the comments under the most recent picture, which was a graphic about the coming Books and Cookies event. "Look, there are fifty likes. No one usually responds to anything. It's not big numbers, but it's a start!"

"When did you get to be the social media expert?" Rosie's bemusement with her daughter hanging out on the phone without her knowledge, and the fact Davon was already plotting before she'd finished a to-do list, was cancelled out by the anticipatory stirring in her belly. Maybe this event could be a turning point.

"Wanna come meet my new friend? She's here with her dad!" Becca pulled at Rosie's arm, dislodging her from her phone as she was trying to scan through the comments. "Come on! Mom!"

"Okay, okay!" Rosie laughed and put her phone down as she followed her daughter out of the office. "I'd love to meet them. Where's your brother?"

"He's still reading in the window," Becca told her. "This is *my* friend. Not Zander's."

"Oh, okay," Rosie said in a joking manner, though she really enjoyed the confidence she was seeing right now. "What's *your* friend's name?"

"Tess. Hey, Tess!" Becca waved to a young girl with mousy-brown hair that hung straight down over her shoulders and looked like maybe it could use a few swipes with a brush. The girl turned and grinned—huge and toothy with a rosiness to her cheeks that looked like she'd just come inside after playing hard. "This is my mom."

Rosie offered a small wave to the girl. "Hi, Tess. I'm Ms. Dean, Becca's mom."

Tess stuck out her hand for a proper handshake and Rosie smiled as she obliged. "Good afternoon, Ms. Dean. I'm Tess Nowak, and this is my dad!"

Rosie's eyes rose to the man standing partially behind Tess as he examined the books on their young adult table display. She was just about to say hello when he cut her off.

"Hello. You're the owner?" The man lifted up a copy of a popular graphic novel that was one of their biggest sellers. "I was just trying to convince my daughter she doesn't need a book with pictures. She needs a book with words. What do you think?"

Ugh. She didn't care that his jawline was covered with the perfect amount of scruff—he was a book snob.

Book snobs were jerks. Period.

Her back straightened as she steeled herself. "Well, actually, graphic novels have been proven to be a fantastic intermediary between picture books and chapter books that help inspire a lifelong love of reading in young adults."

He surveyed her for a moment before responding. "It's still a lot of pictures instead of reading."

"You know, there's an incredible selection around back that might be more to your liking." Rosie demonstrated with her hands that he should walk around the building. "We call it a dumpster, and it's perfect for opinions like 'graphic novels aren't real books.'"

"Mom!" Becca groaned and rubbed her hands over her face.

Davon giggled from the counter and let out a low whisper. "Dayyyym."

Before the previously-sexy-until-she'd-discovered-his-personality father could respond, a clicking noise came from the children's section of the store for a moment before it suddenly descended into darkness. Rosie sighed as she tried to think of whether they had any replacement light bulbs in the back.

"Looks like you've got a light out," the father said, and the small smile on his lips only infuriated her. "I'm Evan, by the way."

"Thank you for your keen observation. I would never have solved that mystery." She laid the sarcasm on thick as she walked over to the dead light bulb and commented under her breath about what a douchebag jerk-face dickhead he was. He might have heard, but she didn't care. Thankfully, Becca and her new friend had already scurried away to avoid the awkwardness of their exchange, so if her language got even more colorful, she wasn't about to hide it.

"I'm pretty tall. I can help you change it," Grumpy Blue Eyes offered.

She cut her eyes at him. Okay, he was tall. Like…very tall and…anyways, that wasn't the point. He was a book snob. "I can manage just fine. This is my store, after all."

He put both hands up in a defensive position. "Understood. Sorry I offered."

Rosie made quick work of grabbing one of the small wooden kiddie stools in the children's section and repositioning it beneath the blown light. She balanced her way to the top step and still found she had to push up onto tiptoe in order to unscrew the broken bulb. Her fingers barely made it around as she worked it out of the socket before Evan's low baritone was right beside her.

"Are you sure you don't need help?" he said, less than an inch away from her now. *When the heck had he gotten so close?*

She startled at the sudden proximity, and suddenly her balance was desperately in question. The stool was no longer firm beneath her feet, and she felt herself tipping closer to the ground. "Ah!"

Strong arms immediately steadied her, however, as she came face-to-face with a chest made out of brick.

"Whoa…are you okay?" Evan's arms were anchoring her to his chest, preventing her from hitting the floor, but also from…breathing. Not because he was holding her too tight, but…jeez, what cologne was he wearing? The musky sandalwood scent she was suddenly enveloped in had her picturing things out of the romance novel she'd finished reading last night, and now was not the time or the place.

"Uh, yeah. I'm fine." She pushed away from him, but he kept his large hands on her forearms. "You can let go."

"Oh." He looked down at his grip, then slowly let go. "Sorry, I thought you were about to fall."

Without a doubt, she'd almost completely bitten it, but she

wasn't about to tell him that. "I'm fine," she assured him, this time holding up the dead light bulb that she'd successfully unscrewed. "Again, I don't need your help."

Unless there was a reality in which he could shut up and just take her in the back and bend her over her desk...

Rosie cleared her throat, pushing the unwelcome thought away. "Really, I'm fine."

He eyed her with one brow lifted, as if he didn't believe her entirely. "Rosie...right?"

She frowned. "Yeah, do I know you?"

"I just, I saw your name on the wall. You own this place?" He seemed to not be able to make eye contact with her now, and the entire exchange was annoying her.

"I do," she confirmed. "Davon can help you and your daughter ring up your purchase at the counter. It was lovely to meet you."

She laid the last part on a bit thicker than she probably should have, and there was no doubt he'd picked up on the inauthenticity of her comment. But she didn't give a shit. Without even a wave or goodbye, Rosie waltzed back to the office and tried to keep Evan and his perfect blue eyes out of her mind.

Like that was even possible.

Chapter Four

Honestly, what were the freaking chances? Evan ushered his daughter to the exit of Fact and Fiction. Right now, all he wanted to do was to get out of this store and away from Rosie Dean. He'd known who she was the moment he'd set eyes on her, even though there wasn't a doubt that his former high school crush didn't recognize him in the slightest.

Hell, in his high school days, Evan had been skinnier than a doorpost and spent most of his time in the outfield playing catch, or in the computer lab programming new video games he was trying to invent. He'd studied and well...that was about it. He hadn't been even remotely in Rosie's league, and the only time they'd spent together was when they'd both been volunteering in the school library. Okay, she'd been the one volunteering, because he'd actually been there as part of his detention for hacking the school's firewall after his friend paid him a pretty penny to change his grades. Now, though, Evan ran on the straight and narrow, and he liked to think he'd filled out a bit since high school. Not only had he grown to almost six feet five, but his frame was wide and strong. He had his morning workouts to thank for the muscular look. He needed that time to release stress and prepare for the day. The rest was just a bonus.

Dark brown hair, bold red lips, and a curvy frame that was only accentuated by her attitude as she jutted out a hip when she was talking back to him was Evan's type down to the very last detail. His late wife, Layla, had been nothing like his type, and everyone had questioned how they had fallen together. He couldn't explain it, but they just had. Rosie, however...no one in his life would question that.

Not that he was considering dating her. Dating was off the table for...maybe forever.

"Dad, isn't it just incredible?" Tess was still talking, and he realized he needed to tune in to what she was saying.

"Yes, absolutely." Evan paused, trying to bring back the last minute of her words, and then decided to just ask. "Wait, sorry. What's incredible?"

"The bookstore," Tess continued. "I told them we'd be back for their cookie event. Grandpa can take me if you don't want to."

"I want to go with you," he replied even quicker than he meant to. "I mean, whatever. Whoever is fine. Let's just hurry up and get home."

Shit, his palms were sweating. *What the heck was happening?* He felt like he was fifteen years old all over again, which made absolutely no sense because he was closing in on forty in a few years and had lived an entire life post–high school. Clearly Rosie had, too. She had kids, to begin with. She was probably married then. She owned a bookstore that was the opposite of everything that made up his personality—heavy on the fun beach reads and magazines and graphic novels. The window display was lined with cat-themed mugs and the wall decor was all vintage animation, like out of an old original Disney movie.

Everything about it screamed whimsical and sweet, while he was practical and steely.

"You can take me?" Tess seemed confused and she

looked down at the graphic novel in her hands and then back up at him. "Really?"

Evan frowned at her confusion, a pit of guilt forming in his stomach as he wondered if he'd done something to make his daughter think he didn't want to spend time with her. "Of course. I love spending my Saturdays with you. You know that."

She nodded. "Yeah, I know. I mean...you didn't really like the bookstore."

He waved a hand like it was no big deal. "Eh, it's fine. You like it. That's all that matters."

Tess grinned and began skipping as she stayed close to him on the sidewalk. "Thanks, Dad! I can't wait to see Becca again. I think we're friends now!"

It was good to see his daughter genuinely smiling and making new friends. Even if they were only here for the summer, he wanted her to feel at home and put down some roots. After all, his parents lived here and eventually he'd inherit their house. He always assumed he'd retire back in Heart Lake one day when he was ready to slow down with his career. Plus, the bookshop might not be everything he would want it to be but it was certainly better than Tess rotting her brain away this summer in front of video games.

"Evan Nowak?" A voice called out from across the street, grabbing his attention.

He looked over to see his old acquaintance Tanner Dean Jr. crossing the sidewalk to make his way over to him. He was hand in hand with a tall blond whose stomach jutted out like she'd strapped a watermelon to her abdomen. He couldn't remember the last time he'd seen Tanner, and he was pretty sure that the pregnant woman by his side had also attended their high school, but he couldn't recall her name.

"Hey, Tanner." He nodded his head and paused on the sidewalk. Tess stopped and looked up at both of them. "How's it going?"

"Great." The buff carpenter grinned and placed a gentle hand on the woman's stomach. "You remember Nola from high school, right? We're due with our first in three months."

"Congratulations." Evan reached out a hand and clapped it with Tanner's outstretched palm. "Of course, I remember you, Nola."

The name brought back memories—these two had been part of the popular crowd back in the day—at least, compared to him. They were still as freaking gorgeous as ever today, and he had no doubt their future child was going to be a knockdown, drag-out stunner.

"Nice to see you again," Nola replied, her own hand rubbing against her swollen belly. She smiled down at Tess. "And who is this adorable cutie?"

"I'm Tess," his daughter introduced herself. "He's my dad."

"Oh, is he?" Nola responded with a small laugh and shook the young girl's hand. "How wonderful. And where's your mom at today?"

Tess's face immediately fell and she paused, as if she wasn't sure how to respond.

"Oh, you probably haven't heard," Evan cut in immediately while placing a hand on his daughter's shoulder. "My wife passed away. Cancer. A few years ago."

Both Nola and Tanner lifted their eyes to his quickly. The looks of pity never got easier to bear.

"I'm so sorry to hear that, man." Tanner responded after a quiet moment. "That must be so incredibly difficult."

Obviously. But he didn't say that. "It's been hard," he

admitted diplomatically, reciting the speech he always gave in these moments. "But we're doing okay now. We're fine."

Everything about his words felt false, but he'd said it so many times that he had convinced himself it was true. Partially. Tess didn't look so sure though, and he tried to squeeze her shoulder as a source of comfort. Instead, she shrugged away from him.

"Well, I'm glad to hear that," Nola said, circling her arm around her husband's. "Listen, it's so good we've run into you. We're having a barbecue at our house on Sunday. Kind of a baby shower, but more just an excuse to get together and drink."

"Nola won't be drinking, of course," Tanner added, and Nola rolled her eyes at him as if that didn't need to be clarified.

"Obviously," Nola replied. "But we'll have plenty for the other adults there, and a whole slew of sodas and juice boxes for the kids—Tess, what's your favorite soda?"

"Orange!" She practically bounced on her heels as she announced this. "I love Fanta, but any brand of orange soda is really good."

Nola grinned and rubbed her hand in a circle over her belly. "Well, we actually just bought some cans this morning at Hobbes Grocery. Sounds perfect for you!"

"Dad, can we go?" Tess was tugging on his sleeve now. "Please? I never get to drink soda unless it's on my birthday. Orange was my mom's favorite flavor, that's why I like it. What was the story about how she laughed so hard that one time that it came out her nose and—"

"Hey, that's enough, honey." Evan ruffled her hair. It was the way Nola was staring at Tess, clearly imagining what it would be like if she died and left her own child behind. She looked so damn sorry. Everyone was always so damn sorry. But sometimes the weight of all that sorrow threatened to crush his chest.

"Great!" Tanner slapped him playfully on his upper arm, clearly trying to lighten the tone. "Your parents have our address, but if you need it, find me on Facebook."

Facebook? But he nodded anyway. "Sure, yeah. I'd bet they know it."

After all, everyone in Heart Lake knew everyone else. They said their goodbyes and continued past Evan and Tess on the sidewalk.

He motioned his daughter forward. "Come on, Tess. We're almost back at Grandma and Grandpa's."

"Okay." She kept walking, but her footsteps fell heavier against the pavement. By the time they rounded the corner, she was basically stomping like a troll beelining for the closest bridge.

Evan felt it impossible to ignore much longer and cleared his throat to bite the bullet. "Tess, honey. You okay?"

She stomped louder, hugging her book to her chest. "I'm fine. We're fine right?"

Damn, she did a great imitation of him, throwing back the words he offered Tanner and Nola a few minutes ago.

"You don't seem that way," he noted as her footsteps continued to punish the concrete. "You seem kind of angry. You know you can talk to me if you're feeling upset about something."

They walked another block before Tess responded, and when she did, she came to a dead stop and put both hands on her hips. "Why don't you like me talking about Mom with people?"

"What?" His eyes widened and he staggered sideways for a moment, as if her words had just pushed him over an invisible edge.

Tess shook her head emphatically and continued walking, now at a faster pace as they closed in on his parents' house up the block. "The only thing you ever say about her is that she died—or *passed away*. Some diplomatic answer that doesn't say anything about her at all—not even her name. We don't talk *about* her. It's like she never existed."

Evan cleared his throat and pressed a hand to his stomach as if to soothe the aching pain that had blossomed in that spot. "Tess, your mother very much existed."

"Really?" Tess spun on her heel and glared at him—the first time he'd seen actual anger in his daughter's eyes, maybe ever. "Because I don't want to forget about her. You might want to, but I don't, Dad. You told them your wife passed away. She wasn't just your wife. She was *my* mom. She was my mom who laughed and drank orange soda until it came out of her nose!"

Evan opened his mouth to respond, but no words came out. Tess shook her head and then turned away from him, and he heard the muffled sound of crying. He reached forward to touch her, hug her, hold her...anything to ease the constricting pain threatening to close in on him in that moment. But she didn't stay still to allow for him to do so. Instead, she broke out into a run and he watched her take the porch stairs up to his parents' house two at a time.

"Tess," he called out, but his voice was a hoarse whisper and he wouldn't be surprised if she hadn't even heard him. She disappeared through the front door, and Evan stayed standing on the sidewalk trying to figure out how to fix this mess—but he felt clueless. It was clear his daughter needed her mom, and while he'd do anything for her, that was one thing he couldn't give.

Chapter Five

"Here's your sugar with a dash of coffee." Rosie's best friend Nola Bennett-Dean placed a large ceramic mug in front of Rosie as they sat on the back deck of Nola's home with their other best friend, Amanda Riverswood. The expansive deck was a recent addition that her brother Tanner had built on Nola's grandmother's home last year when they'd officially moved in. It was one of Rosie's favorite spots now, and the women always held their Saturday morning coffee chats there, since it overlooked Heart Lake. The view of the water, so still in the early morning, was something she'd never get enough of in this place.

Heart Lake was more than just a lake to her, though. This town was her home in more ways than she could count. It felt like part of her, and not just because it had embraced her in a moment when she needed it most. When she'd found herself pregnant and alone, the people in this town never judged her. Her two best friends had been at the lead of any effort to stamp out gossip or speculation. Rosie couldn't help but smile at Nola's swollen belly as she eased herself down into a chair with a cup of decaf hot tea.

"Hey, at least I can have coffee," Rosie teased. "You're stuck with that gross tea."

Nola shrugged. "I still allow myself a cup of coffee a day—no sugar though. Just cream."

"That's how you got into this situation," Amanda joked, pointing at Nola's pregnant belly.

Rosie grinned and sipped the hot beige liquid in her mug. Then remembered Nola was married to her brother. "Ew, Amanda. You're talking about Tanner."

"And?" Amanda spoke her mind and never censored herself, and it was one of the things that Rosie loved about her brazen friend. "I'm just glad I'm the one left without a fetus. Both of your lives are over."

She knew she was teasing, but Rosie shot her a look anyway.

"What?" Amanda took a large swig of her black coffee. "I'm destined to be an aunt to that little cutie in there." She pointed at Nola's belly then to Rosie. "And your twin terrors. Children are not in the cards for me. Not that I have anyone lined up willing to spawn with me anyway."

Nola laughed this time and shook her head. "You've got to let me set up your online dating profile. I keep telling you that I'm really good at those!"

"Absolutely not." Amanda crossed her hands over her chest. "Remember the last time I was on Tinder?"

"The jacket guy!" Rosie tipped her head back and belted out a laugh at the memory of Amanda's date-gone-wrong two years ago with a man she'd met online. He'd shown up at the restaurant they were meeting at wearing a long trench coat and...that's it. Literally. Amanda had barely made it through her first drink before she'd ended up bailing on the entire thing. "Hey, he was nothing if not efficient."

Amanda rolled her eyes and pushed a piece of hair off her forehead that the early morning breeze had unsettled. "An efficient way to end the date quickly, sure."

"Ooh, speaking of being single, Amanda," Nola jumped in. "Guess who just moved back to town for the summer?"

Her friend didn't respond, sipping at her coffee instead. Rosie, however, was interested in the news. "Who?"

"Evan Nowak. Remember him from high school? Tanner and I ran into him and his daughter the other day and, wow, has he changed. Not that he wasn't attractive back then, but he's all man now and I swear I've never seen eyes that blue. Amanda, I think you should call him up."

Blue eyes? A light bulb suddenly went off in Rosie's head as she paired together the man from the bookstore yesterday with the skinny, shy boy from high school—who she might've had a tiny crush on. She hadn't recognized him when she'd seen him yesterday, and to be fair, there was a good reason for that. Evan Nowak had absolutely grown up into a man, and as much as he'd annoyed her yesterday, even she couldn't deny that he looked incredible. Not that he'd been unattractive before—clearly, she'd still been interested in him—but it seemed like over the last twenty years he'd gained thirty pounds in muscle and several inches in height.

"Me? I'm not going to call him." Amanda shook her head at the idea. "Rosie's the one who was in love with him in high school."

"I was not!" she quickly retorted, her voice a little higher than she'd meant it to be. She cleared her throat, trying to pretend she hadn't just squeaked that out. Hiding her feelings was not something she had ever been particularly good at, especially from her best friends.

Nola's eyes lit up as she turned to look at Rosie. "Oh my gosh, how could I forget? Rosie, you absolutely had a crush on him back in high school. And I think his daughter is around the same age as the twins are now, too. This could be a perfect pairing!"

"I've got enough baby daddy drama," Rosie assured her

friend, trying not to think of her own situation with the twins' biological father. "I'm not adding someone's baby mama drama to my life, too."

"You wouldn't be," Nola replied. She frowned, pausing for a moment before her voice became softer. "His wife actually died awhile ago. It's a really sad story. Marvel was telling us about it last night. She found a small mole on her shoulder—seemingly harmless. Literally didn't think much of it at all until it started changing shape and color. Turns out it was melanoma, and it metastasized quickly to her lymph nodes. They did surgery to remove it and she had an adverse reaction to the anesthesia. She went into a coma for two months before the family—Evan, specifically—had to decide to take her off life support."

"Oh my gosh." Rosie felt a tightness in her chest at the thought of the little girl she'd met yesterday losing her mother like that... or the boy she'd once known having to make such a traumatic decision. She felt like a dick, honestly. Particularly after how she'd been so sharp with him the other day. She couldn't imagine what he must've experienced losing his wife in such a dramatic and painful fashion, and she wanted to believe that his gruff personality was more likely a grief response than who he truly was. Either way, he deserved her kindness after such an ordeal. "That's terrible. I'm kind of gutted just hearing that story."

"Yikes," Amanda agreed. "Yeah, that's definitely tragic. Poor guy. Now he's a single dad of a daughter? Man, he must be really going through it. I don't even have kids, but I can't imagine that type of heartbreak."

"It's unimaginable," Rosie confirmed, thinking about her twins. A shiver ran through her as she thought of an alternate future where they lose her and then have no one. Would their biological dad step up? Definitely not. Fear gripped at her heart as she felt the enormity of motherhood and its responsibilities on her shoulders and sent up a tiny prayer that she and her children were never put in a position like that. "I'm not sure I'd survive that. He must have a lot of strength and resiliency."

She decided then and there that she would cut Evan some slack if she ran into him again. After all, this town had banded around her when she'd been struggling as a newly single mom and she was determined to pay that forward. If she'd thought her own story was hard, she couldn't even begin to imagine the mountain he was climbing. Plus, Becca liked his daughter and Becca didn't make friends easily, so she wanted to foster that connection. Even if it meant she had to suffer through book snob lectures from a grieving widower.

"You absolutely would," Nola assured her. "Plus, Amanda and I would never let anything happen to you or your kids. Billy was bad enough."

Amanda laughed. "Oh, God...have you even heard from that dumpster fire lately? How far behind on child support is he again?"

"Behind?" Rosie snorted. "It's been a minute. Maybe four months."

Nola shook her head. "You are so strong to have gone through all of that alone. I'm so grateful to have your brother. This pregnancy has been so hard already, and I can't imagine what it'll be like when the baby is actually here."

"That first year isn't a cake walk," Rosie admitted, though most of her memories from back then were hazy. Sleep deprivation and taking care of newborn twins alone was enough to make any person lose their grip on reality.

"Tanner's going to be a great father, though. If it weren't for him, and all of you guys, I never would have made it through. The twins love him. He'll be a natural at fatherhood."

Her friend and sister-in-law smiled as she rubbed her belly lightly. "Yeah...I know I'm blessed."

They continued talking about postpregnancy plans as they finished their coffee, but Rosie excused herself early to head to the bookstore. She wanted to make sure the shop was cleaned to her liking before patrons began showing up.

Thank goodness she had, because when she pulled up to Fact or Fiction, she found Davon glaring through the store window at none other than Evan Nowak.

"Hey, what's going on?" Rosie asked as she walked in.

Davon's hands were on his hips and he looked ready to rip Evan a new one. "This customer thought he should get a discount on the latest Sarah J. Maas book for his daughter because it's *signed*."

"Well, it's used." Evan held the book up between them and shook it. "I was just asking the question."

Rosie waved off Davon. "I'll handle this."

"Ooh, you're in for it now," Davon said with a little bob of his head and click of his tongue. He headed toward the cash register.

"I'm sorry. I'm not trying to be difficult," Evan continued. "But my daughter is really into reading this summer and we can't just go crazy buying all the new young adult books. Plus, she's into all this cartoon stuff and graphic novels. It's ridiculous, and I cannot justify spending twenty dollars on that."

"I seem to recall someone who loved to read comics when they were much older than Tess. In fact, I ran into you a few times in the back section of the school library where you had fanned out dozens of comic books around you." Rosie tilted her head to one side and repeated a calming mantra to herself in an attempt to stay calm and not snap at him.

"You..." Evan cleared his throat. "You, uh, remember me from high school?"

"And middle school, and elementary," Rosie confirmed. "Why was it okay for you to have read those, but Tess can't read graphic novels?"

"It's not that she can't," Evan countered. He was shifting his weight from one foot to the other now. "It's just, I want to make sure she's a strong reader. That matters, you know, it's a foundational skill."

"But isn't it important to fall in love with stories?" Rosie questioned, but her voice was softer now. "Won't that be what inspires lifelong reading?"

Evan looked uncomfortable now. "I don't know. I'm not sure if I'm great at this parenting stuff. I just want her to succeed."

"What about fun? And being carefree and enjoying childhood?" Rosie picked up a graphic novel from the rolling cart outside the bookstore that people used for returns and giveaways. She handed it to him. "This one is on me. Give this to Tess. She'll love it, and you should read it with her. Life isn't all about work."

"You sound like my wife," he teased, but then the words seemed to get stuck in his throat. He flipped through the pages of the graphic novel slowly. "She always told me I was too serious. Too intense. But I came by it honestly; I mean, look at my old man. The apple didn't fall far from the tree."

Rosie was quiet for a moment, but then reached forward and squeezed his forearm. She felt an ache in her heart as she tried to imagine what he'd been through. As irritating as he our friend from the other day, right?" Tess questioned, ouncing back and forth in her chair. His daughter had cyclopedic knowledge of names after meeting others once.

anner...right." Evan quickly remembered that Rosie anner's younger sister and would more than likely be at other's party. Damn these small towns.

bet that they have a boat," Tess continued. "Dad, do ant to play War?"

picked up the extra deck of cards by his father's elbow ulled them out of the box. The card game War had been rite in their family for years. "Sure, but you know I s beat you in this game."

ss rolled her eyes. "Dad, it's a game of luck. You can't tter at it than me."

ot true," Antoni cut in, grinning slyly. "I always beat ants off your father with that game when he was your 's basically tradition."

an laughed because the claim was ludicrous. "Dad, not even remotely true. I've always been a master "

hat's what I wanted him to believe." Antoni winked at

laughed and they began dealing out cards. They a few rounds, both winning one hand. Even Everly on the competition and began cheering Tess on while attempted to give her tips on how to turn the cards just the right way to make them magically be higher Tess was enamored and laughter rang out over the the next hour as the sun began to lower in the sky.

smiled, feeling whole in that moment. It wasn't ing he felt often since Layla's death, but in quiet

could be—I mean, calling a book signed by the author *used*? Really?—he was also still the boy she once knew under all of that muscle. "I heard about your wife. I'm so sorry."

He went rigid, as if lightning had struck him in that moment. He shook her hand off his arm and shrugged his shoulders. "Nothing to be sorry about. That's life, you know. Things happen. Thanks for the book."

She felt whiplash from how quickly his tone had turned on her as he walked away without a second glance. "Uh, okay...goodbye?"

She was sure he couldn't hear her at that point since he was almost out the door, but her attention was pulled to the two families entering. "Hey, folks! Welcome!"

"Hey, Rosie!" The mother of one of the families smiled at her as they headed inside.

Rosie glanced back out the window to see Evan climbing into the driver's side of his car. She couldn't understand why he got under her skin so much, but his easy dismissal both irritated her and hurt her at the same time. But despite all that, she hurt for him.

She didn't want to feel so soft toward him and yet...here she was.

Chapter Six

"Please, can I go?" Tess had her hands together, clasped in front of her as if she were praying. "They have a boat!"

"Everyone in Heart Lake has a boat," Evan reminded his daughter, and then pointed off the deck to the boat bobbing against his parents' dock a few meters away. "Your grandparents have one right there."

"That thing's mostly decoration at this point." Antoni looked up from the deck of cards he was shuffling for another game of solitaire on the picnic table on the deck. "You can go sit on it, but you're going to need a mechanic to look at the engine if you want it to run."

"See?" Tess turned back to Evan. "That one doesn't work. Becca says that theirs has a flag on the back!"

He smiled a little, but still shook his head to his daughter's proposal to spend an entire day with Rosie's twins at their cabin on the lake. Somehow, they'd gotten it in their heads that they'd have a playdate, but tomorrow he had her meeting with an online math tutor first thing in the morning. The private school she was enrolled in in Chicago was hardcore, and he had to make sure she was staying competitive with the other kids in her grade. "I don't want you to get overtired. Tomorrow, you meet with your tutor bright and early."

"Dad, it's summer. It's time to have fun!" Tess emphasized

as she sat down in the deck chair with an e... ish. "This isn't prison."

His mother glanced at him as she s... spritzer and looked up from the romance n... ing. "Come on, Evan. Let the girl make ... play this summer."

Evan looked at her in disbelief. She'd c... her tune from when he was a kid. When Da... work on math notebooks or write a short es... event in the paper before going to play ball... ride his bike to get pizza, she'd just nod in... and say, "Someday, you'll understand." H... do with the fact that his dad was the son of... moved from Eastern Europe after World W... had very little and fought for everything the...

And as he got older, he did come to unde... internalize the push to succeed. After he h... ized that his dad had wanted him to be ab... he wanted, to value hard work and the pri... the payoff. And now that's what he wante... instill the same values, and what was ha... ents were now wanting him to lay off.

Pressure built in the base of his skull.

What was he getting wrong here?

Evan frowned, trying to push away th... ing a sip of his beer. Okay, he could pr... gently. "Hey, we agreed to go to a ba... house tomorrow afternoon, remember? ...

"I guess. Wait. I just remembered." T... her chair and clapped her hands. "If we ... twins there!"

He nearly choked as he swallowed the...

"Y... now ... an en... even ...

"T... was T... her br...

"I ... you w...

He... and p... a fav... alway...

Te... be be...

"N... the pa... age. I...

Ev... that's ... at war...

"T... Tess. ...

She... played ... got in ... Anton... over in ... scores. ... lake fo...

Eva... someth...

and gentle times like this, it felt so fulfilling. After they finished a last round, he stretched and stood up from his chair. Returning inside, he grabbed some mathematics flash cards from Tess's backpack. "All right, Tess. That was fun, but hey, you know what might be cool? Doing some fractions, get a head start on tomorrow. If you understand these, you'll be light-years ahead of your peers in the fall."

Tess was still holding the deck of cards from their game earlier when she slammed them down onto the wooden table so hard that all fifty-two cards went in different directions. His parents startled and looked up at them, and Tess's eyes seemed like they were trying to cut through him. "Seriously, Dad?! I'm going to bed!" She opened the patio door and slammed it loudly behind her.

Evan glanced down at his watch, but it was still over an hour until the time she'd usually begin getting ready for bed. Honestly, everything about the last thirty seconds had been shockingly uncharacteristic for his daughter until recently. "What the heck," he muttered under his breath.

"Son." Everly began cleaning up the scattered cards. "You should go check on her."

"I don't even understand what just happened," he admitted, feeling frustrated that no matter what he tried to do, it always seemed to be wrong. "I should ground her for that display. She can't act like that!"

Antoni shook his head as he helped his wife and Evan clean up the cards and pick up the knocked-over chair. "Evan, she's trying to communicate with you."

"Not in the best way," Everly added. "But you've got to teach her how to express big feelings. Kids don't know innately how to do that. Especially if they've never seen an example."

He certainly wasn't giving her examples and he knew it. Keeping his emotions in check and hidden under a thick layer of grumpiness and sarcasm was one of his greatest skills. Feelings had been Layla's territory. "Fine. I'll go talk to her."

Evan steeled himself as he arrived at the other side of the door to the guest room where Tess was staying this summer. He tapped on it lightly with his knuckles and then pushed it open.

Tess's body was strewn across the bed, her shoulders shaking with heaving sobs.

"Tess?" He paused in the doorway a moment, trying to figure out what to do. He hadn't expected to find her crying, and something about her tears made his whole body freeze up and his mind go blank. Still, he knew he had to do something, so he crossed the room and sat on the floor at the edge of the bed. He wanted to give her her space, but also let her know that he was there for her. "Hey, I'm here when you want to talk, okay?"

She kept crying and he sat there with her for a few more minutes until her sobs slowed into sniffles. Finally, she sat up and rubbed her palms against her eyes that were now red and puffy, swollen from her tears. "You're never going to be happy with me the way that I am."

"What?" Evan frowned and reached out to squeeze her ankle which was the only part of her close enough to him to reach. "What do you mean, Tess?"

"You're always trying to change me—to make me *better.*" Tess used air quotes with her hands at that last word. "You always want more but I just am me. I can't be more than that and you don't like me."

He felt as if someone had just shoved a knife into his

stomach and twisted it. The very last thing he'd expected to hear from his daughter—literally his entire reason for being on this earth—was that she felt like he didn't like her just as she was. Nothing could be further from the truth.

He pushed himself up onto his feet and climbed onto the bed next to her. He wrapped an arm around her shoulders and she began to cry again, this time turning into his chest and hugging him tightly. He gently caressed her head, smoothing down her unruly curls that reminded him way too much of Layla's. "Tess, I will always love you, but I really like you, too. I'm completely enamored with everything you are, and I always will be. I am so, so sorry that I haven't shown you that."

She didn't respond, but her shaking shoulders slowed and her sniffs soon became light snores as she fell asleep. He gently laid her down in the bed and pulled the covers over her, the exhaustion from her emotions clearly evident on her face. Evan rubbed his hand across the back of his neck, watching her sleep for a few moments as he had the night that Layla died. She'd only been four years old back then, when Evan returned home from the hospital in the middle of the night while his parents had been watching Tess. He'd watched her sleep until morning, until he had to tell her that her mother wasn't coming home.

Evan swallowed hard as he left the room. He went straight to the fridge and grabbed a beer, though he strongly considered breaking into the liquor cabinet for something harder. He was going to have to figure out how to make a shift from taskmaster to parent. He didn't want to destroy his relationship with his daughter and at the rate he was going, he was going to do some serious damage soon. He took his IPA out to the deck and aimlessly scrolled through the local paper when a headline caught his eye and he decided to read the article.

It didn't take him long to read the whole thing, a funny and intelligent commentary on how to build a support system of people around your child if you're a single parent titled "Build a Village, Not a Mob." The columnist was anonymous and just went by the name Miss Mommy, but he found himself agreeing with most of her points. And, honestly, it was an area he was lacking in giving Tess. So often it felt like it was just the two of them against the world, but he knew Tess needed her village. Layla would have given her a village, but his wife had always been the charismatic, personable one. It didn't come as easily to Evan, even though he certainly made friends when he tried. It just wasn't in his nature to reach out first and spark connections the way she had.

When he got to the bottom of the article, he noticed an email address encouraging submissions. Before he could chicken out, he logged in to an anonymous email address he'd created years ago as a catchall for spam emails when signing up for things he didn't actually want to have his real email. He opened up a new email message and began typing:

Dear Miss Mommy,

Any advice for single dads who feel like they're failing? I'm trying to stay calm and not lose my temper, but it's so hard when everything is on my shoulders. My child's entire future, my ailing parents' health, my job…it's a lot and I'm not sure how to handle the stress sometimes. My friends would say I isolate, but I think the truth is I just wish someone cared to notice and find me.

Clueless Dad

He hit send before he could change his mind. Everything about this was unlike him, but what the hell. He didn't have much to lose at this point, and God knows he was already screwing it up on his own.

"Evan?" A small knock on the glass door to the deck pulled him out of his thoughts. He turned to see his mother standing in the open doorway.

"Hey, Mom." He motioned for her to join him outside. Their relationship was complicated in that neither one of them was great at displays of affection, but if there was one thing that he was sure of, it was that he was willing to do anything for his mother. She'd been hard on him as a kid, stood by while his dad set big expectations, but at the same time she also had spent her whole life taking care of him and his father. He found himself wishing often that she'd spend more time and attention on herself, but she wasn't interested in anything outside of his and his father's happiness—except for the occasional glass of wine or fancy cocktail, that is. Today, though, she seemed heavier as she came and sat in the chair next to his.

"You okay, Mom?"

Normally cheerful, her disposition was stoic at the moment. "He's getting worse, you know. Last week, the doctor said if he didn't start taking things seriously, his symptoms would progress more quickly."

"I thought he was taking the medications?" Evan frowned, but then remembered that she probably wasn't looking for a solution right now. "But yeah…it must be hard to be in your shoes, Mom."

"It's overwhelming," she admitted, her voice nearly a whisper. A quiet minute passed between them as they both stared out at the lake. Finally, she cleared her throat. "I'm also worried about Tess, though. It's been really nice having her here this summer. I think it's done her a world of good to be around family."

"I agree." He nodded. "She's really enjoyed her time here."

"Would you ever consider extending your stay? Heart Lake Middle School is a great place, and our guest bedrooms never have anyone else but you two. I know it would be so good for your father." Everly kneaded her brows, and she didn't turn to look at him. It was the most vulnerable she'd ever been, and he felt like he couldn't find the words to respond because he was so shocked by the request. She stood up suddenly before he could say anything and clapped her hands to her thighs. "You know what, I'm being silly. Don't listen to the musings of a tired old woman. I'm going to bed."

With that, she returned into the house and left him sitting there feeling like he'd just been sucker punched in the gut twice in one night. It was a helpless feeling, like he was letting down people in his life that he loved more than the world.

He needed to step up, stop being an island, and figure out a way to be the person others could lean on.

Chapter Seven

"I don't understand," Rosie said as she turned to her son. "You want to put mustard on what?"

"Watermelon!" Zander repeated. "Everyone is doing it on TikTok. It's a new trend and we *have* to try it. Oh, and get out your phone, too, please. I need to record it."

She blinked, trying to piece together the mash-up of words coming out of her kid's mouth that she'd never heard before. But the reality was, she didn't have time to care about what odd food pairings he wanted to try right now. "The mustard should be in the fridge and my phone is on the counter. Don't go crazy."

"Uncle Tanner, do you have mustard?" Zander turned his attention to her brother as he walked into the kitchen.

"In the door of the fridge," he confirmed, then gave Rosie a quizzical glance. "Zander's helping cook for the barbecue?"

She shot him a long look as Zander opened the fridge and found what he was looking for. "He's making a TikTok video."

"Oh." Tanner picked up a bag of hamburger buns on the counter. "Wait, he knows about TikTok?"

"Don't get him started," she joked, but Zander was already out of the room with his mustard and a plate of watermelon. "I'm just finishing up the deviled eggs, but everything else should be ready. How's the grill going?"

Her brother loved being in charge of the grill at any barbecue, but Rosie was always the one actually masterminding the operation from the kitchen. She loved Nola, but there was no doubt in anyone's mind that her best friend couldn't cook worth a damn. So, Rosie was always recruited for Sunday dinner festivities—not that she minded. It felt wonderful to be needed and to have a role that everyone always turned to her for. She preferred to be the one others depended on, rather than vice versa. It's just how she liked it.

After another dash of sweet honey mustard in the deviled-eggs mix—the secret to her famous recipe—Rosie glanced out the window over the sink to check on the guests. Most of the attendees were on the grass playing a rousing game of cornhole or welcoming some other families joining. She paused for a moment and realized that the new guests were actually Evan Nowak and his daughter, as well as his parents.

What was he doing here? Curse these small towns.

Zander and Becca were already in a mad dash across the yard toward Tess. The young girl was bouncing up and down and waving her hands, clearly as excited to see them as they were to see her. Whatever her thoughts were of Tess's father, she was touched to see how the twins had bonded so quickly to the new girl. She'd always made it a point to teach her twins to look for the outsider or the newcomer and befriend them. After living her whole life in Heart Lake, she could only imagine how difficult it must be to acclimate to a small town where everyone was so tight-knit. She might have her finger on the pulse of the community, but she was also a bookworm and had grown up in the library instead of on the football field like a lot of kids in the area. So, she was no stranger to being an outsider, and she was darn well going to make sure her kids included all the bookworms and newbies that crossed their paths.

"Did you invite him?" Rosie asked her brother on his next trip inside the house for a fresh plate of meat patties for the grill.

Tanner scanned the yard, but then looked back at her. "Who?"

"Evan Nowak."

"Oh, yeah." He popped a potato chip in his mouth from the bowl on the counter. "I guess he's back in town for the summer. His parents aren't doing so well—or his father, specifically. Parkinson's. He's helping his mother get him into an established treatment program before they head back to Chicago for the school year. Figured it would be good to show him some hospitality after all he's been through."

"Right. Well, of course," Rosie fumbled a bit on her words, feeling like even more of a jerk than she had the last time she'd brought Evan up to her friends. "I didn't realize he had so much going on."

"Definitely a lot. He needs some friends." Tanner grabbed another handful of chips and then headed out to the grill.

A knot formed in Rosie's throat. Here she'd been boasting to herself about how proud she was of her children for making Tess feel at home in a new town and she'd been doing the exact opposite with Tess's dad.

Well, no more. Time to practice what she preached and make an effort to help him get reacquainted with Heart Lake this summer.

With a finished plate of deviled eggs in one hand and the bowl of potato chips in the other, she headed out to the picnic table they were using to hold all of the food. A mosquito-repellant candle sat in the middle and worked perfectly for warding off flying critters from their dishes. She'd barely put the deviled eggs down before an older man swiped one from the tray and popped it in his mouth.

"This might be the best deviled egg I've ever eaten," he said after he swallowed. "What's in that?"

She beamed. "Honey mustard. That's the key."

"Everly, come try these!" He motioned to an older woman standing at the bar cart pouring herself a cocktail before turning back to Rosie. "I'm Antoni, Evan's dad. I think we've met a few times at some local events. And I've seen you at Saturday's farmers market, haven't I?"

"I go every week for fresh flowers and my favorite goat cheese," she confirmed. "It's my biggest guilty pleasure."

"I know exactly which vendor you're talking about," he agreed. "They have a pistachio goat cheese that will make you lose your mind. Ask my wife."

"What's he filling your head with now?" Everly joked as she joined them, sipping at the edge of a red Solo cup filled to the brim with ice and some light-colored liquor and mixer. "Antoni always was able to find the prettiest lady at the party and talk her ear off."

"That's how I won you over, isn't it?" he joked, wrapping an arm around her waist.

Rosie smiled. "How long have the two of you been married?"

Everly gave Antoni a flirty look. "Longer than you've been alive. We were married right where the pier is now."

"Really?" Rosie lifted her brows. "What was there before the pier?"

"Nothing. Just a sandy beach and a meadow of wildflowers that you could get lost in." Everly had a dreamy, faraway look in her eyes, and Rosie felt a pang of longing for a love story like theirs.

Not that she was interested in dating right now. Absolutely not.

But if it was anything like that...maybe.

"Mom, Dad, do you want to play a round of cornhole?" Evan walked over to them, a glass of water in his hands with a few lemon wedges in it. "It'd be like old times."

"We used to have a cornhole set in our backyard but some kids ran off with it a few summers back," Antoni explained to Rosie, then pointed at the plate of deviled eggs. "Evan, have you tried this woman's eggs? They are the best."

"What?" Evan looked confused for a moment before realizing what his father was talking about. "The deviled eggs? I'm not a big mayonnaise person—trying to eat healthy."

Rosie tried hard not to roll her eyes—jeez, did this man not allow himself any of life's simple pleasures? "It actually has very little mayonnaise. Try it and tell me what you think the main ingredient is."

"I bet it's eggs." He chuckled a little and she couldn't help but smile at his attempt at a joke.

"Besides the eggs," she replied, then handed him one. "Here, try it."

He took a hesitant bite and then nodded his head. "That is pretty good."

"See?" Antoni patted his son on the back. "Evan's always been a very careful eater. We raised him to eat all the vegetables, but as I've gotten older, I've gotten a little wiser. Now I'm the one trying to coax him to have a doughnut."

"Dad, enough already." Evan groaned, clearly not enjoying being the subject of attention. "Come on, let's play some cornhole."

"Not me, kiddo." Antoni stretched his arm then nodded

toward Rosie. "I'm not feeling the best, but this lovely lady could probably give you a run for your money at it."

"You think so?" Evan looked at Rosie, expression maddeningly unreadable. "Want to play a round?"

Determined to make good on her promise to herself to be hospitable, she nodded her head. "Sure. Let's do it."

They walked over to the two angled wooden boards and he handed her a few cloth beanbags.

"What do you say we make it interesting?" He picked up a few beanbags for himself and juggled them in his hands.

She raised one brow "Like a competition?"

"Like a bet." He grinned, and for a split second, there was an ease to him that was almost boyish. It was sweet and endearing and she couldn't help but smile back.

"What are the stakes?" she asked. "You know, just so I am clear what I'll be winning."

"Fighting words." He laughed and tossed one of the beanbags up higher in the air, then caught it in his other hand behind his back. "If I lose, I'll read any book you choose— however silly or cliché you want."

She tried to ignore his judgmental descriptions. "And if I lose?"

"I get to pick the next featured young adult book for the store." Evan wiggled his brows. "And I promise it's going to be educational, maybe something with a STEM message, or about history."

"Yes, because that's what will save my store—kids piling in to grab a story on engineering," Rosie replied sarcastically. "But, fine. You're on. And, you know what else?"

"What do you mean save your store?" Evan seemed stuck on her last comment.

She hadn't meant to be that open about her career

anxieties. "I mean, let's up the ante," she continued without addressing his question. "The twins have been begging me for a playdate or sleepover with Tess. Whoever loses has to host."

"I'd enjoy a night off," he teased, thankfully sidetracked by her additional wager. "Not sure you'd enjoy that many kids at one time, though."

"Oh, I'm sure I can manage." She tossed a beanbag at him and it landed squarely in the center of his chest.

He grinned. "You're on. In fact, I'll let you go first. Ladies, and all."

She rolled her eyes and stepped up to the starting line across from the wooden board with a small hole in the top-center of it. With the ease of someone who'd spent her entire life at Sunday barbecues, she arched the beanbag perfectly onto the board where it hit the wood just above the opening and then slid down and fell through.

"Am I being hustled?" Evan crossed his arms over his chest and watched as she tossed three more beanbags—getting all but one through the hole.

"I mean, I did warn you that I would win," she teased as she stepped back and let him take his turn.

He fared only slightly worse than her, still getting a few beanbags through the hole to score a point. "We're doing first to twenty-one points, right?"

She smirked. "Feeling nervous?"

"I mean, that was just the first inning," Evan replied. "I've still got plenty of time to beat you."

Rosie laughed and shook her head as she walked over to the board to pick up her beanbags from underneath. "Inning? This is cornhole, not baseball."

"It's still called an inning. I looked it up on the American

Cornhole Association website." He was right behind her scooping up his beanbags before walking back to the opposite board. "And officially, it's first to twenty-one points."

She put one hand on her hip and tilted her head slightly. "There's a national cornhole website?"

"It's an association, but yes, they have a website," he clarified.

Rosie laughed and tossed her beanbags at the board, sinking three with ease but missing the last one by a mile. "My God, you're more of a nerd than I remember."

Evan actually laughed, and it was almost disarming to hear him sound so relaxed for a moment. "You thought I was a nerd?"

"I *think* you're a nerd now," she rephrased. "And thought you were one back then, too. But you're like, a cute and buff nerd."

The beanbag he was throwing slipped out of his hand at an awkward angle as he stumbled after hearing her assessment. He straightened and looked at her with his brows high. "Now I'm a cute and buff nerd?"

Shit. Why did her mouth always get her into these situations?

"Slip of the tongue," she tried to walk back her words. "I just mean you're different than your nerdy high school version. You've ... filled out, you know?"

Okay, that was not better.

"I've filled out?" He was egging her on now, his arms crossed over his chest and his shoulders pushed back as he clearly was trying not to laugh.

"That came out wrong," she clarified, pretty sure the heat that she felt in her cheeks was a bright crimson red from his point of view. "I mean, uh, I mean you've gained muscle. You clearly work out now."

Shut up, shut up, shut up. She wanted to crawl into a hole and die at this point. Never in all her life had she dug herself further into word vomit, but here she was wading in it like it was her job.

"I do work out," he replied, stepping forward and tossing his next beanbag directly into the target. "It's nice of you to notice. Always nice to know I'm being appreciated."

"I didn't say I was *appreciating* you," she shot back. "I just mean I noticed."

"Fifteen to thirteen," he replied as he walked past her toward the board to grab his beanbags. He paused inches from her and his voice lowered as he leaned just a little closer. "Thanks for noticing."

Was she on fire? Because it felt like she was on fire.

Both from embarrassment and the fact that when he leaned in so close, she could smell his woodsy aftershave and the heat of his breath against her neck. My God, why did he smell so deliciously like the deep woods when he was from the city? It should be criminal to misrepresent himself that way.

Though it wasn't a misrepresentation at all, was it?

"I'm only two points behind by sheer coincidence." The words fumbled out of her mouth as she tried to find a way to redeem her sanity. "Normally, this would already be a closed game. I'm a little off today."

She tossed her four beanbags quickly and all four made it through the targeted hole. "See?"

"Seventeen, fifteen," Evan updated her then threw his next four beanbags and sunk all four. "Never mind. Nineteen, seventeen. I'm in the lead."

She wiggled her brows and stepped up to the shooting line. "You *were* in the lead. Watch me hit twenty-one right now."

"Tall order," he warned, sitting back on his heels and watching her from the sidelines.

She took a few deep breaths, then did exactly what she promised to do and landed all four beanbags through the hole, hitting the winning total of twenty-one points by a narrow margin.

Rosie threw her hands up in the air and let out a loud cheer. "I won!"

Evan laughed and walked over to her, putting a hand out for a sportsmanlike shake. "Good game. I guess you're picking my next read."

"And you are on babysitter duty for the playdate," she reminded him. "What shall I do with all my free time?"

"Burgers are ready!" Tanner called out to the guests in the backyard.

"I'm going to go grab Tess for food." Evan smiled at her, then headed toward where his daughter was swinging in a tire swing under a tree by the lake.

She waved goodbye, but then immediately put her hand down because it felt awkward. Nola was motioning for her help up on the deck, so she headed in that direction, but she couldn't help but replay the last thirty minutes. That was the most fun she'd had in a while, and it was strange to come to that realization.

She loved her life the way it was, but moments like this made her question . . . did she want more?

Chapter Eight

"Yesssssss. Grandma and Grandpa both said it was okay." Tess had both of her arms wrapped around one of his forearms as she hung on and dragged herself along with him as he walked up the steps to his parents' house. "Please, please, please Dad!"

Evan lifted her up the stairs by elevating his arm high enough to keep her off the ground. "Tess, I already said yes. You can invite Becca and Zander over for a playdate or sleepover on Friday afternoon. We're going to set you guys up in a tent in the back to go camping. I okayed it with their mom."

"You did? You're the best!" She jumped off at the top step and landed with a small thud. "Okay! Camping? Yay! I have to get ready!"

"It's only Sunday! Friday is still five days away, Tess," he reminded her, but it didn't matter because she was already off to her room at a hare's pace.

The words "You're the best" continued to ring in his ears.

He couldn't begin to imagine what she needed to prepare this far in advance, but understanding kids was certainly not his area of expertise. He couldn't lie, however; he loved seeing this side of Tess come out. There was something about today . . . a stirring of long dormant roots. He'd forgotten what it was like to be somewhere where he knew all the houses on a street, or the old maple on the corner, or the people he encountered, and they knew him. He'd taken such things for granted as a kid, but now he was a little older, a little wiser, and the truth was that community could be useful. It was sort of nice to belong, and it was really great to feel more support with Tess, not to be so alone in the whole parenting thing.

Evan's phone pinged with a notification from his pocket as he walked into the kitchen and grabbed a beer from the fridge. He cracked it open and read the new email that just came through.

Dear Clueless Dad,

Being a single parent is a thankless job, and I'm so impressed that you're out there and rocking it. I mean, most likely you're rocking it. I really don't know, because you could be a grade A dick, too. But I'm going to assume that a divorcé who would email Miss Mommy must give two shits about his kiddo.

So, listen: kids like to push our buttons, and they loooove to get a reaction from us because it tells them we care. Bad reactions are still better than no reactions to a kiddo's undeveloped little brain. Find new ways to tell your child you care. Next time he/ she throws a tantrum or has a meltdown, say "I see that you're angry. That can be such a scary feeling to have. Can I give you a hug? That makes me feel better when I'm angry." You're showing that child that you recognize their emotion, you're validating it, and you want to help him/her through it.

Oh, and Clueless Dad... get out there. Meet someone. Make friends. You deserve happiness as much as your child does. People notice you, but they're waiting for you to welcome them in. Open yourself up. We're here when you're ready.

All the best,
Miss Mommy

PS: I'll attach some of my favorite parenting Instagram accounts and websites below—definitely check them out!

Evan laughed to himself as he read the columnist's response. There was a release attached to allow her response and his email to be published in this week's paper, which he quickly signed and sent back. Honestly, the response was a million times better than he'd expected. She'd been honest with him, and her advice on validating Tess's feelings... shit, how had he never thought of that?

It seemed so obvious now, reading it in black and white, but in the moment when he felt like his buttons were being pushed, it was harder to see that. But that was the reality, wasn't it? Tess's recent outbursts weren't about him at all.

They were about her.

His daughter was hurting from the loss of her mother, and maybe in some ways... had she felt like she lost her father, too? Evan swallowed hard at the thought, placing the beer down on the counter with a *thunk* that made it fizz up and pour over the top by a few drops. Damn, he felt like the biggest asshole in Michigan right now. Layla would have known all of this stuff. Emotions and communication had been her expertise, and he had no doubt that she would have been able to navigate every high and low Tess might have thrown at them.

A pang of sadness plumed in his chest at the memory of his late wife. He missed her. He always would. But something felt a bit more distant, and not in a bad way. It was as if the pain was still there, but it was just a bit further away. He had prayed for that space for years—any relief from the pain—but now that he was actually feeling it…he felt like he was betraying Layla.

Rosie's face came to his mind, and the guilt settled in harder in the pit of his stomach.

"Hey, kid." Antoni walked into the kitchen and made a beeline for the fridge. He grabbed a beer and knocked the top off. "Can I join you?"

Evan motioned to the chair in front of him at the kitchen table. "Sit, Pops."

He did, but it took him a few moments to settle and get comfortable. He sighed after a long swig from the bottle. "Your mom been talking to you about me?"

"She worries about you," Evan replied, not directly answering the question, but not hiding from it either. "You know how much she loves you."

Antoni smiled in a wistful kind of way that seemed more sad than joyful. "She really does. That woman has been my whole world for longer than I've known what life was like without her."

"You guys have a great thing going. You always have," Evan agreed. He'd always been enamored with his parents' relationship, and he'd thought he'd found the same thing for himself once. Layla and he could have been end game. They could have been old age, sitting on the front porch and looking out at the lake together.

"Your mom is going to need your support, you know. After…" Antoni gestured toward himself and then took another swig of his beer. "Well, I don't know how much longer I've got—at least as the man I am now. I don't want your mom's last memories of me to be as my caretaker."

"Dad, she's been your caretaker for the last forty years," Evan tried to tease, though the entire conversation was making him uncomfortable.

Antoni laughed. "You're not wrong there."

They let a quiet moment pass between them, sipping their beers and reflecting on the topic.

"I've got Mom," Evan finally said, his voice quieter this time. "She's not going to be alone."

Antoni cleared his throat and looked away. Evan could see a sparkle of tears lining his lower lids. He didn't respond, but finally nodded his head and then tipped his beer bottle toward Evan. They clinked the tops of their bottles together and went back to sitting in content silence.

After Antoni finished his beer, he headed back upstairs and Evan pulled out his phone. He opened the email from Miss Mommy again and read it over. He had sent the release form back to her editor already, but something made him want to respond directly to her. He wasn't sure what the protocol was on that, but she'd answered one question, so why not another?

Dear Miss Mommy,

Your response was really helpful and I definitely am going to work on validating my daughter's emotions more. Thank you for being so thoughtful in your response. In fact, I wanted to ask another question— any tips on teaching a dad how to do his daughter's hair? Especially when it's so tangled? My daughter

*has been asking me to help her French braid it, and
I've jumbled it up each time.*

*Also, thanks for encouraging me to get out there
more. Maybe soon.*

Thanks,
Clueless Dad

He placed the phone back down on the table and finished
the rest of his beer. Standing up, he headed out to the back
porch to place it in the recycling bin, except a scratching
noise coming from below made him pause.

Scratch, scratch.

"Hello?" he called out, though he wasn't sure what he
would have done had something or someone answered him.
It was pitch-dark out and the only things he could see were
the tree line and the shimmer of the moon on the lake. He
reached inside and flicked on the porch light, basking the
area in a dim hue.

Nothing stood out to him, but then he heard the scratching sound again and this time, what sounded like a whim-
per along with it. Evan placed his bottle in the recycling bin
and climbed down the stairs into the grassy yard, surveying
beneath the deck. He took out his cell phone and turned on
the flashlight, illuminating the bare dirt space beneath that
was closed in by a wooden lattice.

"Oh!" His flashlight beamed over a tiny face sticking out
through the holes in the lattice. Evan leaned in closer and the
smallest little meow came out of the stuck kitten. "What are
you doing here, fellow?"

He stepped closer and moved the flashlight around to
examine the situation the little kitten had found himself in.

It appeared that one of his claws was stuck in the wood and his head was between the lattice—which should have been easy to get out of, except the kitten was clearly panicking and thrashing about, causing himself to get more stuck.

Evan pulled at the top edge of the lattice by the porch. It came loose pretty easily and he made a mental note to fix that tomorrow. Reaching one hand down, he grasped the kitten's abdomen and gently unhooked his claw from the wood.

"Shhh, it's okay, buddy," he spoke softly, trying to comfort the little guy as he freed him and lifted him out from under the porch. He held him against his chest and the kitten began mewing loudly. Evan pet him gently and then quickly scanned the rest of the area under the porch with his phone's light for any more stowaways. Finding no one, he headed back up to the house with the new friend shivering against him.

First things first, he found an old nail brush and combed the dirt and fleas out of the kitten's fur in the downstairs bathroom. With a soft, warm wet wipe, he cleaned him up and checked for any injuries. He seemed healthy, but skittish, for sure. Evan wrapped him in a warm blanket and brought him back up to the kitchen where he dug out a can of tuna and opened it.

The kitten chowed down on the tuna faster than he'd ever seen someone eat, and he smiled as he sat at the kitchen table and watched it devour the food on the floor by his feet.

"WE HAVE A KITTEN?" Tess ran into the kitchen screaming at top volume with her arms stretched wide. "LET ME KISS IT!"

"Tess!" Evan put his hand out and motioned for her to lower her volume. The kitten had run under the cabinets the moment she'd set foot on the tile out of sheer terror. "You can't be loud around little animals. It frightens them."

He got down on his hands and knees to find the kitten.

"Oh, no! Mr. Wallace, I'm so sorry I scared you!" Tess was whispering loudly now, almost in an exaggerated way.

"Who's Mr. Wallace?" Evan asked as he scooped the kitten out and cuddled him to his chest.

"My cat." Tess pointed to the kitten in his hands. "Mom said that one day we could have a cat and she'd name it Mr. Wallace."

A lump formed in Evan's throat as he suddenly recalled his late wife's college professor who'd been her mentor throughout a hard time in her life. He was a lovely old man who had four cats in a small townhouse in Chicago, and Layla had been distraught when he passed. She always said that she'd learned the most about life from him, and she'd told Evan more than once that he'd be well served by opening himself up to letting others in.

"Mr. Wallace, huh?" Evan placed the cat back in front of the tuna and encouraged Tess to slowly introduce herself to him with the tip of her fingers.

Mr. Wallace sniffed her warily for a moment, then rubbed his chin against her hand. She held in a squeal, but Evan could see it ready to burst out of her.

"Oh, Dad, please, we have to keep him," Tess said, now stroking the cat's back with one gentle finger. "Mom brought him for me. I know it."

"We'll have to check with your grandparents," Evan replied, even though he knew without a doubt that they'd give a resounding yes to anything that made Tess smile like this.

Admittedly, he was enjoying seeing it as well. Owning a pet hadn't been on his upcoming to-do list, but he couldn't deny that the poor thing had already wormed its way into his heart just as much as he clearly had into Tess's.

"We have to take him to the vet," Tess began, counting off things that she wanted done on her fingers. "Also, we need a cat bed, food, a water bowl, and some toys. Oh, and a litter box. But can we get the kind that cleans itself? Because... gross."

Evan laughed and shook his head. "We can get all that tomorrow, but you know, if we get a pet, then you're going to need to help take care of him. That means cleaning the litter box sometimes."

Tess wrinkled her nose, then looked back at Mr. Wallace who was now grooming himself in her lap. She shrugged. "All right. I'll do it. As long as we get to keep him."

"For tonight, however, he should stay in the bathroom in case he makes a mess before we buy everything he needs," Evan said, mostly thinking out loud.

"I'll get my sheets and blankets and make a bed!" Tess tucked the kitten against her chest and stood up. "I'll sleep in the bathroom with him."

"You want to sleep in the bathroom?" Evan raised his brows. "Tess, that's not going to be comfortable."

"Dad, he cannot sleep alone in there!" Tess's mouth fell open as if the idea was preposterous. "I'm going to keep him safe."

Evan thought about it for a moment and then shrugged. "All right. Let's get him and you set up in the bathroom. I'll bring a bowl of water, you grab your blankets."

Tess was already in the hall and headed upstairs with the cat cradled in her arms as Evan filled up a bowl with some water and picked up the plate that still had tuna on it. He passed his father in the hallway on his way up.

"We got a cat?" Antoni asked, half a smirk on his lips.

Evan grinned. "Surprise?"

Antoni shook his head, then nodded in the direction Tess had run off to. "Nice to see her so happy. I think we've got an old box in the shed and some wood shavings. I'll put together a makeshift litter box until we can go to the pet store."

He felt his heart swell in his chest at his father's kindness and support. "Thanks, Dad. That would be great."

By the time he got to the bathroom, Tess was sprawled out on the tile floor on a mound of blankets and the kitten was in front of her playing with a loose hair tie. Evan stopped at the door for a moment, just watching them, and something felt whole.

Maybe Layla did send them this cat. Maybe she was saying it was okay to move on, because she'd always be here. Maybe Mr. Wallace was the key to bringing their little family back together.

Chapter Nine

Rosie pried her eyes open once she felt the sun beating down on her face through the window by her bed. She groaned and rolled onto her side, but all that did was show her that it was already seven o'clock in the morning and she had precious little time before the twins would be bouncing in here and demanding breakfast. Normally on a Monday morning she'd be carting them off to school and heading straight to work, but since it was summer, they'd be tagging along with her for the day. It wasn't easy wrangling them, but far easier than calling in a favor with someone, asking a friend to watch them.

No. Never. She'd just have to tolerate them running around the store.

She grabbed her cell phone off the nightstand and scrolled through social media briefly—a habit she knew she should break, but she couldn't help herself from enjoying a little bit of Instagram before starting her day. She frowned at a photograph that her friend Amanda had posted that was simply a faraway view of the lake with the caption—*changes are coming.* Cryptic. She made a mental note to ask her about that later.

Opening her email, she found a new response from Clueless Dad in the top of her inbox. She'd gotten an email from him to her Miss Mommy column not too long ago, and admittedly, she was a bit excited to see that he had responded. She wasn't sure why his message had stood out from the dozens that she got each week, but something about his felt very real and genuine.

Also, knowing he was a single dad didn't hurt matters. Good to keep her finger on the vein of the single-parent market around this area. You know, for research.

She opened his email reply and read it over quickly. A warmth crept onto her cheeks when he called her thoughtful, and she couldn't help but laugh at herself for reacting so much to this complete stranger. The image of her and this mystery man sharing similar struggles of raising kids alone over a glass of wine down at the Olive or Twist bar off of Main Street made her stomach do flip-flops, and she felt silly and excited at the same time.

Rosie hit reply and began typing up a message to Clueless Dad about leave-in conditioner and detangling spray, but she only got about halfway through before her own little bed-head daughter came waltzing into the room.

"Mom, I'm going to make waffles for breakfast," Becca announced as she twirled around and dropped herself, back first, onto the comforter. The blanket puffed up around her and then settled back down on the mattress.

"You're going to make waffles?" Rosie repeated her daughter's claim as if she hadn't heard her right the first time.

"Yes. I'm going to make them for you, Zander, and me for breakfast." Becca sat back up. "I'm old enough now."

Rosie was normally the cook, but she was more than willing to give herself the day off if her daughter insisted. "Well, go ahead. I just bought some new chocolate chips. They're in the pantry."

"I know," she replied, pushing off the bed. "Zander already ate a handful."

Rosie groaned and rubbed a hand over her face as she watched her daughter skip out of the room. Her son was growing up fast, and no matter how much she fed him, he seemed to be a bottomless pit. Thank God the kid was the most active little person she'd ever met, so it wasn't something she had to worry about much.

She took her time getting up and dressed for the day, combing through her modest closet for something cute to wear today. Normally, she didn't put more than a second's thought into what she wore to work, but for some reason, she found herself glancing through her small collection of sundresses.

Rosie pulled out a black sundress that had bright yellow sunflowers splashed across it and held it up in front of her body in the mirror. Forcing herself not to second guess her decision, she quickly changed into the dress and pulled on a pair of strappy heels to finish the look. As she was buckling the side of her heel, a loud banging noise came from the kitchen and she heard the twins begin fighting.

She sighed and ran her fingers through her hair as she walked out of her bedroom ready to start her actual duties as mom and house manager.

"Why are you guys fighting?" she called out. "It's time to go! Finish your waffles and let's get in the car."

"Do we have to go to work with you today?" Becca asked as she rounded the corner with a waffle in one hand that she was biting into like a piece of toast. "I want to stay home."

"We're going into the bookstore together, then Marvel will pick you guys up and take you fishing the rest of the afternoon," Rosie reminded them. "She had a doctor appointment this morning so she couldn't come earlier."

"Fishing!" Zander jumped up from the stool he was sitting on, grabbed three waffles off his plate, and shoved two in his mouth at once. He then grabbed his backpack and swung it over his shoulder as he headed toward the front door. He called back to his sister in a garbled voice, "Come on, Becca!"

Fifteen minutes later, Rosie was pulling into her usual parking spot next to Fact or Fiction Bookstore. The storefront was dark, and she wondered if Davon was running late to open. The kids piled out of the car, both of their noses stuck in a book, and followed her as she unlocked the front door and began throwing on the lights.

The bookstore was homey and comfortable, and as all the lights began to illuminate the shelves, she found herself feeling more at home than she had felt…at home. There was something about being around a stack of books, that smell of paper, the softness of a reading nook…it felt like part of her.

"Sorry I'm late!" Davon announced as he came in through the front door behind her in a whirl. He looked like he hadn't slept at all, but the grin on his face was undeniable.

Rosie lifted one brow as she assessed her friend and employee. "You've got a story to tell."

His grin widened and he glanced at the twins—neither of whom were paying attention.

"Kids, can you guys go turn on the lights in the back office?" she requested, giving them an excuse to walk away so she could hear Davon's new gossip. They walked off without much of a word, still reading their books.

"Okay, so, he slept over last night." Davon's voice was hushed as he pushed his bag into the cubby under the register and took off his coat. "And…oh. My. God. Rosie!"

"What?" She laughed as she leaned her elbows on

the counter where she stood across from him. "Do you like him?"

"Like him?" Davon shook his head. "I am *in love*. That man did things…oh, I can't even say or I'll have to take a sick day."

Rosie chuckled and shook her head. "Well, I'm glad you're happy. You better tell him I said he has to treat you right, or he'll have to deal with me."

Davon rolled his eyes and clicked his tongue. "Please, like you could even scare a fly."

She shrugged defensively. "I'll have you know that I killed a spider last night all by myself."

"Oh, did you now?" He laughed. "What a daredevil."

The bell hanging over the front door chimed as someone pushed it open.

"Are you open?" Evan asked as he stuck his head in and looked around.

Rosie felt her stomach tighten at the sight of him so early in the morning. Somehow, he managed to look even sexier with his hair slightly askew and sleep lines still across his left cheek.

His daughter charged in a moment later with an eager smile. "Are Becca and Zander here?"

"They're in the back." Rosie pointed toward where the twins had just gone and Tess skipped after them. "Yes, Evan. We are open. You're here quite early though."

He pushed his hands into the front pockets of his jeans as he sidled up to the counter. "Yeah, Tess needs a new journal. It was her top priority today. Do you sell those?"

"Got a whole table of them over there," Davon replied for her, pointing to a nearby stand with an assortment of different blank journals for all ages and styles.

"Great." Evan headed toward the stand, but his gait was slower than normal. Almost as if he was looking for a reason to stick around the counter longer. Something about him seemed . . . jumpy? Nervous? She couldn't quite put her finger on what was going on.

"Journaling is great for kids," she added, unsure what else to say but knowing she wanted to ease the tension she was feeling from his procrastinating movements.

He turned back around to face her and quickly stepped closer. "That's what I thought. Very productive activity."

She shook her head with a small grin. "It doesn't have to always be about productivity, you know. Maybe it's just about expression."

Evan gestured to the book stacks. "That's what all these are, right? Expressions of something or someone."

Rosie hadn't thought of it that way before. "I suppose that's true. What books do you normally read?"

"When I get a chance, I like to stick to biographies, World War II history, and memoirs. And—occasionally—a spy thriller or mystery." He grinned at the last admission, almost as if he was embarrassed.

"Oh, I love mystery books! Have you ever read a cozy mystery?" Rosie walked over to a nearby shelf and grabbed one of her favorite paperbacks. She returned and handed it to him. "*To Kill a Mocking Girl* by Harper Kincaid. Five stars. Here, you can have this."

He put his hand out to take it but paused. "Cozy?"

"It's like the PG version of a mystery novel," she explained, knowing that that was probably the last thing he would have picked for himself to read. "No violence or gore or any of that. Just good old-fashioned suspense and crime solving in a small town with a colorful set of characters."

Evan lifted one brow as he looked at her, turning the book over in his hand to read the back. He was quiet for a moment as he read, then glanced back up at her. "There's a nun in this."

Rosie beamed. "It's a really great book."

He chuckled lightly but tucked the book under his arm. "Well, I guess I have to take your word for it, don't I? Besides, I lost at cornhole, so, I have to read this."

She gave him a gentle pat on his upper arm, trying to pretend that she hadn't felt how hard his bicep muscle was under his collared shirt. "Look at you—going outside your comfort zone. Well, my goodness, Evan Nowak, I'd dare say you're growing."

"Don't get used to it," he joked. He grabbed a couple of journals for Tess and then she checked him out at the counter—the black credit card he was using certainly didn't go unnoticed.

Whatever job he was doing in Chicago, he must be great at it, Rosie thought.

"Thanks, Rosie," Evan said before going to fetch Tess.

As he returned with all the kids in tow, Rosie's phone chimed. She glanced at her phone as she walked beside them. "Oh, shoot, Marvel had to cancel. She needs to make an emergency dentist appointment."

"If they can't go fishing, Dad, can Becca and Zander come with us to the adventure trail?" Tess was pushing up on her toes and rocking back and forth, the way she always did when excited. "I told them all about the fort in the trees!"

Rosie's twins were standing at a slight distance, but clearly listening for an answer. She looked between them and their new friend, knowing that she wouldn't be able to say no.

"Uh, I think you have to ask their mom," Evan told his daughter. "I mean, I don't mind. We're going to this adventure trail in the woods. Zip-lining, climbing around a ropes course in the trees...not the safest thing out there but it is fun, and great exercise."

Zander just heard the word zip-lining and nearly took off like a rocket toward the door. "Mom! We have to go! Please! Please!"

"Whoa! Hold on." Rosie grabbed him by the arm and kept him upright as she looked up at Evan. "Are you sure you don't mind? I have to stay here and work in the store."

He shrugged. "The more, the merrier."

"Yay!" Zander was already pushing the front door to the store open and the girls were inches behind him. "Bye, Mom!"

"Well, have fun," Rosie offered, grateful that they were getting out and doing something fun.

Evan held up his new cozy mystery book. "Oh, I will."

She grinned as she watched them leave. Despite her initial misgivings about the man, she couldn't deny that he was a great father. There was no doubt how much he loved Tess, and his willingness to take on the twins for the day for her was all the proof she needed.

"Smitten kitten." Davon leaned his elbows against the counter next to her where she stood watching the now-closed front door. "Looks like that daddy has gone from dreary to dreamy—"

"What?" Rosie's mouth fell open and she pushed back on her heels. "Quit it. Just doing customer service—got to reel them in, right?"

"Oh, you're reeling." Davon laughed and shook his head, and she caught her reflection in the mirror behind him. Her cheeks were stained crimson and her eyes looked like they were sparkling. Damn it. "I'd say you're full-on swooning over him, honey," Davon continued. "But don't worry. I won't say anything about your little crush."

She huffed and flipped her hair over her shoulder. "I don't have time for gossip. I've got work to do in the office."

"Just put a sock on the door if I shouldn't come in!" Davon called out after her.

Rosie rolled her eyes as she retreated to the office and sat down at her computer. There was no merit to Davon's claims, and she wasn't going to let him get in her head about it. Sure, Evan was…well, he was…improving…if she really admitted it. But that didn't matter. She wasn't interested in dating right now anyway.

Forty-five minutes later, Rosie had completed the invoices for the day and decided to put some time into her Miss Mommy column. She pulled up the handful of submissions she'd gotten since last week and began to read through them to find ones that she wanted to answer. She was halfway through a letter about potty training when her cell phone began vibrating in her pocket.

Rosie quickly pulled it out, initially worried something had happened at the adventure park with the twins. Nope, it was an unknown number calling from Detroit. She frowned as she considered whether to answer it or not. There was still a possibility it could be the kids trying to reach her on a pay phone, or maybe a police officer found them on the side of the road? Her mind started to race to worst-case scenarios and she quickly accepted the call.

"Hello?"

A man cleared his throat on the other end of the line. "Rosie Posie?"

She recoiled at the familiar voice and the nickname that only one person had ever called her. "What do you want, Billy?"

"Can't a baby daddy check in every once in a while on the one who got away?" He chuckled lightly, and she could picture him with a cigarette on the corner of his lips and a lighter rolling across the back of his knuckles as he fidgeted. At least, that's the way she remembered him when she thought back to the man who'd gotten her pregnant and then disappeared.

"It's been months of radio silence."

"I've got some news, Rosie Posie." He sighed then, and there was a sadness in the lilt of his voice. "My father passed away last week."

She didn't respond for a moment, memories of Big Earl coming to her mind. Billy had grown up without a mother, and he'd lived with his father at the time she'd known him. The man was kind and gentle, and it had always struck her as odd that someone so selfish could have come from a good man like Earl. "I'm sorry, Billy. Earl was...he was a good man."

"Yeah, he was," Billy agreed before clearing his throat again. "Listen, I've been thinking that it's time I met the twins. I know you've been sending Earl photos of them all these years, and man, did he love seeing them grow up. I don't want to let him down, you know? I should have a connection with my children. It's only right."

Rosie furrowed her brow. "Billy, you've always known where we've been and I've never stopped you from seeing the twins. You're the one who has been missing in action for almost a decade."

"You don't have to be petty, Rosie baby," he replied, and

she seethed slightly at his words. "I know I've made some shit decisions in the past. But I'm not the same man I was back then. I just lost my father. I *am* a father. I'd like to see my children."

"I have to think about this," she finally responded. "Give me your number and I'll talk to the kids. If they're open to it, then I'll let you know."

"That's all I ask, Rosie," he responded, then gave her his phone number and the address where he was staying.

She hung up the phone and immediately placed her head down on her desk. She'd guessed that this day might come eventually, but after so long, she'd just let him fade to the background of her mind. She didn't need him. She'd managed everything alone. She was an island unto herself. But he was still their father.

Rosie sighed. This was going to be an impossible decision.

Chapter Ten

Evan wasn't sure how he'd been roped in to becoming the town summer babysitter, but somehow, he'd spent the last three days as the chaperone for the Dean twins and his daughter as the kids gallivanted all around town together. The first day had been zip-lining, which had gone relatively well until the end when Zander got a bad case of motion sickness and puked on the instructor. The next day had been spent on the lake fishing and swimming while he was on lifeguard duty, and today the kids had spent the day playing board games on the back deck. Despite all of that, he *still* had found himself agreeing to hosting a sleepover tonight for all of the kids in his parents' basement.

Not that he really minded, to be honest. He'd taken the week off of work after Tess's blowup last weekend, when he'd realized it was time to make a change. He'd started doing some internet research on parenting sites and now had a piece of paper folded into his wallet. Written on it were parenting mantras he needed to reflect on:

It's not meant to be easy.
Tess and I are exactly where we need to be.
My child will remember most the time I spent with her.

He was starting to see that he needed to let go of his academic ambitions for her for the summer and instead focus on ensuring that she had time for fun. She deserved it.

Maybe they both did.

Rosie was working at the bookstore, so he didn't mind letting the twins tag along since it made Tess so happy. In fact, he was growing a bit fond of the rambunctious duo and the way they brought out Tess's playfulness.

His phone vibrated in his hand and he looked down from watching the kids playing on a makeshift hopscotch course in the driveway. Rosie's name lit up his screen with a new text message.

Are they still doing okay? I can come get them if it's too much.

He smiled lightly but felt silly for doing so. Instead, he cleared his throat and responded quickly. Enjoy your night off. The kids are fine.

Thanks! Her reply was fast and he tried to think of something else to say to keep the conversation going but came up short.

"Dad, are the burgers ready?" Tess came flying toward him as she ran barefoot through the grass with a huge smile on her face. "I just showed them the cat! Now we're hungry!"

Evan lifted the lid of the grill and checked on the progress of their food. "Looks pretty close to it. Why don't you guys all go inside and wash your hands, grab some plates, and then meet me out here?"

"Wash hands! Food's ready!" Tess yelled to the twins who were still on the hopscotch course.

They chased after her into the house as Evan made quick work of turning over the vegetable kabobs he had lying next to the burgers. He threw a few slices of cheese on the patties and broke apart the hamburger buns. Five minutes later, all the children had plates piled high with burgers and vegetables and were crowded around the outdoor patio table together.

Evan took a seat at the far end and dug into his burger as he listened to the kids trade stories.

"You have bunk beds?" Tess's eyes nearly bugged out of her head at Becca's admission. "I've always wanted bunk beds! Dad, can I get a bunk bed?"

He frowned. "Who'd sleep in the second bed?"

"Friends! Becca, Zander! Visitors, Dad!" Tess made it seem like it was obvious, and to her it surely was. "They can come visit us in Chicago. Or we can stay here!"

"Yeah!" Zander nodded his head. "You guys should stay here. Heart Lake Elementary is really fun. I can show you around to everyone."

Evan chuckled but didn't intervene. He scarfed down the rest of his burger as the kids fantasized about going to school together. The twins told stories of their life at home and Evan couldn't help but find himself leaning in a little to hear what life was like for Rosie Dean behind the scenes. If the kids could be believed, it was anything goes over at the Dean house, and humor and fun were top priority for them. He saw the value in that to some extent—he knew Layla certainly would have—but he wondered about their grades and discipline.

"Your mom sounds so cool," Tess admitted. "My mom died."

The way she just bluntly laid out the facts like it was the most normal thing in the world caused Evan to nearly choke on the pepper he was trying to swallow.

"My mom told us that," Becca confirmed, her mouth full of chewed ground beef. "Our dad isn't around."

"It's like opposites," Tess commented, pointing at the twins. "You guys need a dad and I need a mom."

Evan cleared his throat and quickly tried to scrounge up something to change the topic. He could see where their minds were going and he wasn't about to be Parent Trapped into anything. "Did you guys hear the story of the lock-picking nun?"

"A nun?" Tess's head turned to her father, and the twins clearly had their interest piqued.

He nodded, then added a mysterious lilt to his tone. "Yep. Her cousin was accused of . . . *murder*."

The kids gasped, and he knew he had them hooked on the story from the cozy mystery that Rosie had given him a few days ago. Not that he'd finished reading it or would admit to even having started it.

Evan widened his eyes and spread his hands out as he spoke. "Yes, *murder*. The nun has to help her cousin clear her name and in doing so . . . they find the real killer."

"Who was it?" Zander took a sip of the cola he'd been drinking. "I bet it's the boyfriend. It's always the boyfriend. Was there a boyfriend?"

He laughed at the kid's assumption and stood up to grab the book from the kitchen counter inside. "Well, I guess I could tell you the whole story, but I think I'd need a little help."

"Ooh, a story!" Tess clapped her hands and lifted her feet onto the chair in front of her, tucking her knees to her chest. "Can you read it to us?"

Evan nodded and took his seat again as he opened to the first page and began reading, "Quinn Caine may have traveled all over the world . . ."

He kept reading, and the story had the children enthralled—hell, he was, too. By the time he took a deep breath and looked up, he realized that it was getting dark outside and the sun was almost completely down. "Whoa, guys. It's getting late."

"But we were just getting to a good part!" Zander stood up from his chair and yawned, despite his desire to keep reading.

"How about we read more over breakfast tomorrow?" he suggested. "Plus, if we go inside now, you guys can spend a little more time playing with Mr. Wallace before bed."

"Let's do it!" Tess shot up out of her chair.

"I want a cat now." Becca was on her feet and following Tess inside along with Zander. "I actually think I want six."

Uh-oh. That might not go down so well with Rosie. Evan realized he was chuckling as he watched the kids crowd around the fluffy cat bed he'd been goaded into. Once it looked like they were going to be gentle, he left them to play and he headed down to the basement to grab the sleeping bags out of storage, along with some pillows and blankets. The basement was large and mostly empty, but carpeted and warm. He'd set up a projector to play movies on the wall and the kids had chosen a film called *Raya and the Last Dragon*. Once everything was set up for the kids to watch a movie and fall asleep, he headed back upstairs to find Zander holding Mr. Wallace and giving him kisses on his head.

Tess was telling her friends about her new duties as a cat owner and regaling them with a dramatic story about cleaning the litter box with three pairs of gloves. He didn't burst her bubble and tell them that she'd yet to actually clean the box once, but he laughed along with her story anyway.

Hell, it actually felt like, for once, he was doing everything right. This whole parenting thing seemed . . . smoother? Maybe that was because he'd taken the time off of work, or maybe it's because he'd taken columnist Miss Mommy's advice and was trying to be present and relate to his daughter. He'd surprised himself to see he actually really related to the twins as well. In fact, he got a huge kick out of them both. They were silly and fun, and both were beyond fearless in a way that he couldn't remember from his own childhood.

After he'd helped them get settled into their sleeping bags to watch the movie—Mr. Wallace happily on Tess's lap, of course—Evan retired upstairs to his makeshift office to catch up on emails he'd missed throughout the day. Thankfully, his out-of-office reply had redirected most of his work requests, but he quickly scanned through the rest and responded to what he could. He typed up a fast email to his boss to let him know that he'd be working irregular hours next week. He was still going to get his work done, but he wasn't going to be a nine-to-five stickler like he'd been in the past. He wanted to bend the rules—not that there were really set hours in his job. It was more so that, as long as the work got done by deadlines, they didn't care how.

And he always got his work done.

But next week, he wanted to spend more time with Tess during the day and really dig into being a present father. As soon as he hit send, he saw a new email pop up in his inbox from Miss Mommy. He'd forgotten that he'd sent her a response asking her about detangling Tess's hair but found himself excited to read her response. She'd sent him a list of products to purchase that could help and told him to be patient and focus on bigger things than how his daughter wanted to wear her hair. He laughed as he felt a lightness enter his chest. He noticed that the icon next to her email was lit up showing that she was online and available for direct chatting. He hesitated a moment and then clicked the chat button and typed in a quick thank-you message.

Thank you, Miss Mommy. I actually had quite a few parenting wins today, and I'm sure you're partially to thank.

A little notice came up to say that she was typing on the other end. Just partially?

Evan grinned, not having expected her to write back so promptly. Maybe more than partially.

I'm glad to help. Us single parents have to stick together!

Miss Mommy was single? Evan found that piece of information intriguing. Not that he knew much about Miss Mommy except what she wrote in her column to other parents, but he hadn't expected a single parent, like himself, to have so many answers that he struggled to find.

He decided to go with some light banter instead. It's a challenge, right? I mean, how do they expect us to date when we're chasing after a child?

Haha, we don't! Maybe when they turn eighteen, she responded quickly.

Finally, someone who was reminding him that he deserved happiness. After losing Layla, it had been the last thing he'd wanted to do. About two years after her death, he'd had a brief, physical-only fling with one of Tess's teachers, but that had fizzled out faster than it started. He hadn't been able to give the woman the commitment she wanted because he just felt so numb, so unable to open himself up to her. He kept thinking about Layla.

A few more years later, he was thinking that maybe it was time to try again. Slowly, and at his own pace. If—and only if—it felt right.

Well, in the meantime, I've got a ton of frozen cookie dough and I'll bake that to keep me warm at night, he joked.

Although, it wasn't really a joke because he was famous in his family for his chocolate chip cookies. So much so, in fact, that he always kept extra dough in the freezer for his mother when she wanted a fresh batch.

Miss Mommy responded quickly. You'll have to send me your recipe. I've been meaning to pick up a new hobby.

I can't tell you all my secrets, he wrote back. Maybe I'll make them for you one day and you can guess the secret ingredient.

Her icon appeared that she was typing and then disappeared. He frowned, wondering if he'd overstepped in his last comment about meeting her. Was it too flirty? Too forward? Evan groaned as he realized that he should absolutely not consider dating anytime soon because his flirting game clearly left a lot to be desired.

Maybe one day, Clueless Dad.

Her final message came through before she logged off and her icon showed as being offline.

Maybe his flirting game wasn't as bad as he thought.

Evan glanced at the clock and realized that the kids' movie should be almost done at this point. He headed downstairs to check on them and, sure enough, the ending credits were rolling across the screen and all three kids were snoring in their sleeping bags. He turned off the projector and smiled as he looked at them all in a line, puffs of hair sticking out of the top of little human burritos. Zander was on the end closest to him, and there was no mistaking his mother in his face. He had her nose and her long eyelashes.

Not that Evan had noticed Rosie's eyelashes.

A thumping began pounding louder in his chest and he felt a serious tug to reach out to Rosie again. Maybe just an update. He snapped a quick picture of the kids all sleeping in a line and texted it to Rosie to let them know that they were all safe and sound.

She responded instantly, Oh, thank goodness! No trouble?

Perfectly behaved, he wrote back. Hope you enjoyed your night off.

A picture loaded on his screen and he realized that it was from Rosie. The image was of painted red toenails pressed against the side of a bathtub full of bubbles. A glass of red wine was held out in front of the camera, and he could just barely make out her reflection in the silver tub faucet. Not clearly enough to tell what he was looking at, but he knew it was her. In a bath. She was sending him a picture while she was naked... and drinking.

He felt a stirring that seemed entirely out of place, and yet, not entirely unwanted.

Oh, I'm having the time of my life, was her caption on the photo.

Looks like a good time, he wrote back, even though he wanted to say a lot more. Hell, he wanted to say that a glass of wine and a warm bath sounded pretty damn good, and even better if it was with a beautiful woman. But Evan Nowak didn't say things like that. Evan Nowak wasn't interested in dating or meeting any other woman.

At least, that's what he was trying to remind himself.

Chapter Eleven

For her third Books and Cookies event, Rosie was thrilled to see how well the town had embraced what was turning into a regular Saturday festivity. The store was already so crowded that she'd had to pull out extra chairs from storage. She'd even convinced a local chef to come sign one of her newest cookbooks, and if the store's Instagram was any indication, people were literally ready to eat up the new offering.

What she hadn't planned for, however, was Marvel backing out at the last minute with her cookies for the event. Not that she could blame her, since Marvel had twisted her ankle at her clay studio the other day and was using crutches for a few weeks as she recovered. Rosie had insisted that she'd handle the cookies and Marvel should just rest and heal. Which she certainly meant, but when she'd pulled the cookies she'd made out of the oven this morning and realized that they had somehow flattened into rock-hard flying saucers, she felt defeated.

Why were cookies her own personal Waterloo?

Thankfully Evan would be here any minute to drop off the twins—apparently the sleepover had been a huge hit and the kids had had the best time—and she begged him to pick up some cookies at the grocery store on his way over. Not exactly the homemade, kitschy vibe that she'd been aiming for, but, hey, she had to start somewhere.

The bell over the front door rang and Rosie turned to see Zander pushing through. He was holding a large Tupperware bin that he could barely see over the top of.

"Mom, I've got the cookies!" Zander teetered to the side and almost toppled over, but Becca grabbed his arm and righted him. "Where should they go?"

"Ah, thanks, kiddo!" Rosie scooped the box up from him and carried it over to the small banquet table she'd set up to serve the food and drinks. She opened the bin and inspected the cookies inside to lay them out on a platter, but...these were not cookies from a grocery store. "Did you guys make these?"

"I did." Evan's voice caught her off guard, and she looked up to see him standing next to her with a second Tupperware container full of cookies. "You said you needed them for the event."

"I...I thought you were going to buy them at the grocery store," she stumbled over her words as the scent of warm cookies hit her. If those tasted as good as they smelled...

"Eh, I already had some cookie dough in the freezer ready to go." He shrugged as if it were nothing, but the man had baked at least three dozen cookies for her at the last minute.

"I don't know what to say other than thank you, Evan," she replied honestly, carefully arranging the cookies on a tray. "That was incredible of you to do that. Really, truly kind."

He grabbed a cookie off the tray and snuck a bite. "You can make it up to me after. How about lunch? Your treat."

"You want to get lunch?" She nearly choked on her tongue as the words tumbled out of her mouth. Was Evan Nowak asking her out on a *date*? "Like a...you mean like a—"

"Like a meal?" He frowned, his brows furrowed. "The kids have to eat. I'm sure they would love grabbing something from Dickie's Deli and eating down at the lakeside with us. But if you're busy..."

"Oh!" She let out a big sigh...but it wasn't of relief. Or was it? She wasn't sure, and she didn't have time to figure it out right now. "You meant all of us have lunch together. Yeah, we can certainly do that. Actually, my friend Amanda will probably come with us if that's okay. She's bringing her goddaughter to this event."

"The more, the merrier," he repeated, before walking away from the table as he left her to finish placing everything the way she wanted.

Rosie quickly unpacked the cookies and arranged them, mentally kicking herself the entire time for being so silly to think that Evan was actually asking her out on a date. What if he had? Would she have said yes? The thought seemed stuck in the front of her brain and wouldn't let go.

"Hey, Rosie!" Amanda pulled her out of her thought spiral as the leggy brunette pushed a young girl toward her. "You remember Lizzie, right?"

"Of course!" Rosie greeted the girl with a hug. This wasn't the little girl she remembered when Amanda had been taking care of her last summer. Lizzie was a full-blown teenager now, and the black clothes and thick black eyeliner told Rosie that Amanda might be having a hard time. "You've certainly gotten big, Lizzie. How old are you now?"

"Thirteen." Lizzie's mouth barely opened when she spoke and she kept her eyes down as she picked at the skin on the edge of her cuticles—her nails, of course, were painted black as well.

"Ah, thirteen. That's a big year. I remember that age, and it was...well, puberty is rough." Rosie bit her lip to keep from continuing her babbling. "Sorry. I mean, I'm sure it's fine. You've probably already started your period, right?"

Christ, why couldn't she stop talking? If this is what she had to look forward to when Becca became a teenager, she needed some practice. Actually, a lot of practice.

"Gross." Lizzie rolled her eyes and then glanced toward the back of the store. "I'm going to go find a book. Got any thrillers?"

"Oh, sure." Rosie pointed to a section toward the left. "Check out those shelves. I'm sure you'll find something that will suck you right in!"

Lizzie walked away and Amanda and Rosie exchanged a glance.

"Wow..." Rosie shook her head. "She's...different than last year."

"Tell me about it," Amanda let out a low moan. "Were we like that when we were teenagers?"

"If you listen to Tanner, he'd say we were worse," Rosie joked. "But then he always was the good one."

Amanda shook her head. "Yeah, you're probably right. It's just a phase, and anyway, I take her home to her mom's at the end of next week."

"Want to join us for lunch on the lake? We're going to pick up some sandwiches from Dickie's for us and the kids," Rosie offered as she sorted a stack of books that needed to be returned to the shelves.

Her friend's eyes narrowed. "Who's *we*?"

She could feel her cheeks heating, but she hoped that they didn't turn crimson and give her away. "Evan Nowak and his daughter. The twins have become good friends with her."

"Just the twins?" Amanda wasn't buying it. "Or is there something happening with Evan?"

"Of course not!" Rosie assured her friend, but she realized too late that her voice had gone very high-pitched. Not believable at all.

"Uh-huh." Amanda grinned like she'd just caught her in a lie. "Yeah, I'd love to be the third wheel for lunch."

Rosie rolled her eyes. "There are no wheels. First, second, or third. It's just lunch. For the kids."

Amanda nodded her head a little too emphatically. "Sure, sure. I'll come find you after the event and then we can head out."

She tried to ignore her friend's insinuation by throwing herself into the Books and Cookies event. Luckily, that wasn't too hard. People were storming the shelves and Davon needed her help at the cash register once the line started wrapping around the store. By the time she was ready for a lunch break, she'd already sold more in one day than she had all week, and all of the cookies had been gobbled up. If she was able to keep up this pace, she wouldn't have to reduce Davon's hours at all. Hell, she might have to hire more help!

"I finished that book, you know," Evan told her as they met up on the sidewalk in front of Fact or Fiction. The kids were a few yards ahead, walking together toward the deli, involved in an animated conversation about the book he was mentioning. "And I read it to the kids, but we didn't get through all of it. They're probably going to want to know how it ends—not that it wasn't obvious. I figured it out right away."

Rosie lifted her brows. "Really? Well, I'm impressed you actually read it."

"Because I wouldn't know how to read?" he teased.

She laughed. "Because you are a book snob."

"What's a book snob?" He looked confused, pushing his hands in his pockets as they walked side by side.

Rosie sidestepped and pushed her shoulder against his arm, giving him a small nudge. "Someone who thinks reading has to be productive and educational only, not enjoyment and heart-filling."

"I mean, heart-filling is a bit of a stretch. Though I really did like the dog in that book." He grinned at her, returning to walking in a straight line after balancing himself from her nudge. "There's nothing wrong with education, though."

"There's nothing wrong with fun, either," she bantered back. "In fact, I think that's really something you could use more of in your own life."

"Me? How so?" He glanced sideways at her.

She shrugged. "Name the last thing you did just to have fun and enjoy the moment."

Evan was quiet for a moment, matching his voice when he finally spoke. "This is pretty fun right now."

Rosie swallowed hard, refusing to look at him because she was pretty sure her expression would give away the butterflies currently somersaulting in her stomach. "I . . ."

"Hey, Rosie! Hey, Evan!" Amanda walked out of the front door of Dickie's Deli sandwich shop with Lizzie in tow, just as they were approaching. "I ordered a bunch of sandwiches for everyone. They're prepping them now, and then I figured we could carpool to the lake?"

She was beyond thankful for the interruption. "Oh, thanks. Evan, do you remember Amanda Riverswood from high school?"

"How could I forget the girl who painted a mural of a goat on the side of the gym?" He reached a hand out and Amanda shook it. "That was the strangest senior prank ever."

Lizzie's brows raised as she looked up at Amanda, and Rosie could swear she actually saw a modicum of enjoyment on the teenager's face.

"It wasn't a senior prank," Amanda countered insistently. "It was design. That school was so drab. I was just spicing it up."

"Okay, but...why a goat?" Evan countered, crossing his arms over his chest.

Amanda ran her hand across her face and laughed out loud. "It was supposed to be the elementary school mascot."

"That mascot was a buck." Evan's brows scrunched together as if confused. "Not a goat."

She grimaced. "Well, no one told me bucks weren't goats."

Rosie laughed, having heard this story more than a few times but enjoying it just as much at each iteration. Hell, she'd been there right alongside Amanda as her lookout to make sure no teachers caught her. She had, of course, failed, since two teachers found them and they were both suspended for a week.

"Maybe we were more of a handful back then than we thought," Rosie teased.

Amanda gave her a knowing look. "It would appear so."

"Mom! Sandwiches are ready!" Zander walked out of the deli with a large brown bag in his arms. Becca was behind him with another bag, and Tess was holding a bunch of sodas, attempting to balance them all. "Can I ride with Aunt Amanda?"

Rosie looked at her friend for approval.

"Sure, kiddo! I can fit four more in my car. Why don't I just take the kids?" Amanda's smile said she knew exactly what she was trying to make happen. "I'm sure Evan can give your mom a ride, right?"

"Oh, sure." Evan nodded his head. "We can follow behind you."

"Take your time," she assured him as Rosie shot her friend death stares. "I'll probably take the scenic route anyway. Kids, come on!"

Rosie watched the kids pile into Amanda's crossover, leaving her and Evan standing alone on the sidewalk. She glanced up at him—had he always been this tall? The sun was behind him and she was nearly blinded just trying to make eye contact. "Uh, I guess we can take your car? Mine's back at the store."

"Sure. I'm parked on the street about a block back." He motioned behind them and turned to head in that direction.

She did the same, but then he stopped and moved around her until he was walking on the sidewalk between her and the street. "What was that for?" she asked.

He frowned. "What?"

Rosie pointed to him. "You just randomly circled me."

"I want to stand on this side of you," he replied, his tone making it sound like he didn't understand why she was asking the question. "That's all."

What the heck. "Okay . . . but why?"

"What if a car came up on the sidewalk? I'd want it to hit me first." He gestured to the very-empty street, then to where they were standing. "It's just the gentlemanly thing to do."

"It's the gentlemanly thing to die for me?" She laughed at this, but the truth is she was beyond flattered at the chivalry. How had no man ever done that for her before? Not that she'd been out with many to give them the opportunity, but still. She hadn't even known that to be a thing until this moment, and now she felt . . . taken care of, but in the best way.

Evan grinned. "I guess it's a little old-fashioned."

"No, I like it," she encouraged him. "I guess I'm not used to a lot of gentlemen around here."

"Are the Tinder matches not so great?" He was clearly joking, but he wasn't that far off.

She shook her head. "There's no online dating in a small town like this. Everyone knows each other, and you can only match with your brother so many times before you realize that organic is the only way."

"Holy shit." He shook his head, his smile widening. "Yeah, I guess Chicago has a few more options."

"I'm sure you take full advantage of that," she kidded, but the thought made the butterflies in her stomach drop like concrete:

"Not me," he assured her, and the butterflies slowly returned to life. "Ever since Layla…it's been hard. I tried to get out there once or twice—brief things, but nothing felt right. After having been so in love, being with someone who I was truly meant to be with…I don't know how I could go back to just casual flings after that."

She was quiet for a moment as they reached his car and both climbed inside and put on their seat belts. "I wish I knew what that felt like," she admitted as he pulled away from the curb. "I…I haven't really had that."

"Not even with their father?" he asked. "Sorry if that's too personal a question."

"It's fine." Rosie shook her head ruefully. "Billy has been out of the picture since before they were born. He was casual—too casual."

"I'm sorry." Evan's voice was softer. "They're really great kids, you know. You've done an incredible job with them."

"Thank you." The words almost got stuck in her throat

as a lump was quickly forming. Complimenting her kids was basically mommy porn. She made a mental note to include that in her next Miss Mommy column on dating and parenting.

Evan pulled the car into the parking lot by the small marina off the lake. Most of the town gathered in the grassy park area by the water to watch the boats or throw around a ball, and on a Saturday afternoon, it was always packed. She spotted Amanda right away thanks to a fully-dressed-in-black Lizzie next to her. Something seemed off though.

She frowned as she watched Amanda step in front of the twins, her hand back as if telling them to get behind her. Rosie's eyes traveled past her friend to the adult man who was walking toward her kids.

The butterflies turned back to concrete. Her hand flew to her mouth as she realized she might throw up. "Oh my God."

"What?" Evan turned to look at her, alarm in his expression. "Rosie, are you okay? You look suddenly very pale, like you just saw a ghost."

She swallowed hard, trying to nod her head. She couldn't get words out, but just wrenched her seat belt off and climbed out of the car as fast as her feet would move. Evan was calling out to her, but she couldn't think about him right now. She had to get to her children.

She had to get to them before their father did.

Chapter Twelve

Evan had been under the impression that things had been going well, but the moment Rosie hauled ass out of his car like it was on fire, he began to doubt that assessment. He called after her, but she was nearly running toward where the kids were gathered for a picnic. Everything looked normal? At least, he thought? Picking up the pace, he hurried after her only to see her run directly past all the kids and to a man walking their way.

He stopped at the kids' picnic blanket and looked at Amanda. "What's going on?"

"It's Billy." She grabbed his arm and pulled him away just enough to keep her voice unheard by the kids. "That's the twins' father."

Evan's gaze flew back to where Rosie was standing in a wide stance with her arms across her chest as she spoke to the tall man in leather pants and a frayed cut-off shirt. She looked ready for battle, and while he couldn't hear what they were saying, she was clearly keeping him away from the kids. Everything in him wanted to go over there and make sure she was okay—give that asshole a piece of his mind. Who just shows up randomly like this? But he knew that was the last thing Rosie would want. Instead, he turned his focus on the kids.

"Hey, what about we go get some ice cream to follow

those sandwiches?" he asked the kids. "There's a new place up the block from here, isn't there?"

"Crazy Cool Cow?" Zander jumped up, a bite of the sandwich he'd been eating visible in his mouth still. "Yes! I want cookie dough ice cream—two scoops!"

"You got it," Evan said with a chuckle. "Come on, everyone. Let's go."

Amanda shot him a grateful look and helped round up the kids to follow him. "I haven't been to Crazy Cool Cow yet! What should I get, Becca?"

The young girl seemed thoughtful, then smiled wide. "Butter pecan!"

Amanda wrinkled her nose. "Pass. What about mint chocolate chip?"

Becca shrugged. "Okay, but I'm getting butter pecan."

"I'm going to get double chocolate," Evan volunteered. "Or triple chocolate if they have it."

"Oh, me too!" Tess bounced on the balls of her feet as she walked along next to him. "Dad, can I have sprinkles, too?"

"Sure, kiddo," he agreed. "Sprinkles for everyone."

Fifteen minutes later, everyone was sitting on the picnic tables outside of the new ice cream shop eating their treats with only two complaints of brain freeze so far—both from Zander. Evan was entertaining the kids with the rest of the book he'd started reading to them last week, and they were all trying to make guesses of who the bad guy was. He spotted Rosie walking slowly toward them—no man with her—and he wanted to run to her. Something about her expression looked torn to pieces, and he had the strong urge to go hug her and tell her how incredible she was. But as he watched her approach, he saw her resolve steel as she pushed down everything she was feeling and replaced it with a big, determined smile.

"Hey, kiddos! Where's my ice cream?" she called out as she got closer.

Zander turned to his mother. "You can have some of mine! Oh, wait. I ate it all. I can get a second ice cream and you can have some of that!"

She ruffled his hair with her hand and laughed. "Sneaky way to get more ice cream there, Zander."

He grinned, and Evan gave Rosie a knowing smile.

She dodged his expression, her cheeks flaming red. Was she embarrassed by the whole scene? He hoped not. He'd like to think that they knew each other well enough at this point that she felt like she could talk to him about serious things.

That was a strange thought. Evan frowned to himself as he realized what he was saying. Since when was he interested in being anyone's confidant...or more? He pushed the thought away. That wasn't an option.

"Hey, we just rented a bunch of new movies on demand," Amanda volunteered a few minutes later. "Lizzie and I were going to do a movie marathon tonight—do you kids want to join?"

Tess immediately looked at him, a pleading expression in her eyes.

"Uh, what movies?" he asked, not wanting to say no, but also feeling like he was supposed to ask those kinds of questions, right?

Amanda named off a few animated films he'd never heard of.

"All great movies," Rosie assured him, probably sensing his reluctance after her insistence that he never did anything fun. "You should let Tess go. They'll have fun."

"The twins are going to go?" he asked.

Rosie nodded. "Why not?"

The twins cheered and immediately turned to Evan as everyone waited for his answer. He smiled and nodded. "Okay, have fun. I'll pick you up before bed."

"Thanks, Dad!" Tess threw herself at her father for a big bear hug.

As soon as the kids were done with their food, Amanda wrangled them all back into her car and they waved goodbye. Evan found himself standing alone on the sidewalk next to Rosie...again.

"Do you want a ride back to the store?" he asked, since they'd taken his car here.

She looked up at him, that same fragile determination he'd seen before had appeared again. "Do you want to go get a drink with me?"

"Uh...sure." He hadn't been expecting a proposal like that, but he wasn't about to turn down a stiff drink on a Saturday evening when he was child-free. "Where to?"

"Let's get out of town." She looked down the street, but her mind seemed miles away. "I want to be...somewhere else."

"Okay, uh, well, let's get in the car and see where we end up?" He rubbed his hand across the back of his neck, trying to scan his memory for bars in nearby towns. The only one he could come up with was Wish You Were Beer in Kalamazoo where he'd once used a fake ID to try his first beer when he was seventeen. "I know a hole-in-the-wall place that might be nice."

She was already walking toward his car with a confident stride. "Let's go there."

Twenty minutes later, after a quiet car ride that somehow didn't feel awkward but rather just peaceful, he pulled his car into the small lot behind the bar that had clearly not had a remodel in a few decades. He ushered her into the bar, finding them a high-top by the back wall that was out of the way from the crowd of college students gathered around the bar watching a sports game on the television mounted to the wall.

Rosie placed her cell phone down on the tabletop along with her purse. "Order me an amber ale. I have to go to the bathroom."

"Sure." He watched her walk off toward the restrooms before he ordered them two beers and a plate of french fries from the bar. Whatever she was going through, he figured fries might help.

When he sat back down at their table, Rosie's phone lit up and a new email notification appeared on the screen. He did a double take when he saw the email address was missmommy@heartlake.org. Leaning over a little closer, he tried to read the subject line, but everything was hidden except the address. He touched the screen, but it immediately asked for a passcode—which, of course, he didn't have.

He wasn't going to find out the answer unless he asked her. But why was Rosie emailing Miss Mommy? Or...the other possibility could be that Rosie *was* Miss Mommy. Evan chuckled and pushed the thought out of his mind. It was impossible. He didn't know Miss Mommy, but from talking with her, he knew she was warm and funny. Not that Rosie wasn't, but she had a bit more of a tough exterior. Plus, she was insanely busy with her bookstore and two kids; there was zero chance she had time for an extra side gig.

The bartender walked up with their drinks at the same moment Rosie returned from the bathroom.

"Thanks for ordering," she said as she sat down and took a sip of her beer. "Thanks for...everything, actually."

"It's no big deal," he assured her, though he wasn't really sure what she was thanking him for. "I also ordered some french fries."

Rosie grinned. "It's like you read my mind."

"Well, I figured it might have been a rough day." He shrugged then took a sip of his beer. "Carbs always make me feel better."

"A man after my own heart," she replied. "Carbs can fix anything. Well, almost anything. You probably have a lot of questions for me about earlier, huh?"

He shook his head. "No. I mean, Amanda filled me in a bit, but it's really none of my business. We all have a past, you know?"

"Yeah, that's true." She took another gulp of her beer. "But you've never made a mistake like I did, you know? Life happened to you, and it was terrible. Shitty. Horrible. I welcomed shitty into my life when I met Billy. It's hard not to feel like it's my fault, you know?"

Evan furrowed his brow. "What do you mean? What's your fault?"

"The twins not having a father around." She sighed, leaning forward on her elbows. "My best friend is pregnant right now, and they have the perfect family setup. My own parents—they gave my brother and me the perfect life growing up. Until my mother passed away, that is. Not that that was their choosing. I always wanted to give a life like that to my children one day, and yet that's the only thing I never provided—family."

He considered her words for a moment, then shook his head. "I don't agree with that. I mean, the sentiment is valid. I hear your feelings, and I appreciate you sharing that with me...but I've spent a lot of time getting to know your twins.

They're not lacking for anything, especially family. Hell, Heart Lake is like one giant family in all the best and worst ways. You're a big part of that."

Her cheeks darkened a bit and she looked down at her glass. "Yeah?"

"Not a doubt in my mind," he continued. "But, as a single dad, I can understand the feeling. All that negative self-talk around, 'Am I enough for her? Can I be both her dad and mom? Can I give her the life we once dreamed of for her, even if I'm the only one here now?' It's heavy. And it's real, but it's all a giant cognitive distortion. The fact is, statistically, all children need to be successful and happy is one caring adult in their life. That's me for Tess, and that's certainly you for the twins."

Rosie's brows had lifted and the corners of her lips quirked. "Cognitive distortion?"

It was Evan's turn to smile now, and he shook his head with a small chuckle. "Some leftover verbiage from therapy," he admitted. "After Layla died, I spent a couple of years in a shrink's office. I think it was the best thing I ever did for myself, but even more so, for Tess."

She was quiet for a moment, but then Rosie reached her hand across the table and placed it gently on top of his. "Thanks for sharing that with me. I think that's really brave that you went to talk to someone about everything you went through."

He shrugged, feeling tension in his gut at having opened up so much. Vulnerability wasn't his strong suit, and he wanted to douse the moment with humor. "Well, it certainly was...productive."

Rosie laughed so loudly that it was almost like a sharp bark. "Oh my God...yes. You are nothing if not productive."

He grinned, the tension easing. "You're not the first to notice. Layla used to tease me about that as well. She'd always tell me that I needed to let loose more and have fun. She and Tess would have full-blown dance parties in the kitchen and force me to join them…"

His voice trailed off and he felt a lump forming in his throat. He paused for a moment, trying to allow the memory to wash over him and his feelings to pass. Rosie squeezed his hand a little tighter.

"Sorry." He cleared his throat. "I'm not usually so… emotional."

"She was your wife," Rosie responded. "You're allowed to be emotional."

"I know. But it comes in waves, you know?" He let go of her hand to pick up his beer and take a long swallow. She pulled it back quickly and did the same, but for some reason he suddenly felt like he'd done the wrong thing. Like he'd hurt her feelings or pulled away. Like she'd been holding his hand as more than just a friend comforting her widowed high school acquaintance.

"What I mean is, I've moved on," he continued. "The loss of my wife, my daughter's mother… that's always going to hurt. Hell, it's always going to be the most painful thing I've experienced. But I'm learning that it doesn't have to limit the rest of my life. Layla wouldn't have wanted that. I don't want that—at least, I'm trying to not want that."

"That's great that you know that about yourself," Rosie said with a nod. She was fidgeting with her fingers as her hands rested on the table. "Billy doesn't feel… in the past. I wish he did, but when he showed up today… well, he wants to take the kids on vacation with him. Apparently, he owns a boat—or as he called it, a mini yacht—and wants to take them on a trip to get to know him. Hasn't paid his full share of child support their entire lives, but apparently his songwriting career has been able to buy him a boat and a home on Lake Superior."

"Wow." Evan shook his head. "I can't imagine how that must have felt to hear today."

"I already knew, actually." She swigged down the rest of her beer, then motioned to the bartender. "I'm going to need another one of these."

"Did you ever push for child support?" Evan wasn't trying to sound accusatory, but he couldn't imagine how expensive taking care of twins had been all by herself all these years. "He owes you. Hell, he owes his kids."

"He does," she agreed as the bartender dropped off another round of beers for the both of them. "But I never asked again after the first time he said no when I was still pregnant. To be honest, I didn't need it, and so it really felt more like I'd be fighting just to fight. The truth is, Billy's father sent us a check every month. I don't know how Billy came from that man, but his dad was a good, good man."

She paused for a moment, and it seemed like she was swallowing back tears.

"He sounds wonderful. I'm glad the twins have a good relationship with their grandfather," Evan said. "That's so important."

Rosie shook her head. "They never met him. He said he couldn't go around Billy like that, but that he wanted to know his grandchildren were well cared for. He's passed now, so, that door is closed forever."

Evan felt conflicted hearing that. It was so... practical. Something he was very used to being. And yet, it felt wrong. Having had a chance to know the twins and not taking it felt wrong. They were good kids...hell, great kids. He pitied the man for going to his grave without having gotten to know them.

He was a little surprised at how strong his emotions were on the topic. He'd just met this little family of three, and yet, he felt more connected than he'd realized. He pushed away the thought, attributing it to the fact that these were Tess's friends. It meant a lot to him to see her feeling so at home here in the place he'd grown up. He'd forgotten how much he'd missed it after moving down to Chicago.

"A vacation sounds like a big step," Evan finally answered, trying to sidestep his emotions and return to the original topic. "Maybe something smaller first, right? I get wanting to know his kids...but that seems like a lot in one go. I don't know if I could do it if I were you."

Rosie nodded emphatically. "Right? It's insane! I told him that maybe a supervised dinner was something we could work out—if the kids are open to it. I still have to talk to them about all of this. Christ, I don't even know how to broach that conversation."

"That's tough." Evan shook his head. "Maybe ask a therapist?"

She laughed. "Wow, they really converted you, huh?"

"Well, it worked!" Evan shrugged and then joined her in laughing at himself. "I mean, life's tough as a single parent. Sometimes we need to lean on someone else. Or pay them to let us lean on them."

"It's a bit easier said than done. Leaning is hard." *You could fall.* Rosie grinned and then finished her beer. "Come on. We should probably head out before they come looking for us."

Evan glanced down at his watch, realizing that several

hours had gone by, despite feeling like they'd just got there. He motioned to the bartender for the check. "Yeah, Tess needs to get home and finish her chores. That cat we adopted has become all my responsibility somehow."

"I heard about Mr. Wallace," she replied, shaking her head. "There's no way you were naive enough to think that you wouldn't be the one changing that litter box."

He handed his credit card to the bartender as she came by with the check. "A single father can dream."

"Thanks for paying," she commented a moment later as they were walking toward the front door.

Evan pushed the door open first and held it for her. "Not a problem. I...I really enjoyed myself."

Her pace slowed as she approached his car, allowing him to step around her and open the passenger door for her. "It was actually really nice to talk more, really get to know you."

His hand lingered on the doorframe as she looked up at him, and something about her gaze felt wanting. He felt his stomach flip-flop in his abdomen and he took a step closer to her without even thinking why. She didn't move back, and she seemed to be holding her breath. Evan wasn't sure if it was the two beers he'd had, or the intimacy they'd shared in talking about their lives, or maybe admitting for the first time out loud that he was ready to find love again. He was ready to meet someone new and add them to his life—not to replace his past, but to add to his future.

"Rosie..." His voice was low, gravelly, and barely above a whisper. One hand still on the car's open doorframe, he moved the other one to her upper arm and tugged her gently against him.

She leaned forward, flush against his chest as her hands rested on the front of his sweater. He hadn't realized she was so much shorter than him, but in this moment, looking down at her long lashes and the way her lips parted softly, made him feel on fire.

"Yes?" she breathed.

"I want to kiss you," he admitted, almost not believing the words he was saying. *Was that him? Did he really mean that?*

A resounding yes thumped in his chest.

Rosie didn't wait, and she pushed up on her toes until her lips were pressed against his. His grip on her arm tightened slightly, securing her against him as his mouth opened and they explored one another. It started gently, curiously, but a flame ignited between them faster than he knew how to tame. Her hands were in his hair, pulling his face closer to hers as he pushed her back up against the car. His hands found her hips and pulled her up until she had her legs wrapped around his waist. It was a seamless motion, like they'd been here before... and yet, it was all brand-new.

She groaned against his lips and he slid one hand up to the back of her neck, pulling her hair just hard enough to open her wider for him. He devoured her mouth, tasting the hops from the beer she'd recently consumed and wanting to taste so much more.

"Evan," her voice was a throaty panting sound. "Oh, God..."

His mind was flooded with emotion, but when she reached behind him and cupped his ass, he was pretty sure he would never look back. Until her cell phone began ringing loudly, vibrating between them.

"Oh!" Her eyes widened and they pulled apart just enough to allow some sense to return to the moment.

It was like they were both suddenly back in their bodies and realizing how far things had just progressed between them. He lowered her down until her feet were back on the ground and then stepped back, trying to readjust himself.

"I, uh, I should get that," she said, patting her pockets and pulling out her cell phone. She looked up at him sheepishly. "It could be the kids, you know?"

"Of course." He nodded, then pulled the door open again and motioned for her to get in the car. When she did, he closed it behind her and did his best to take as many deep breaths as possible as he walked around to the driver's-side door. He paused at his side for a moment, looking up at the sky and trying to remind himself that he was leaving to go back to Chicago at the end of the summer. He wasn't here for a fling, and Rosie certainly deserved more than that.

So, why did he feel sick to his stomach at the thought of her being with someone who could give her that? Someone that wasn't…him. He pushed the thoughts away and climbed into the driver's seat.

"That was the kids," she said. "They're ready to go home."

"Where to?" he replied, smiling nonchalantly like they hadn't just completely changed the dynamic of their relationship up against the side of his car.

Chapter Thirteen

A notification popped up on Rosie's phone, and she glanced down to see two new emails received in her Miss Mommy email account. Putting down the beach-read romance novel she was reading at the counter at work, she swiped across her screen to open the most recent one.

From: Clueless Dad

Thanks for the recommendation on those kid-friendly summer reads! I've actually been reading more myself as kind of a stress reliever. Ice cream has been a good stress reliever, too! What's your favorite ice cream flavor?

She finished reading the short message and began typing a reply before Davon interrupted. "Wow, who are you talking to that is making you smile like that?"

Rosie looked up at him, startled. "What?"

Davon lifted one brow, a grin on his face. "You're smiling like the dang Cheshire Cat over here. Who are you texting?"

"I'm not texting anyone," she insisted, a little too defensively. She hadn't even realized she'd come across so eager in her nonverbal cues, but admittedly, she had been going back and forth texting with Clueless Dad for over a week now. In fact, she was trying to work up the courage to ask him out to coffee... but that seemed like a big step. Hell, she still didn't even know his name. But she knew he loved to read, just like she did. He loved being a father, and he was a romantic soul, even though he hadn't said anything in that vein yet. She could just tell that there was a softness about him, and that felt really good to be on the receiving end of.

Her mind flitted to Evan and their heated exchange last night up against the side of his car. She could feel her cheeks burning at the memory, but that had certainly been a mistake—right? Clueless Dad was certainly more compatible for her than Evan, who was leaving town at the end of the summer anyway, and who didn't appreciate a good book, or letting go of the reigns of control in his life. She wasn't sure how they'd ended up tangled together in a mass of limbs, but she'd be lying if she didn't admit that her entire body pulsed when she thought of the way his mouth had devoured hers. If there was one good thing she could say about him, it was that the man was talented when it came to how he used his lips. She wouldn't be devastated to fall into that position with him again.

No. She needed to get it together and stop thinking with her... Rosie cleared her throat and looked back at Davon. "It's just a work email. Nothing scandalous."

"I've never smiled like that when you've emailed me, but okay," he joked as he wiped down the countertop with a soft cloth and some cleaning spray. "Don't you have to get going for your girls' night? I'm closing up today, so why are you still here?"

She glanced up at the large clock on the wall where every number was represented by a book—one of her favorite pieces of decor in the store. Sure enough, it was almost time for her to head home to meet Amanda and Nola for their weekly girls' night happy hour. They took turns rotating whose porch it was on every week, and today was her turn to host. It was never anything fancy—just a couple hours of chatting and relaxing with a glass of wine. Or in Nola's pregnant belly's case, a cup of iced tea or a cool seltzer.

"Good call," she replied. "I'm headed out. Can you handle inventory on the latest shipment in the back?"

"Already done," he assured her with a wave of his hand. "It's all logged in to the system and put on the shelves already."

Rosie put a hand on her chest and smiled at him, truly grateful to have his help around the store. She wouldn't be able to do it without him, and the idea that only a month ago she'd been about to let him go made her sick. Thankfully, the weekly Books and Cookies events had been revitalizing her customer base and she was sailing away from the pit of despair she'd been in last quarter. "You're the best, Davon."

Thirty minutes later, she was locked in a negotiation battle with the twins to get them down for bed while Amanda set up a charcuterie board in her kitchen for them. Nola was late, as usual, but they always gave her a pass now that she was pregnant. After several more rounds of back and forth, Rosie finally acquiesced to thirty minutes of quiet reading time in their beds before it was lights out.

"Christ, those kids drive a hard bargain," Rosie said to Amanda as she entered the kitchen after closing the door to the twins' bedroom. "Can you imagine what I'm in for when they hit puberty?"

Amanda grinned as she placed a piece of ham folded into the shape of a flower in the center of the wooden board already full of different types of cheeses and fruits. "If they're anything like Lizzie, you're going to need a lot more wine."

Rosie laughed and picked up the decanter filled with red wine she'd been letting breathe for a while. She took a sniff, enjoying the peppery aroma the red zinfandel was giving off. "Perry Mott gave me this bottle before he moved a few weeks ago. It smells heavenly."

"I'm going to miss seeing him around Heart Lake," Amanda admitted, talking about their old high school wood-shop teacher who'd been a staple in the Heart Lake social scene. He'd moved to Florida to be with his partner after he retired, and his absence was certainly going to be noticeable this coming winter when he wasn't here to throw his annual holiday party. "Okay, the charcuterie board is ready."

Amanda lifted the board with a smile of pride on her face and carried it out to the porch. Rosie followed her with two freshly poured glasses of wine. The front of her cabin was small and mostly faced the trees, but it was secluded and quiet and nice to sit on in the summer when the breeze was just right. She had a wooden swing and a rocking chair on one side of the porch and a long padded bench on the other.

"Ah." Amanda placed the board of snacks on the small round table by the swing and then took a glass from Rosie as she sat down in the rocking chair. "I'm glad to be off work next week."

"Still going to that retreat?" Rosie took a sip of her own wine as she eyed her friend. She leaned against the banister, not ready to sit down just yet. "What's it called again?"

"Designing Our Lives," Amanda replied, gesturing her hands over her head in the shape of a rainbow. "It's going to be five full days of immersive soul work for the designer within."

Rosie tried not to smile, since she knew her friend took her new age stuff very seriously. Still, it sounded a little out there for her taste. "Well, that sounds...fun."

Amanda shot her a look, one brow raised. "Please. I know you're making fun of me in your head right now."

"What?!" Rosie laughed. "Was it that obvious?"

Before Amanda could respond, a loud engine came up the driveway through the trees and she saw her brother's pickup truck pull to a stop. Tanner was behind the wheel, but he jumped out of the car quickly and circled around to open the door for Nola and help her step down.

She wobbled slightly on the dismount, trying to find her balance with her protruding belly, but then looked up and waved at the girls. "Hey, ladies!"

"Nola!" Amanda waved back.

"Hey, this is a girls-only wine night," Rosie declared loudly for her brother's benefit. "Go home, Tanner!"

He grinned at his sister and rolled his eyes. "Chill. I'm just the chauffeur today. I'll pick my girls back up in a couple hours."

Nola pushed up on her toes and planted a kiss on her husband's mouth, then rubbed her belly. "Say goodbye to Daddy!"

Rosie loved how happy they were, but sometimes new love was nauseating. She would see if they'd still be smiling when that baby was puking up on them at two o'clock in the morning.

"Is this what happens when you have kids?" Amanda asked, taking a larger gulp of her wine.

She shook her head. "I think that's just Nola."

"Don't be haters," Nola joked as she eased herself onto the swing on the porch. Tanner was already reversing down the driveway.

Rosie stepped back inside for a moment to get her a glass of iced tea before rejoining them. "I have a lot to update you all on."

"Is this about Billy?" Amanda immediately asked, leaning forward and resting her elbows on her knees. "From the park the other day?"

"Wait, what?" Nola's eyes widened as she took the glass of tea from her. "Billy, as in . . . the twins' father, Billy?"

She nodded. "One and the same. He contacted me awhile back saying he wants to meet the twins. His father passed away and I guess that has him reevaluating his life choices. Whatever that means."

"The man has hardly paid a dime in child support over the years, or even called to ask about them." Nola was shaking her head, clearly heated about the experience. "Are you going to let him see them?"

"I mean, I can't *not* let him. He is their father, and he still has rights." Rosie groaned then swigged down the rest of her glass of wine. "I'm going to need a refill for this story."

Amanda lifted the decanter and poured her another glass.

"So, he wants to take them on a trip on his yacht," Rosie began. "Which, obviously, I said no to."

"His yacht?" Amanda lifted her brows. "The audacity."

"I know," Rosie agreed. "But I said no. The twins aren't ready for that. Hell, I'm not ready for that. After some thought and discussion with other parents, I've decided that I'll tell Billy he can come here for a weekend and see them—supervised."

"A whole weekend here?" Nola glanced toward the house.

Rosie shook her head. "No, he can't stay *here* here. He can get a hotel or bed-and-breakfast or something. But if he wants to spend time with them that weekend, and the twins are open to it, I'm okay with a test drive."

"I'm happy to chaperone if you need someone," Amanda chimed in. "He won't get away with one goddamn thing on my watch."

She laughed at her friend's fierce loyalty. "Thank you. I might take you up on that. I will be there for the initial meeting, of course. But after that... it might be better to give them their own time with him without their mom hanging around. I'm worried they'll feel like they have to split their loyalty or something like that."

"That's fair," Nola agreed. "We can be impartial third parties."

"Well, I wouldn't call us fully impartial," Amanda joked. "I'd skewer his balls for kabobs in a second flat."

Rosie nearly spit up the wine she was swallowing. "Oh my God, Amanda. You're insane."

Amanda laughed. "But seriously, what about the movie in the park event next weekend? That might be a neutral meeting place—and the entire town is there. You know everyone will protect those twins within an inch of their lives."

She had no doubt that that was true, and it really wasn't a bad idea. Any first meeting definitely was going to need to be in a public setting. "You guys are both going to be there?"

"Absolutely," Nola replied. "Unless I go into labor or something."

Rosie grinned, but before she could shoot back a witty response to her friend, she heard rustling in the woods next to her house. Set far into the trees, she didn't get much traffic around except for joggers on the trail about a hundred feet west of her property line that led straight to the lake. A moment later, a figure in tight black jogging pants burst through the tree line and paused in her yard, as if he had no idea where he was.

"Evan?" Nola spotted him as soon as Rosie had and called out to him. "You out for a run?"

He spotted them on the porch and smiled sheepishly. She was pretty sure he was lost given the way he was looking around in surprise. Finally, he waved and walked toward them at a slower pace. "Hey, ladies."

"Did you get lost?" Rosie asked, trying to keep her eyes on his face despite the fact that the man wasn't wearing a shirt and his pants were oh-so tight. Jesus, did he have an eight-pack? She swallowed hard, reminding herself to reign it in.

Evan's cheeks darkened slightly. "Uh, I think I did. I was following a trail through the woods, but now . . . I'm here."

"If you miss the right turn by my property line, you end up straight in my yard," she replied, pointing back toward where the trail veered off in the other direction. "It's easy to miss."

He rubbed his hand across the back of his neck, then pulled a water bottle out from the runner's belt strap behind his back. He went to take a sip and then frowned. "Shit, I'm out of water. You mind if I fill up in your sink?"

"Sure." Rosie stood up, placing her wine glass down on the table next to the charcuterie board. "I'll show you to the kitchen."

Amanda cast her a sly smile, but she ignored her. Evan bounded up onto the porch, skipping several steps with his long legs as he followed her inside.

"The sink water is fine," Rosie said, pointing to the faucet but then walked over and opened the fridge. "But I also have filtered water in the fridge you're welcome to."

He stalked over to her with determined steps until he was right in front of her. "I'll take the filtered water, thanks."

She swallowed hard, acutely aware of the sheen of sweat across his bare chest and the musky smell of hard work and pheromones. She quickly turned her back to him, leaning down to lift out the jug of water while simultaneously trying to calm her breathing. "Here you go."

He took the jug from her and filled his water bottle slowly. When he finished, he handed it back to her and she returned it to the fridge. She fully expected him to walk away at that point, but he hadn't budged.

Evan leaned against the kitchen counter and took a swig from his water bottle. "Should we talk about last night?"

His voice had a scratchy, husky quality to it that made her skin stand on edge and her insides clench.

"Uh…" She wasn't sure how to answer him, because she hadn't figured out what the hell last night had been about for herself enough to explain it to him. "Well, I mean…I don't want you to think I'm expecting anything. It was just…we got caught up, you know? It was nothing. We can forget it." She was rambling at this point, but even in her nervousness, she hadn't missed the dark flash that crossed Evan's expression. "Oh, uh…what?"

He shook his head slowly, then placed his water bottle down on the countertop. "I don't want to forget it."

The words had barely left his mouth with enough time for her to process them when he stepped forward and closed the gap between them. Evan's hand slipped behind her to the base of her neck, nestling his fingers in the roots of her hair just taut enough to make her chin lift and her head tilt back at his firm tug.

His mouth covered hers and every bit of breath in her lungs seemed to dissipate. She wasn't even conscious of how her hands had found their way to his chest, and then his neck, and now she was cradling his face and pulling him closer to her as if they weren't already completely merged. Evan broke their kiss for a split second, long enough for them both to fill their lungs before diving in for more.

"Mom!" Zander's shout cut through the heated moment like a switch. "Mom, can you come tuck me in again?"

Rosie jumped back, untangling from Evan like he'd just scorched her. And in many ways, he had.

"Uh." She cleared her throat, trying to find the pieces of her mind scattered across the room. "Yes, yes. I'm coming, honey."

"I should get back to my run," Evan said softly, a husk still on the edge of his voice. "It'll be dark soon."

"Right," she agreed, nodding her head a little too adamantly. "Well, uh, good talk. Bye."

With that, she turned and headed down the hallway toward the twins' bedroom. *Good talk. Bye?* She wanted to rewind the last fifteen seconds and change everything about what she'd said, but instead she walked confidently into the kids' room and pretended like none of that had just happened.

She smiled at Zander and pulled back the covers on his bed as she heard the front door of her house close. "I can't believe you're still up. Was the book good?"

"The best!" Zander exclaimed, bouncing into bed with too much energy for this late at night. "Can I get the next book in the series tomorrow?"

"It's not out yet," Becca reminded her brother from where she was already tucked in with a faux-fur eye mask over her face. "Mom, can you *please* tell him to go to sleep?"

Rosie gave Zander a knowing smile and wiggled her brows. "Bedtime. Can't keep your sister up."

Zander pouted, but then giggled and curled into his pillow. The moment he shut his eyes, she could hear his soft snoring begin to settle in. Lucky child. She wished she could fall asleep like that, but there wasn't a doubt in her mind that she'd be up long into the night thinking about tonight's kitchen encounter.

Chapter Fourteen

"She's not here, you know."

Evan was startled by the voice suddenly to his left and turned to see Davon standing there with a stack of books in his arms. "What? I mean...who?"

"Who? Who?" Davon did a terrible owl impersonation. "Rosie. It's just me manning the shop today."

He glanced around the interior of Fact or Fiction as he turned the book that he'd just pulled off the shelf over in his hands. "I wasn't here to see Rosie. I just needed a new book. This one looked good."

"The Cupcake Killer Chronicles?" One of Davon's brows went up as he read off the title from the spine. "You don't seem like the typical cozy mystery reader."

"Aren't you not supposed to judge a book by its cover?" He could feel warmth flooding his cheeks but jutted out his chin defiantly. "It's a more recent interest," he admitted. "But I actually do enjoy them. They all have fun puzzles, but also a heartwarming cast of characters. Anyone would want to be friends with them, you know? That level of close-knit comfort must be nice to have."

"You mean like what you and everyone in this tiny town have?" Davon shook his head. "Come off it, man. You're all doe-eyed over my boss, and I don't blame you. Rosie's incredible. But just be prepared. Even if you can play the local card, everyone in Heart Lake will pick her side if you all go south."

"What?" Evan balked, trying to find a response.

Davon continued. "I know you're from here, too. But this town adopted Rosie when her ex walked out on her while she was pregnant with the twins. And after her mom died and her brother left for college? There's nothing this town wouldn't do to protect her."

"I don't plan on hurting her," Evan clarified, but his words were slower now. His brain felt like it was going a million miles an hour and he wasn't even sure how he'd stumbled into this conversation. He'd just been on his way back from grabbing a coffee when he saw the bookstore front and decided to grab the next book in the series he'd finished. He'd told Miss Mommy about the book this morn-ing and she'd urged him to get the next, so here he was. But now it felt like he'd stumbled into something bigger. "I mean, there's not anything happening between us anyway. I return to Chicago at the end of the summer, and I don't think either one of us is the *fling* type. I mean, I am not the fling type."

Davon shrugged and stacked the books he was holding carefully on the shelf. "Suit yourself, but don't say I didn't warn you."

"Thanks, man." Evan pushed the book back onto the shelf, deciding to come back later for it. "I've got to head out to meet up with a friend, but I'll be back to grab the book another time."

"See you, Romeo!" Davon called over his shoulder.

He made his way to the front of the store and pushed open the door, hearing the bell ringing above him to announce his departure. If he was being truthful, he had considered the possibility of running into Rosie when he'd walked in. Last night had been…surprising. The way her body had responded to his…hell, the way he'd taken charge and initiated things…it felt like a new chapter. It felt comfortable and right, and that wasn't something he'd felt since Layla.

His late wife's face crossed his mind so vividly that he had to stop in the middle of the sidewalk for fear he was going to run right into her memory. His chest felt tight, like it was hard to take in a full breath. He reached for the brick wall of the store next to him to steady himself, a dizzying feeling nearly pulling him sideways. *What the hell was happening?*

Evan slowed his heart rate with a few deep, calming breaths. Things around him began to stabilize as he reminded himself that these feelings were going to pass, but it had been since the dark days after Layla died that he'd had a panic attack. He'd struggled with anxiety in high school and then again in college when he'd felt pressured to get straight As and be good enough to stay on the university baseball team. It was actually Layla who'd insisted he go to the college counseling resource center for help, and he'd spent a year learning about coping skills, mindfulness, and breathing techniques to help him get through those darker moments. Even if he still could fall in the hole, he had tools to pull himself out.

His phone rang in his pocket, pulling him from his thoughts. He slipped it out and answered when he saw Tanner's name on the screen. "Hey, Tanner."

"You coming?" Tanner said from the other end of the line. "I've got a cage on hold for us at the community center."

"Almost there," Evan confirmed their plans to go hit

baseballs in the batting cage this afternoon. "I was just running a quick errand."

"Okay. I'm going to hit a few. See you soon."

When Tanner hung up, Evan got back into his car and took a few more deep breaths before turning his car down Main Street and toward the community center. He'd spent most of his high school years in that building practicing for college ball, and so when Tanner had invited him for some batting practice, he couldn't say no.

"There he is!" Tanner pointed the end of his bat toward Evan as he walked over to the batting cage his friend was in. "Grab a bat, Nowak."

He pulled on a rental helmet that smelled like a few too many people had worn it before him, then grabbed one of the bats leaning against the wall. They hit balls for a while, waging bets about who could hit them farther or aim for a certain spot on the far wall.

"You've still got that talent," Tanner admitted as they switched spots. "Have you thought about coaching any? I know Heart Lake would be happy to have you."

Evan shook his head. "Nah, I don't have time for that. Tess needs me, you know? Plus, I'm headed back to Chicago at the end of the summer."

"I'm surprised your parents haven't tried to convince you to move back yet," Tanner joked.

He grinned. "Oh, they have. My mother, especially. She's . . . she's got a lot going on with my dad, you know?"

Tanner nodded, aware of Antoni Nowak's Parkinson's diagnosis. "How's he doing with that?"

"Some days are better than others." Evan hit the next ball harder than the last. The thought of his father's health declining wasn't something he was ready for. The summer was nearly halfway over and he didn't feel ready to leave...but he had to. His life and job were in Chicago. Tess's life and friends were all in Chicago. It was his home with Layla, and it was his home away from...Heart Lake. Although, he felt less like running away from this small town than he once had. His dad had put a lot of pressure on him in high school and his mom had stood silently by his side. Evan had done a lot of work in therapy on forgiving them for that. His anxiety was certainly a direct reflection of their pushing, but his mother had apologized to him a few years back. They'd been mending their relationship ever since, which was why this summer trip was even possible in the first place.

"Well, you know Nola and I are happy to help anytime your parents need it," Tanner said as he switched places with him. "We're going to be lifers in this town."

Evan laughed, then teased his friend, "Your sister seems to be a confirmed resident, too. Something about your family... can't get away, huh?"

Tanner shrugged between pitches. "I keep telling her she could get a writing job at a paper. But you know Rosie. Stubborn to a fault. She's never going to give up on the bookstore even if it takes all of her time."

Evan frowned, trying to piece together the connections that Tanner was so nonchalantly dropping. "Wait...Rosie is a writer?"

His friend looked up at him. "She used to write for the school paper in high school. Some sort of gossip thing, remember?"

The recollection slammed into his consciousness. Pirate Parley had been the most popular column in their school paper back in the day—named after their mascot, a man dressed up like Blackbeard who went by the name of Maverick Mac. There wasn't a lot of sense behind it, but the school had loved it just as much as they loved the witty column by enigmatic Pirate Parley that answered burning gossip questions from other classmates. "Yes, Ms. Wilma was seen at the park holding hands with the science teacher," had been the type of articles run.

"Pirate Parley was Rosie?" Evan asked, unsure how he'd never pieced that together before now. Hell, no one had. The writer's name had been kept anonymous all these years, and when they were teenagers, they were more interested in the gossip than the truth. "Am I clueless or is that one of Heart Lake's best-kept secrets?"

Tanner dropped his bat after hitting a fast one. "I mean, I don't think people really care all that much. It's not like we're Hollywood tabloid material out here."

Evan chuckled lightly, but his mind was turning over faster than he could keep up. He thought back to the bar when he saw that Miss Mommy email notification on Rosie's phone. Was it possible? Miss Mommy was Rosie? Now that he had that thought stuck in his head, it was hard to unstick it, and it suddenly seemed all too clear to him.

If it was true…he knew who she was now, but Rosie had no idea that they'd been communicating back and forth all these weeks. And after last night…

Crash! Evan's foot caught the edge of a mound of dirt and landed directly on his face. He groaned and rolled to his back, finding himself staring up at Tanner.

"The hell, Nowak?" Tanner lifted one brow then reached down to help him up. "You all right?"

"Yeah," he assured his friend. "Just…you know, distracted for a minute there."

"Well perk up," Tanner continued, handing him his bat. "I want to beat you fair and square, not because you injure yourself."

He laughed and they played a few more rounds before calling it a day. When he arrived home, he walked into the living room to see Tess standing on the hearth in front of the fireplace holding a spatula to her mouth like a microphone. She was belting out lyrics from some recent pop song about crying on the bathroom floor after a breakup that she'd made Evan listen to way too many times. But none of that would have surprised him except for the fact that his father was holding a wooden spoon up to his mouth and repeating the lyrics after her—though not very well.

"What the heck is going on in here?" Evan asked, his hands on his hips as he watched the impromptu performance.

Tess waved at him but didn't stop singing. She did, however, turn the music up louder on the stereo. "Come on, Grandpa!"

Antoni moved his hips from side to side in a rickety manner that had Evan stepping a bit closer to him just in case he toppled over. "What's the chorus again?" Antoni asked his granddaughter.

She repeated a few lines to him and then they both belted it out together when the refrain ended.

Evan just shook his head and walked past them into the kitchen where his mother was trimming clippings from a small herb garden in little round white pots on the windowsill.

She looked up at him with a handful of parsley and smiled. "Didn't know your dad could still sing like that," she joked.

"He can't," he assured her with a laugh as he grabbed

a pitcher of iced tea from the fridge and poured himself a glass. "How long have they been going at it like that?"

"I think this is the grand finale. It's sweet seeing him like that again. I'm glad you both are here." His mom was watching them in the living room with a wistful look in her eyes, almost a mistiness. "It's nice seeing some life in this house again."

"Mom, don't sound so morbid," Evan countered, but the truth was that he understood what she meant. Ever since Layla had passed away, he felt like he'd just been . . . existing. Getting through, day-to-day, and trying to be a good father and make good choices—but none of that was really *enjoying* life. But watching his daughter teach Olivia Rodrigo songs to his father? That really felt like living.

Almost as much as he had felt alive when his arms had been around Rosie yesterday, or the way her lips had felt against his. He swallowed hard at the thought that he'd been missing all of this just as much as his mom had been, in her way.

Tess called him and his mother in to finish listening to their concert, and Evan had every intention of staying focused, but he found his mind continually wandering back over the conversations he'd had with Miss Mommy . . . and with Rosie. He wished she were here right now, because he knew she'd karaoke the hell out of this moment. She didn't seem the type to let a good dance-off pass without joining in—but was Miss Mommy? Rosie and Miss Mommy both seemed like such different people, and yet . . . it all seemed so clear to Evan that they were also one and the same. But should he ask her about it? Should he confront her and tell her who he is? Admit to being Clueless Dad?

Absolutely not. At least, not until he knew what he wanted out of all of this.

Rosie wasn't a fling, and despite their spontaneous physical dalliances as of late, he didn't want to treat her like one. He needed to figure out what he wanted, and he needed to figure it out fast. Because if there was one thing he did know, it was that he didn't want to hurt her.

Chapter Fifteen

Trapping the twins in a boat in the middle of the lake seemed like the best method for breaking the news to them that their long-lost father wanted to meet them. At least, that's what Rosie had convinced herself of when she'd come up with this plan. But now, as she sat with her fishing line cast out in front of her and the twins in the middle of Heart Lake in a tiny rowboat, all she wanted to do was dive in and swim back to shore and pretend none of this was happening.

"Mom, your line!" Zander pointed at the end of her fishing line that was now moving in the water near where his was cast. It pulled tight and she felt a tug against the grip she had on the rod. "Reel it in, Mom!"

Rosie quickly began pulling back the rod, but a quiet snapping sound filled the air as her line broke in two and disappeared under the water's surface. "It broke my line!"

"That must have been a big fish. Maybe it wasn't even a fish," Zander mused, peering over the edge of the boat into the water. "Hey, can lakes have mermaids, too?"

Becca rolled her eyes at her brother, even though Rosie knew she was just as into the mermaid-themed chapter books they were both reading right now. "*Nowhere* has mermaids, dummy. They're not real."

"No name calling," Rosie reminded her daughter. "And

I'm sure mermaids can exist wherever they choose. But, uh, listen, guys...I have to talk to you about something."

"Oh, man." Zander returned to his seat next to Becca and gave her a knowing look. "What did we do? Is this about the brownies? I didn't know they were for the store when I ate them."

Becca looked back at Rosie, ignoring her brother. "What's going on, Mom?"

"I know you guys have been curious over the years and have asked questions about your father..." Rosie felt like her tongue was drying up in her mouth as she spoke and was pretty sure she might just choke on it right then and there. She cleared her throat and tried to start again. "What I mean is, well, is that something you're still interested in?"

"Knowing who our dad is?" Becca frowned with skepticism, but Zander was leaning forward with wide eyes.

"Yes!" He practically shouted his response. "Can we meet him? Where is he? Is he coming for dinner?"

Becca shoved Zander hard and he had to rebalance himself so that he didn't fall off the boat entirely. "Shut up, idiot!"

"You're the idiot."

"I'm rubber, you're glue, whatever bounces off me sticks to—"

"Hey, hey!" Rosie put a hand between the two of them, separating them the best she could in a tiny rowboat with nowhere to go. "Guys, no fighting. Those were mean words."

Her daughter crossed her arms over her chest and looked irritated as hell. "I don't want him to come over for dinner. We don't even know him."

"No one is coming over for dinner," Rosie clarified, trying to calm the situation. This was quickly going off the rails, though she wasn't sure what other response she could have expected. "But your father...he'd like to get to know you both."

"Why?" Becca shot back.

Rosie paused, trying to figure out the best way to respond to that since she didn't really have the answer either. "Well, I think he has some regrets about the choices he's made. I think he's realizing how important family is."

"We already know how important family is," Becca replied. "And we're kids."

She nodded understandably. "That's fair. He is a bit behind the eight ball on that one. You guys are advanced for your age, you know that."

"Tess knows how important family is and she's the same age as us," Becca argued, not letting up for even a moment. "Why doesn't he know? He's a grown-up."

Zander put a hand on Becca's forearm and squeezed it. "Maybe we can ask him?"

Her tough expression faltered for a moment as she glanced at her twin brother. "He better have a good answer. I'm *going* to ask him."

"Good," Rosie replied, trying hard not to chew on the edge of her cuticles like she did when she was stressed. "I'm glad you're going to ask him. He said he's ready to answer your questions, whatever they might be."

Becca jutted her chin out defiantly and looked toward the shore. "Hey, look, it's Tess and Mr. Nowak."

Rosie followed her daughter's gaze to the dock jutting off the shore in front of the Nowaks' house. She hadn't realized that they'd drifted this far out to make it to his parents' house, but she was admittedly happy to see them. "Maybe we should go say hi?"

Zander was already waving and picking up one of the oars to begin rowing to shore, but since she hadn't begun rowing on her side, the boat just spun in a circle.

"Becca, help your brother, please," Rosie instructed as she moved to the opposite side of the boat and tried to straighten them out with her oar. Finally, after a few minutes, they were pulling up alongside the long wooden dock where Tess stood at the edge waiting for them.

"Hi, guys! I'm building a tent in our backyard." She pointed back toward the house where a pile of canvas and sticks was sitting out on the grass. "Dad said we can go camping tonight! Want to help me set it up?"

"Yeah!" Zander took her hand as she helped him and then Becca out of the boat and they ran up the dock.

Evan appeared behind her and reached a hand down to Rosie. She took it gratefully and stepped up onto the dock. He had been sitting in an Adirondack chair at the end of the dock, a beer in one hand and a book in the other.

"What are you reading?" She eyed the novel sticking out of his back pocket, but it was too scrunched up for her to see the cover. Book homicide was what that was, but she tried to remind herself that everyone reads books differently and that just makes them well-loved.

"Just browsing," he replied, not giving her an answer at all. "Want a beer? It's a nice day to sit out on the lake."

"Sure," she agreed, following him over to the chair he'd been sitting in and plopping herself down in the empty one next to his. There was a small cooler in between the two chairs and he opened it, pulled out a beer, popped the top off, and handed it to her.

"You look like you need one," he joked.

"You don't even know." She took a sip gingerly, testing

it out before she committed. She didn't mind a cold beer. Especially on a hot summer day like today. "I told the twins about Billy."

Evan sat in the chair next to her, leaning forward to prop his elbows on his knees as he angled his body toward hers. "How did they take it?"

She grimaced. "It could have gone better. Becca got pretty defensive. She's protective of Zander, you know."

"I think she's also protective of you," Evan added.

"That's probably true." She lifted the beer to her lips to take another sip when she felt something dripping down her hand.

"Jesus, Rosie, you're bleeding." Evan took the beer from her and placed it on the armrest of the chair, then grabbed her hand and stretched it out to look at it better. "What the hell happened?"

Sure enough, there was a long red slice across the side of her palm that was beginning to drip blood down her wrist. "Oh, wow. I don't know. My line broke when we were fishing. I might have cut it on that, but I don't even remember."

Truthfully, she'd been so nervous the entire boat ride that she probably wouldn't have noticed if an anvil had fallen on her head.

"I've got a first aid kit out here." Evan opened his fishing box at the edge of the dock and pulled out a small white plastic kit with a red cross on it. With deft hands and quiet skill, he cleaned the cut and carefully placed a bandage over it. She didn't try to protest his help, and she found herself a little mesmerized watching him take care of her in that moment. He was so focused on making sure she was okay, the look of concern on his face so genuine that she felt her heart pounding in her chest. This wasn't the norm for her.

She rarely accepted help and she never needed anyone to take care of her. Needing others were dangerous when they could let you down.

But right now, she wanted nothing more than to continue letting him. It felt so good, so freaking comforting, to have his hands on her skin. She could get used to that, and it was a little too dangerous.

"I'm all better," she said, pulling away even as her cells called out for more touch.

When he was done, he looked up at her. "How's that? Does it still hurt?"

She swallowed hard and shook her head. There was zero chance she'd be able to form a sentence right now, so she didn't even try.

He didn't push her to speak, but instead just kept looking at her for a moment. Their eyes searched one another's, and she was acutely aware of the fact that her hand was still in his. After what seemed like forever and not long enough, he let go and sat back in his chair. They both picked up their beers and took a few swigs, and she wanted to ask him what he was thinking but she was afraid she'd like his answer too much.

"So, are you going to let them meet?" Evan broke the silence. "Billy and the twins?"

She cleared her throat. "Yeah. I mean, I have to. I should. It's the right thing to do."

"That's up to you to decide," Evan replied. "You're their mother. You've been there their entire lives, and you know what is best for them. If that's getting to know Billy, then you decide that. Not whatever rules make things the right or wrong thing to do. You're the expert on those kids, Rosie."

Rosie looked over at him, examining the sincerity in his

expression as she mulled over his words. *I'm the expert on the twins.* It was something she'd never thought of before, but there was a lot of truth to that. When Becca's first grade teacher hadn't been able to get her to speak in class, Rosie had known how to coax her out of her shell. Not the teacher. When Zander became sick with a virus when he was an infant, she'd been the one to tell the doctors what was wrong and how to help him. They hadn't known. The fact was that, despite all the specialists or other influences in the world, she *was* the expert.

A new idea for her next Miss Mommy article popped into her head, and she found herself thinking of Clueless Dad for a moment. It had been a few days since she'd responded to his message and she felt a bit of guilt. Here she was with Evan—and it felt so good. It felt like they were a team. Not only was the physical attraction there, but the way he spoke to her, the advice he gave her…it made her feel cared for and collaborative. As if she could maybe consider letting someone into their little three-person unit one day.

She pushed the thought from her head, trying to remind herself that Evan was leaving at the end of the summer. Clueless Dad—whoever he was—was local, and clearly the better fit. "You're right, Evan. Thanks. I appreciate the advice."

"Mom!" Zander came racing down the dock toward her with Tess right on his heels.

Rosie could see Becca still up at the tent area, trying to pitch it all by herself. "What's up, Z?"

"Tess's grandma said that she is making bologna sandwiches for lunch! Can we have lunch here? Please, Mom? Please!" Zander waved his hands over his head, and Rosie couldn't help but laugh at his theatrics.

"Sure, kiddo. If that's okay with them." She looked over at Evan. "Do you mind?"

"Of course not." Evan stood and rubbed a hand over his stomach dramatically. "Actually, I could use a good bologna sandwich right about now. In fact, let's race! First one to the house gets two sandwiches."

Zander didn't need a second to consider the invitation, bolting immediately back toward the house. Rosie laughed as Evan ran beside him, clearly pacing himself a bit so that he wasn't beating Zander. She felt her heart swelling in her chest, thumping against her rib cage like it was going to burst right through.

"Dad's racing?!" Tess gasped as if she was shocked, but then clapped her hands and chased after them. "Dad, I'm coming, too!"

"Come on, Tess!" he called back.

Tess laughed uproariously as they all charged toward the house. "I'm going to get there first!"

Rosie picked up her beer and walked more slowly up to where Becca was still working on the tent. "Honey, want to come in for lunch?"

Becca shook her head. "No, I've got to set up this tent."

"The tent can wait, B." Rosie tilted her head to get a better look at Becca's expression, which was stern and focused. "Let's go eat."

"It can't wait!" Becca burst out in a shout that startled Rosie. "What if we need it? We have to have some place to live when you don't want us anymore."

"What? Becca, what are you talking about?" Rosie's eyes widened as she tried to absorb her daughter's words. She placed her beer down on the picnic table next to them and then sat cross-legged on the grass behind where Becca was working. "B, come here. Come sit with me."

She ignored her at first, but after Rosie repeated herself,

she finally put the stakes down and walked over to her mother.

"Sit, please." Rosie motioned both to her lap and the grass in front of her.

Becca chose her lap, sitting on her legs and leaning sideways into her chest. Rosie wrapped her arms around her daughter so tightly that she was almost worried it might hurt her, but she just couldn't let go. "Tell me what's going on, B."

"What if he takes us?" Becca's voice was quieter now.

Rosie felt the ache in her chest deepen. "Are you talking about your father? Billy?"

Becca nodded. "What if you don't want us anymore after you see what it's like without us?"

Tears formed on the bottom ledge of her lashes, and she was grateful that Becca was against her chest and couldn't see her face. She rocked slightly back and forth, making a soft cooing sound then kissed the top of her head. "B, that's never going to happen. Absolutely never."

"How do you know?" Becca was sniffing, her shoulders trembling.

"I know because I'm your mother," Rosie replied. "I'm not here because I have to be here. I'm not your mother because I didn't have another option. I'm your mother because I wanted you. I chose you, and I chose your brother. I choose both of you every day and I will keep choosing you both every day for the rest of my life."

She was quiet for a moment, then her small arms snaked around Rosie's waist. "I love you, Mommy."

"I love you more, baby girl." She kissed the top of her head again. "Do you believe that?"

Becca nodded, looking up at her with glistening eyes.

"I'm okay with hanging out with our dad. But I love you more, Mom."

She pushed a stray hair off Becca's forehead, wishing she could take the fear from her daughter. She couldn't imagine what it must be like to find out about a father that was never around before. She knew the revelation wouldn't go perfectly, but she hadn't anticipated the fear and pain in her daughter's eyes. "It's okay if you love your dad one day, too, Becs. Your heart is big enough for everyone to fit inside, and so is mine."

"Maybe I'll just spend more time with him first," Becca responded. "Before I decide if I love him or not."

Rosie smiled and took Becca's face in her hands, giving her a big kiss on her nose. "You're an amazing kid, B."

"Can I still have a bologna sandwich?" she asked, pushing up out of Rosie's lap and looking toward the house.

"Of course," Rosie said, standing up too. She grabbed her beer off the table and took a long·swig as she followed her daughter, trying to steady the swell of emotions in her chest at the conversation they'd just had and the sight of Evan through the kitchen window helping Zander build his own sandwich.

It was all so... wonderful.

Chapter Sixteen

It had been over two weeks since Evan had last seen Rosie or the twins. He'd texted her a few times about meeting up, but she'd been busy—at least, too busy for him. First, there was an event at the store, and then, the twins were meeting Billy. He was interested to hear how it all went, but as the days went by, he began to feel the familiar anxiety rising in him. If things had gone badly, he'd have heard about it by now. That wasn't what he was worried about.

What if things had gone well—really well? Not that he didn't want that for the twins. He definitely did. But he'd be lying if he said there wasn't a part of him that was afraid Rosie might see the man she once cared about and fall head over heels again. That maybe the few moments of passion between them had been just that—a quick moment in passing.

"Next!" the cashier called out as Tess led them up to the counter to pay for their ice creams. He took a step forward and mentally shook his head. He needed to trust what was happening with Rosie, not sell it out over some fear.

It was weird being in Crazy Cool Cow without Rosie and the twins there, too, and it was making it nearly impossible to push away the thoughts he was having. Despite a strong self-protective instinct whispering for him to run back to Chicago and not take the risk of letting his heart be broken, a thought had started sliding into his mind, sticky and sweet like fresh honey.

What if he stayed in Heart Lake?

Tess could see her grandparents more. He could help out.

And it would be a chance to see if this thing with Rosie was something real. When he'd seen her holding her daughter on the grass, clearly deep in conversation, as he helped Tess and Zander make sandwiches inside that day…his heart had pulled in a way he didn't think would ever happen again after Layla. He knew in that moment, then and there, that he was ready to try, and he was willing to put his entire heart out there for this woman.

And then she'd dropped off the face of the earth the next day.

"Dad?" Tess pulled on his sleeve, trying to get his attention.

He glanced down at her, noting that his ice cream cone was melting and beginning to run down his hand. "What?"

Tess pointed at the cashier. "He's asking for money."

"Oh." Evan smiled apologetically at the cashier, and grabbed his wallet from his back pocket, handing over a few bills for their ice creams. "Sorry about that."

He followed his daughter outside to the tables and chairs lining the sidewalk in front of the ice cream store. She picked a seat near the end and he sat down across from her, wiping his hands off with some of the napkins from the dispenser on the table.

"Hey, kiddo, I've got a question," he said as he swallowed a mouthful of ice cream.

She looked up at him expectantly, a line of chocolate across her top lip. "What?"

"If we didn't go back to Chicago in the fall, would you be sad? Would you miss your school?" Evan wasn't sure how else to bring this up aside from just straight-out asking the question. He didn't want to consider any next steps that she wasn't also on board with, and he was pretty concerned about the transition and how it might impact her schoolwork and social life.

"What do you mean?" Tess asked. "Like staying here? Or going somewhere else?"

"Nothing is set in stone," he clarified. "I'm just thinking about the possibility of maybe, you know...staying in Heart Lake. Staying with Grandma and Grandpa a little while longer."

"Can Mr. Wallace stay, too?" Tess asked, immediately concerned for her cat.

Evan chuckled. "Mr. Wallace goes wherever we go, of course."

She seemed satisfied with that answer. "Okay, then let's stay."

"Just like that? You don't want to think about it? What about your friends at school?" He'd expected a bit more resistance, but she seemed completely nonplussed.

Tess shrugged. "We can write letters. Be pen pals! And they can come visit. Or we can visit there. I don't need to see them every day. I'd rather see Grandma and Grandpa every day. And Ms. Dean and Zander and Becca. Can I see them every day, too?"

"I think you have to ask them about that one," he replied, biting into his ice cream cone now that he'd eaten the top off. He swallowed the sugary bite. "What about your school-work? I'm worried switching schools will put you behind your peers."

She rolled her eyes. "Daaaaad, stop. I'm in fourth grade. It's not that complicated."

Evan snorted a laugh and shook his head. "Well...that's good to know. I'll keep that in mind, but nothing is certain right now. Can we keep this between us for now? I don't want to get your grandparents excited if it doesn't end up happening."

Tess nodded conspiratorially. "I am a vault of secrets."

"I hope not," he replied, amused at her seriousness. "We don't keep secrets in this family."

"You keep secrets," Tess replied, popping the last bit of ice cream into her mouth.

"I do not," he protested.

"Then why didn't you tell me you're dating Becca and Zander's mom?" Tess lifted one brow as she stared him down. "I saw you guys looking at each other like...like you used to look at Mama."

Evan felt like he'd been walloped in the chest with a rubber hammer. "Tess...I'm so sorry. I don't know what to say. It's not a secret. I just, I don't know what it is yet. You know no one could ever replace your mom, right?"

Tess nodded and folded her arms on the table in front of her. "Dad, I'm not worried about that. I know all that already. I'm worried about you—or, I was. But not anymore. Not now that I see you with Ms. Dean. You look really happy."

He wasn't sure how to respond to that, but he looked down at the remnants of his ice cream cone and tried to swallow the emotion building in his throat.

"I like her," Tess continued. "But I don't like secrets. Promise no more secrets?"

Evan smiled at her and put his hand out. "I promise, kiddo."

She shook his hand then jumped up and waved to someone behind him. "Hey, it's Becca!"

He turned to see the twins walking up the sidewalk with a man in a leather jacket between them. Zander was in the middle of telling the man an animated story, and Becca was smiling brightly. He didn't see Rosie at first, but then he spotted her behind them. She seemed to be giving them a bit of distance, and he realized that this was the same man he'd seen at a distance in the park awhile back.

Billy.

A stab of jealousy hit him unexpectedly and he quickly looked away from the little family of four. "Tess, we should probably get going."

She completely ignored him, however, and walked up to the twins to say hello. He followed behind more slowly, unsure how to even introduce himself to this man. Admittedly, he was handsome in an edgy, punk rock kind of way. The edges of his dark hair were dyed neon colors and a tattoo crept up the side of his neck. If Evan had still been in his twenties, he might have considered this guy pretty cool. Now, however, he just seemed like he was in some sort of extended adolescent period.

When Rosie's eyes met his, she lit up with a smile and whatever jealousy he'd felt for a moment disappeared. There was zero chance that the woman he knew today was interested in a man like Billy. Not when she looked at Evan like that—with a hunger in her eyes that made him stand up straighter and smile back.

"Hey, guys," Rosie greeted them. "Billy, this is Tess and her father, Evan. The twins and Tess are close friends."

He noticed that she didn't state the relationship dynamic between her and himself, but he didn't blame her for that. Hell, he wouldn't know how to describe it either.

"Good to meet a friend of the twins," Billy responded, giving them a small nod. His voice was higher-pitched than Evan had expected. Billy extended a hand to him. "You too, man. We were just going to grab some ice cream. Want to join us?"

Evan shook Billy's hand. "Not this time. We just finished our cones, but thank you."

"Can I help them pick out a flavor?" Tess asked, her arm already slung around Becca's. "I'll be right back, Dad!"

He nodded as she went inside with the twins and Billy, watching her through the wide windowpane.

Rosie sidled up next to him, barely brushing her shoulder against his. "Hey, stranger."

"I'm the stranger?" He lifted the corner of his lips into a small smile and let his hand drop between them, grazing the back of her hand with his knuckles. "You're the one who's been hard to pin down these last few weeks."

"Sorry about that," she said. She intertwined one of her fingers around his so quickly that he almost wasn't sure it had happened. "Things have been crazy busy at the store, and with the kids and Billy."

"How is that going?" He nodded toward them. "They seem to be getting along really well."

She nodded, and he noticed her shoulders drop as she let out a sigh. "It's going better than I imagined, to be honest. Billy is . . . well, he's a bit annoying. Kind of like he hasn't aged a day since I first met him. It's weird, because I feel like an entirely different person than who I was back then. But not Billy. Same old, same old."

"The kids seem to respond well to that, though," he said, unsure how to take that explanation. He felt a wriggly feeling of jealousy stem across his chest again.

"He's really trying," she agreed. "I appreciate that a lot. It's nice seeing the twins get to know him."

"Where's he staying?" He was a bit embarrassed to even ask that, but the nervousness in his gut wanted to know.

"He's got an Airbnb in the next town over. He's only here until the end of the weekend, then he goes back out on tour." Rosie crossed her arms over her chest. "I'm letting him take them alone to the summer festival tomorrow. I figure it's the safest bet since everyone in Heart Lake will keep their eyes on him. But I could use a distraction. Do you want to do something?"

"Sure," he accepted quickly, not even thinking it through. "Tess is going with my parents to the festival tomorrow, so, I'm free. Want to spend the day on the lake?"

"I'll bring the wine," she replied. "You bring the food."

"Sounds like a date." Evan turned his body partially in her direction, trying to look for any sign on her face that she wanted that.

She grinned up at him, gazing at him from under thick lashes. God, he loved them. And when had her eyes turned so dark? They almost seemed reflective, like he could see the flame flickering between them burning deep within her. "It *is* a date, Evan."

"Oh." He swallowed hard. Why wasn't he smoother than this? He felt like he was about to forget how to speak entirely. "Well, okay then. It's a date."

Just then, the kids tumbled back out onto the sidewalk with hands full of ice cream cones and a proudly smiling Billy behind them. Even Tess had another ice cream cone in her hand.

"Two?" Evan asked her, laughing as he shook his head. "You're going to be hyper today, huh?"

Tess nodded enthusiastically. "Dad, they are going to the summer festival tomorrow. Can I ask Grandma and Grandpa if we can all go together?"

"Sure, Tess," he told her. "I'm going to stay home tomorrow though. I've, uh, I've got work to finish."

He didn't miss the sly smile on Rosie's face or the sparkle in her eyes at his subterfuge. Turns out Billy didn't miss their silent exchange either.

"Oh...okay." Billy nodded, winking way too obviously at Rosie and him. "All right, I'll be the babysitter tomorrow. You're welcome."

He could feel his cheeks heating and Rosie stammered. "Oh, well, I might come say hi."

"No secrets, Dad," Tess called him out, then pointed at Rosie and back at him. "You promised, remember?"

"Uh, yeah." Shit. This wasn't how he'd pictured announcing things between them. "Well, Rosie and I might have lunch tomorrow while you guys are out at the festival."

"Just a quick lunch," she clarified, looking equally as caught off guard as he was. She rubbed a hand across the back of her neck and tried to change the subject. "How's the ice cream, guys?"

"I got rocky road," Zander announced, and it seemed he hadn't picked up on anything from their innuendoes.

Becca, however, was clearly understanding with the way she was suddenly eyeing Evan with open curiosity. "I got butter pecan," she said.

"Cool." Evan nodded, shoving his hands in his pockets. "That's a good flavor."

"I got rainbow sherbet, in case you were wondering," Billy added, holding up his cup of colorful ice cream. "It's damn good."

He found himself laughing slightly; honestly, Billy was a bit charming. Definitely not responsible father material, but certainly had the part of fun uncle down pat. He was glad that the twins would have that, even if he still wished for more for them—and for Rosie.

Chapter Seventeen

Rosie stared at the shelves of wine bottles in front of her at Hobbes Grocery Store as she tried to decide what to pick out for her date with Evan in an hour. She'd just dropped the kids off at the festival with Billy and wanted to grab some supplies before heading to where they'd agreed to meet at the lake, not too far from where she lived. Her cabin didn't have a lake view, but it wasn't far, either, and just a quick jog through the woods could bring her to the lake's shore.

"Can't go wrong with the red zinfandel," Marvel announced, sidling up to her in the store aisle. "Perfect date wine."

"Date?" Rosie cringed. "What makes you say that?"

"The way that Nowak boy looks at you, it better be a date," Marvel joked. She grabbed a bottle of red off the shelf and handed it to her. "Here, this one is basically an aphrodisiac. Thomas and I love it."

Thinking about her father's romantic life wasn't exactly a turn-on, and Rosie found herself grimacing slightly at the mental image. "Well, uh, thanks for the recommendation."

"He's a good guy, Rosie," Marvel continued. "Give him a chance, huh?"

She could feel her cheeks getting warm. "I appreciate the dating advice, Marvel, but I'm still very much single." Though even as she said it, it didn't feel entirely true. Her mind flitted to Evan, and then to Clueless Dad. "I'm actually talking to several guys right now."

"Damn." Marvel let out a low whistle. "Good for you, girl. Make them work for it. Maybe get two bottles to celebrate."

With that, Marvel flounced away and turned down the next aisle. Rosie pulled her phone out of her pocket and opened her emails, scrolling back to the last one she'd sent Clueless Dad. She'd asked him about his favorite quick dinner recipes that his kid would eat and suggested maybe they get together for a coffee. She hadn't heard from him since then, which was a bit embarrassing since he'd been pretty steadily responding to her up until that point. Clearly, he didn't want to get coffee.

The rejection stung a bit, but it had given her a good idea for her latest Miss Mommy column—"What to do when you're the only single one in your mom groups." It had gotten a higher number of views on the website than usual and had clearly resonated with other single parents out there, particularly the section she wrote on how to cope with rejection.

Maybe she should get two bottles of wine, now that she thought about that possibility happening again today. She'd basically demanded that today be a date—what if Evan hadn't wanted it to be a date? What if he'd just been trying to be nice and distract her on the first day she was letting Billy take the twins alone? Maybe he was just a nice guy, and that was it. A friend. She rubbed her hand against her cheek, trying to calm herself.

Intrusive, anxious thoughts were swirling in her mind, and she grabbed a second bottle of zinfandel to be safe. She quickly paid at the checkout and tucked the wine into the trunk of her car before pointing her way back home. When she came up her drive, she spotted Evan's truck parked in front of her garage, but no one was in the front seat from what she could tell. She pulled her sedan up next to it and turned off the ignition. A few deep breaths later, she got out and grabbed the wine from her trunk before heading up her walkway.

"Hey." His voice was low and subtle, but there was a rumble to it that she felt on her skin.

Rosie looked up to see Evan sitting on the top step up to her porch. He was wearing dark blue jeans that hugged his thighs in a way she couldn't *not* notice, and a loose black T-shirt that did the same to the bulging biceps on his arms. Her response was just as breathless. "Hey."

He lifted up a wicker basket that had a lid over it—the quintessential picnic basket. "I brought lunch."

Rosie held up the grocery bag. "I brought wine."

"Seems like we're ready," he replied, pushing up to his feet and meeting her at the bottom of the steps. "Want to head down to the lake?"

She nodded, and neither one of them said anything as they walked down the wooded trail side by side until they came out at the shore. It was a small inlet from the much larger Heart Lake, but it was entirely secluded and one of the reasons why Rosie loved where she lived so much. The closest neighbor was near the mouth of the inlet, but she rarely saw them. Here, she had her own little dock jutting out into the water with a canoe tied to the end. She'd had a rowboat at one point, but Tanner had borrowed it awhile back and somehow forgotten to return it.

In front of the dock, however, was a large stretch of grass that ended abruptly at the water's line where a five-foot drop lined with stones separated the land from the cold water. Her brother had thought that was the main reason not to live out here, since it wasn't an easy incline into the water like so many other houses in Heart Lake, but Rosie liked the steep drop-off. The dock and rickety stairs still allowed her plenty of access to the water, but she never worried about flooding, and she always had an incredible view. There was a small storage area at the beginning of her dock, and she opened it to pull out some outdoor blankets and a bug-repellent candle.

Evan helped her fluff out the blanket and lay it flat on the grass, then lit a match from his basket to light the candle. It had a citrus smell she didn't love, but it was better than being lunch for mosquitoes.

"So, what did you bring?" she asked as she pulled the bottles of wine out of the grocery bag and placed them on the blanket's surface. Thankfully, both were screw tops, but she realized that she hadn't brought any glasses with her. "Because I definitely forgot cups."

He grinned and sat down cross-legged on the blanket and began pulling items out of the basket—a log of cheese, sliced salami, grapes still in a bunch, a loaf of bread that she could already smell was freshly baked, and a small jar of artisanal jam. "I decided to go for an amateur charcuterie board. Minus the board, which didn't fit in the basket."

She laughed and pulled a grape off the stem, popping it into her mouth. "No board, no cups, but plenty of food and wine," she kidded. "Sounds like quite the match."

His eyes seemed to darken for a moment as they scanned over her, and she swallowed the grape so fast that she almost choked on it. Rosie coughed, sputtering as she tried to clear her throat.

"You okay?" he asked, putting a hand on her knee as she sat next to him on the blanket.

She nodded. "Just forgot how to eat for a second there. You must have that effect on me."

His smile returned and he reached forward and picked up the loaf of bread. He ripped off a piece and handed it to her, then did the same for himself. "I have an effect on you?"

"If mild annoyance is an effect, then yeah." She let him spread some jam onto her bread and then took a bite. "Mmm, is this Everly's?"

He nodded, chewing on his own bite then reaching for one of the bottles of wine. "Yeah, my mother loves jamming season. I think we have enough to last us ten years. Let's have a toast."

She watched him screw off the lid and hold up the bottle. "I forgot the glasses, though."

"We can drink out of the bottle like we're still in high school," he teased and then took a quick swig. "Actually, I don't think I ever drank wine this good in high school."

"Two-buck chuck was all I drank," she joked, taking the bottle from him and drinking a few sips. The spicy aroma filled her nose, and her throat felt the peppery burn. "Or that bottom-shelf vodka from the ABC store—you know the kind that you had to mix with a million things to not feel like it was poison?"

Evan chuckled, leaning back on one elbow and stretching out his legs. "I was the Red Bull mixer type. What about you?"

"Fruit punch."

He laughed at that. "Fruit punch? With vodka?"

"What?" she teased. "It was very yummy! Sometimes I'd mix in a little Sprite or ginger ale to give it that extra kick. The juice really masked the flavor of the vodka."

Evan shook his head. "I should have hung out with you more in high school, huh?"

"Why didn't you?" She didn't look at him as she asked this, and while her tone was playful, the question felt very real once it was out there. She took another few sips of wine, hoping maybe he didn't hear her.

"High school was a hard time for me," he stated, confirming that he had heard her. "My parents and I had a rocky relationship back then. There was a lot of pressure on me to be...I don't know, different? Different than them and what they did with their lives. They wanted me to get that full athletic scholarship for baseball, graduate college, move to the big city—make something out of myself. My father always said he regretted not having done the same."

Rosie frowned. "Really? Your father had one of the most popular barbershops in the state. People came from all over Michigan to get their hair cut by him."

"I know." Evan looked out at the water, a sadness in his eyes. "When he had to close it after his Parkinson's diagnosis, he took it really hard. At least, that's what my mom said. He began showing symptoms about a month before Layla died. I was so consumed with my own grief back then, I didn't even notice what he was going through. Or what they both were going through. My mom was his rock back then—still is."

"They have a pretty wonderful marriage," Rosie commented. She didn't know the ins and outs, but they'd always been a couple she'd admired over the years. "They seem solid."

He nodded. "They are. Still in love after all this time. Still in Heart Lake, growing old and living peacefully together. It doesn't seem like such a bad future, does it?"

"Not at all," she admitted, having really imagined the same for herself for a long time.

"I always wondered why they didn't want that for me," he continued. "Why did they want me to move away and make a lot of money when their life here has been so happy and full of love?"

She didn't have an answer for that one, since her own parents had never put that type of pressure on her. In fact, they'd always encouraged her to do anything, as long as it made her happy. But, as a mother now, she suspected that Evan's parents' motives had been pure. "I think about that with the twins sometimes. I don't think it's about them, or them not living up to a standard I want for them...I think it's about me. I think it's my insecurity that this isn't going to be enough for them—or, more accurately, that I'm not enough for them."

"Hmm." Evan was quiet for a moment, a soft hum in his throat as he reflected. "You're saying maybe my parents weren't worried about who I would be, but rather, who they weren't?"

"Yeah." Rosie picked up a piece of salami and chewed on the edge. "I know Heart Lake gave me a wonderful life, and I love it here. I love it for myself. But I'm one person and I always feel like I'm falling short on giving the twins everything they deserve. Part of me does want to push them to go far, get out, explore more...find all the things and people and lessons that I can't give them. Go beyond me. They deserve more than me."

Evan moved the back of his fingers down her upper arm, a soft caress that made her shiver with anticipation. "I can't imagine anyone more deserving than you." His voice was softer now, and she found herself leaning closer to him, mentally begging him to kiss her. "Rosie, you're an incredible mother."

She swallowed hard, her gaze now fixed on his lips. She found herself biting the corner of her own bottom lip as she contemplated just making the first move herself. So, she did. Leaning into him, she placed her hand against his chest, feeling the firmness of it, and with only a moment of hesitancy, she kissed him. He didn't move at first, letting her be the one in the driver's seat. She took control slowly, deepening their kiss as he parted his mouth for her. Her hand slid up over his collarbone, and then his shoulder, wrapping around the back of his neck as she pulled herself against him.

A low groan in his throat encouraged her, and his hand slid around her waist, pinning her to him. Suddenly, he was on top of her and pushing her down against the blanket as he leaned over her. Her leg was wrapped around him, bent at the knee and keeping their bodies locked together. His tongue tasted hers and everything in her mind seemed to go blank.

But not her body. Her body felt like it was on fire, and while she couldn't form an actual cohesive thought in her foggy brain, her body moved as if on autopilot. It knew what it wanted, and who. She could feel his body respond to her, a hard length pressing against her beneath his jeans, straining to be free. Her hips pushed up off the blanket to create further friction, wanting to feel him against her...inside her.

They were wearing too many clothes.

"Evan," she whispered his name in between kisses that were becoming frantic and frenzied. "I need you."

His hand slid beneath the hem of her skirt, pushing it up around her waist. He felt her core, and there was no doubt for either of them that she was ready for him. With quick hands, he unbuckled his jeans and freed himself, pressing against her entrance without actually moving farther.

His restraint was killing her. "Evan, please," she gasped, trying to move her hips to pull him into her.

He pulled away farther. "Rosie, hold on..."

"What?" She swallowed hard, trying to form a thought in her head aside from how desperately she needed him right there and then.

"Are you sure about this?" His voice was soft, concerned. The look in his eyes begged her to stop him, and yet, keep going at the same time. "I don't...I don't know what this will mean."

"It doesn't have to mean anything." Even as she said that, she didn't believe it. She saw on his face that he didn't either. "I'm on birth control. I'm clean. It's fine."

"I am, too, but it's been...awhile. I don't usually do this," he admitted. "Not, uh, not like this..."

"Me neither," she admitted, her hand touching his cheek and cupping his face. She held him still to look at her, and he seemed so vulnerable in that moment. She wanted to ease his anxieties and tell him how much he meant to her, how much this meant to her. How she had completely been lying when she said it didn't have to mean anything, because it already did and they both knew that. "But I want to be with you, Evan. Only you."

His mouth found hers again and there was no stopping the momentum they had started this time. He groaned against her, and she felt the rumble in his chest as he pushed her back down onto the blanket and covered her body with his. She hiked her leg back up, anchoring her knee against his hips as she held herself to him.

When his fingers slid across her core, the daylight slipped

away and was replaced by a crimson darkness behind her eyelids that felt like home and ecstasy all rolled into one slow, rhythmic movement.

"Oh, God...Evan." Her groan was louder than his, and she devoured his mouth to keep from shouting out as he brought her to the edge of an internal cliff and tossed her over without a second thought. She moaned against his mouth as her body trembled in a way she didn't even recognize. Everything about the way he was touching her felt brand-new. She felt brand-new. She felt...perfectly used.

Neither of them were prepared for the sharp sting of her cell phone coming to life from somewhere in the caverns of her purse only inches away. They froze and the moment broke as if someone had just caught them. He pulled away, straightening his back and clearing his throat.

"I should probably get that..." She pulled at her skirt, covering herself, and then reached for her bag. A frantic search while the ringing continued finally brought her face-to-face with Billy's name across her screen. "It's, uh, it's Billy. It could be the kids..."

"Answer it," Evan urged her with a nod.

She appreciated his understanding, despite how awkward things felt. She answered and held the phone to her ear. "Hello? Billy?"

"Listen, I don't want to alarm you," Billy began from the other end.

That was not the way to start any sentence when speaking to a mother. Her stomach felt like it was closing in on itself, clenching and turning at the same time. "What? What's going on? Are the twins okay? Is someone hurt?"

"Yeah, it's fine, we're all fine," he assured her. "But, uh, well...we had sushi. I didn't know Zander was allergic to edamame."

"What?!" Rosie gasped, her hand at her chest. "I gave you an entire list of their allergies! Soy was literally the first thing on his list!"

He scoffed, and she was damn glad that there was an entire town between them because if he'd been standing in front of her right now, she was pretty sure she would throttle him. "Okay, I read that list, but how was I supposed to know edamame is soybeans? It's basically a trick question. The list didn't say anything about edamame."

"Billy!"

"Sorry! We're at the Heart Lake Hospital emergency room. Just come whenever you're ready. No rush. He's doing fine. Becca gave him the EpiPen shot at the sushi stand. She's a smart one, that girl." He laughed slightly. "She probably gets that from you."

"No shit," she responded. "I'll be there in fifteen minutes. Do not go anywhere."

She hung up the phone and looked up to see Evan staring at her wide-eyed. "Is everything okay?"

"Zander had an allergic reaction. I have to go..." She was already beginning to put her stuff back in her purse, but everything felt cluttered and confused and like she was moving so much slower than normal.

"Holy shit." Evan jumped to his feet and began tossing things in the basket. "Come on. I'll drive you."

"Are you sure?" She pushed to her feet, trying to figure out how to actually stand up without completely collapsing. Her knees felt like noodles and her heart was pounding so loudly in her chest that she could barely hear his voice over it. "I need...yes, I need a ride. I shouldn't drive right now.

Okay, let's go. We're going to Heart Lake Hospital. You know how to get there?"

Evan took her hand and squeezed it, slowing them both down for a moment. "Rosie, I've got you. You've got Zander. We're going to be fine."

Tears sprang to her eyes, and God, she believed him.

Chapter Eighteen

The last time Evan had stepped foot in Heart Lake Hospital, he was sixteen years old and had broken his big toe in a boating accident in a stupid dare with his friends. He'd been in a walking boot for weeks after that, benched from his baseball games, and on his parents' shit list for "squandering his talent," as he recalled. But the last time he'd stepped foot in any hospital had been when he'd said goodbye to his wife. That had been in Chicago, but honestly, walking through one emergency room was pretty reminiscent of any. He'd lost Layla on the oncology floor, though, and there was a peace in that wing that wasn't found anywhere else in a hospital. Emergency rooms were chaotic and rapidly moving, but when he'd entered the oncology floor, there was soft music and whispered voices and the feeling of loss around every curtain.

Evan tried not to hold on to that memory as he followed Rosie down the emergency room halls, winding around the curtained-off rooms to the number the charge nurse had said her son was in. He wasn't here to think about himself. She needed him, and he was absolutely going to do whatever he could to make this situation better for her.

What did that mean for how he felt about her? Evan wasn't sure if he was ready to say, but a quiet four-letter word tugged at the back of his mind and played on his heartstrings.

"Zander?" Rosie called out, gripping the curtain in front of them and sliding it open to reveal the young boy sitting on the edge of a hospital bed holding a deck of cards splayed in front of him.

"Hey, Mom!" He looked up at her with a smile like nothing had even happened and held up the cards to her. "Go fish!"

"What?" She shook her head, storming past the thin man in a leather jacket who was also holding a set of cards. "You're playing Go Fish?"

Evan had noticed Billy immediately but said nothing because he wasn't sure he'd be able to utter anything half-way civil right now. The thought of this man waltzing in after all these years and potentially hurting the twins...it made Evan's stomach roll with a fierceness he'd only felt before when he thought about Tess.

There was that four-letter word again.

"I'm winning," Zander clarified.

"I think he's hustling me," Billy replied, punching Zander on the shoulder with a light swing. "Kid has won three rounds in a row."

Zander grinned at his father and Evan felt a swelling of protectiveness in his chest. "Dad! I told you I've played this game before!"

"Guys, stop!" Rosie crossed her arms over her chest and made a ceasing motion then grabbed her son's face and carefully examined him. "What is going on? Where is the doctor? Zander, are you okay? How do you feel? Can you breathe?"

"He's fine, Rose," Billy interrupted, and the way he called her by her full name so casually made Evan clench his jaw. "The doctors already fixed him all up. As soon as they get his insurance card, he's good to go."

"You're waiting on his insurance card?" Rosie's gaze cut to Billy and it was eviscerating in her anger. "It would be great if you could be the kind of person who had those kinds of documents, too."

Billy shrugged defensively. "I mean, that's what moms are for, right?"

"Jesus take the wheel." Rosie was speaking through gritted teeth now, still holding Zander's face in her hands. "Baby, how do you feel?"

He nodded his head. "I'm okay, Mom. My face was all puffy before and my throat felt super scratchy, but then Becca stabbed me."

Rosie looked over at her daughter who was sitting in a folding chair off to the side, her knees up to her chest and a book laying open in front of her. "I'm so proud of you, Becca. You saved your brother."

The girl shrugged, but Evan could see her cheeks turning dark red at the compliment. "I mean, it's nothing. You taught me how to do it like eighty-seven times."

Rosie let go of Zander long enough to go envelop Becca in a huge hug, practically lifting her off the seat. "I love you, kid."

"Mom!" She struggled to push her mother off of her, her face even more crimson than it had been a few moments ago. "Stoooop."

Rosie kissed the top of Becca's head and then let go of her. "Okay, let's get out of here. I'll go talk with the doctors. You guys stay here for a minute, okay?"

The twins both nodded in agreement.

"Do you need help?" Billy asked.

She didn't even respond to him but gave him a scathing look before walking past the curtains toward the nurses' station.

"Man, she hasn't changed much, huh?" Billy turned to Evan and bumped his side with his elbow and let out a laugh. "Still as dramatic as ever, am I right?"

It took everything in Evan to not punch Billy in the face right then and there, but the twins were watching. They loved their father. He wasn't going to be the one to knock him off their pedestal. Instead, he took a deep breath and turned to look at the young man. "I understand what she's feeling. Parenting is hard. Single parenting is even harder."

Billy avoided eye contact and cleared his throat at that comment. He got the message Evan had been delivering. "Yeah, right. I bet. Uh, well...maybe I should head out? It's getting late, you know? Can you tell Rosie I took off?"

Evan leveled his gaze at Billy. "You're leaving?"

The man looked nervous and was fidgeting with the edge of his jacket. "Well, yeah. I mean, everything is fine. You guys have got this. You don't need me. Right? I mean, I'm just in the way."

Something about the way he said that pulled at Evan, and he felt a tiny bit of compassion seep in. He couldn't imagine how hard it must be to try to come back into a fully formed family like theirs. Did he just call Rosie and the twins his family? Something about that felt...right. It felt true.

Evan reached a hand out and placed it on Billy's shoulders. "You've always got a place here."

"Yeah?" Billy looked up at him, a vulnerability that only another father could recognize in the inexperienced man's eyes. "I appreciate that, man. I'm glad Rosie has someone."

He didn't respond to that, but there wasn't a doubt in his mind that Rosie had him. She had all of him. That four-letter word pulled at him and he looked back toward the twins, who were now conversing about a part of the book Becca was reading. Rosie wasn't the only one who had him...her entire family did.

He was in love with Rosie. Head-over-heels infatuated. But he also deeply loved these two kids sitting in front of him. It felt so obvious, and he couldn't believe it was only just hitting him right now.

Evan looked at Billy and nodded. "I've got them."

Billy shook his hand, then headed out after a quick round of goodbyes, leaving him alone with the twins as Rosie was still at the nurses' station asking the charge nurse a bunch of questions. Becca was sitting on the hospital bed behind Zander now, holding the book up to him so that he could read. She smiled at Evan and he smiled back.

"You guys okay?" he asked, stepping closer to the two of them.

Becca nodded, speaking for the both of them as she usually did. "We're okay. Zander feels better. And...we're happy you're here, especially with our mom."

Zander looked up at him and nodded in agreement. "We like Billy. He's fun. But..." Zander looked at his sister, as if for permission. She nodded in approval. "But we're really glad you're here."

Evan felt a lump swelling in his throat and he batted the tears from his eyes as he tried to clear his throat. What the hell was even happening right now? He hadn't expected to feel this surge of emotion hearing their acceptance of him in their life. It felt heavy in the best way, full of responsibility and pressure that he wanted to dive further into.

"I'm glad I'm here, too," he replied and reached forward to squeeze Zander's knee.

"Okay, I got it all settled," Rosie said, storming back into the room like she'd never left. She looked around for a moment, clearly feeling the vibes happening between them. "What's going on? Where's Billy?"

"He, uh . . . he had to go." Evan rubbed his hand across the back of his neck, feeling like a jerk for relaying that news. "He said to tell you goodbye."

"Great." Rosie didn't seem surprised at all, and she seamlessly moved into mom mode. "Zander, do you have everything you need? We're being discharged, but we'll follow up with the pediatrician on Monday."

"I have to go back to the doctor?" Zander whined, pushing off the bed and standing up.

Becca was beside him. "You like the doctor," she reminded him. "They have lollipops."

"Oh, yeah!" Zander pumped a fist in the air. "Okay, let's go."

"I'll go pull the car around," Evan offered. "Meet you guys in the bay out front?"

Rosie nodded. "That would be wonderful. Thank you."

"Can you turn the air-conditioning on so it's cold when we get in?" Becca asked. "It's so hot outside."

He laughed lightly and Rosie rolled her eyes. "Sure, I can do that."

"I'm so sorry," Rosie joked. "These kids are clearly high-maintenance."

"Or they're great at advocating for themselves," he said, reframing her thought. "Wonder where they learned that autonomy from?"

Rosie's cheeks darkened and she bit the edge of her bottom lip, a small smile and teasing lilt in her voice. "Just go get the car, Nowak."

Fifteen minutes later, he was headed back to Rosie's house with the entire gang in the back seat. He called in to check on Tess and his parents—all of whom had had an incredible amount of fun at the fair that led to a sugar crash for Tess. His mom told him she was already fast asleep in bed, despite it barely being past dinnertime. Turns out four funnel cakes was maybe three too many. His mom encouraged him to take his time and have fun, since they didn't expect Tess to be up again until tomorrow morning.

"Do you want to come in?" Rosie asked him as she leaned against the car, looking through the open passenger window as the kids were already scurrying their way up the porch steps and into the house. "One glass of wine?"

There was zero way he could say no to that offer. "Sure. One glass."

There was a small smile on the edge of her lips that said otherwise, but he turned off the car and stepped out. Evan followed her up the porch stairs and tried to stay out of the way as she instructed the kids in their bedtime routine.

"Do you want to open the red in the cabinet?" she called out to him, sticking her head out of the bathroom where she was supervising teeth brushing. "It's above the fridge. The opener is in the drawer next to the dishwasher."

Evan agreed and made his way about her kitchen to find the wine, some glasses, and a wine opener. None of the items were where she'd said they'd be, but he managed to find them all anyway. He set everything up on the coffee table in front of the couch, the living room light dimmed, lit by a string of lights that went from one corner of the room to the other. It added a spontaneous ambience to the room, but everything about Rosie's house was a reflection of her quirks. The armchair covered in a newspaper print was pointed at a television that still had bunny-ear antennas on the top, and the couch was a deep, dark blue that pulled him into the cushions as he sat back and waited for her to be done with the twins.

"Sorry about that," Rosie said as she walked back into the room. She dropped down on the couch next to him with a loud plop and leaned back into the cushions with her arms stretched out like she was about to fall asleep. "Those kids have an amount of energy that I will never understand. They're both asleep now, though."

Evan laughed and handed her a wine glass half filled with red wine. "Sounds like you need this more than I do."

She accepted the glass with a grateful smile. "Thanks. And...thanks for everything today. You were quite the sport. I'm sorry things went so haywire from what we'd planned."

He shrugged and took a sip from his glass. "That's what parenthood is. I was just glad that I could be there for you guys today. That was pretty scary there for a minute."

"Right?" Rosie gestured in agreement. "Can you believe Billy just bailed like that?"

"He's in a hard spot," Evan admitted, not sure why he was defending the guy. What the hell was he saying right now? "I mean, I just think he's in a position where he can't really win no matter what he does. It's got to be hard coming into a fully formed family like that."

Rosie studied him for a moment, her eyes searching his. "You think we're fully formed?"

"You and the twins?" he asked. "You guys are one of the healthiest family units I've ever seen. You all get each other. Those kids look at you like you're their entire world."

"They are mine," Rosie replied, her voice barely above a whisper. "And I can do it myself. There is nothing I wouldn't do for them." She turned on the couch to face him and leaned farther into the pillows. "Is that how you feel?"

"Like Tess is my entire world? Abso-freaking-lutely." He turned his body toward hers on the couch as well and decided to be more brazen as he ran his fingertips down the side of her cheek. He tucked a few stray hairs behind her ear then let his hand fall to her lap. "But you don't need to do everything alone. You are allowed to ask for help sometimes."

"I guess I can try." She intertwined her fingers in his. "I think for me it's almost like if I don't ask for help, then things aren't ever too hard. I just can push my feelings down in my internal trash compactor and get on with my day."

"Look, I'm not an expert in psychology or anything, but that doesn't sound particularly healthy. You can let people in more, you know. Grow your heart, your family."

"Do you feel like it's hard to become part of my family?" she asked suddenly. "Does it seem like we're missing something... missing someone?"

The implications of her words hit him like a ton of bricks and he had to place his wine glass down on the table for fear he might drop it. He grabbed hers from her hand and did the same, and then, as if on autopilot, he pulled her onto his lap. Rosie moved seamlessly with him as she straddled him and her hands cupped against his jawline, tilting his face to hers until their lips found each other.

"Evan," she whispered against his mouth, and his arms wrapped around her back pinning her to his chest. "Can we go to my room? It's just... if the kids wake up."

Good point.

He didn't answer, just groaned his agreement, pulling her up and off her feet and carrying her into the room, placing her gently on the bed. His jeans felt so tight that he was pretty sure he was going to burst through them, but all he could focus on was the feeling of smooth skin on her legs as his hands ran up and down her thighs. Her hands moved down his chest until they found his belt buckle, and she tugged at the restraints until he was free and her hand slid around him.

Evan's breath was trapped in his lungs. "God, Rosie... you feel..."

"Shh," she whispered and placed him at her entrance, pushing her underwear to the side. "I can't wait."

He couldn't either, and when she pressed down on him, he felt like he was going to come undone. Warm, wet, sweet, she pulled at him and he gave her everything he had until they were both panting and thrusting against each other. He never wanted to leave. This felt like home. She felt like home. The way her body responded to him was intoxicating and he never wanted to be sober.

"Rosie... are you close?" he asked between gasps of air.

She nodded furiously, her grip on his shoulders tightening as she moved up and down on his lap. "God, yes," she groaned. "Evan... I..."

Her words trailed off as he felt her body begin to tremble around him. He wrapped his arms tighter around her, plunging as deep as he could and finding his own ecstasy in the middle of her waves of pleasure. Evan muffled his groans in her neck, trying his best to stay as quiet as possible despite the way fireworks were exploding in his mind's eye.

It seemed to take forever, but eventually his body seemed to come down from the ceiling and he found himself leaning forward. His forehead was on Rosie's chest, both of them sweaty and panting as they tried to find themselves again. He didn't want to let go, and so he wrapped his arms around her and moved them until she was lying flat on the bed beneath him. His arm wrapped around her and cuddled her back to his chest like the perfect little spoon.

After a while, her breathing slowed and he could tell that she'd fallen asleep in his hold. He kissed the side of her head, behind her ear, and found himself lingering.

"I love you, Rosie," he whispered, knowing she couldn't hear him.

He closed his eyes and held the woman he loved tighter. Tomorrow, he would tell her when she was awake. He would tell her how much he had fallen for her, and how he wanted to stay in Heart Lake. He wanted to be part of her family. He wanted her and the twins to be part of his family with Tess.

He was done pushing away the fears about what might happen...he was in love. And he was going to embrace it.

Chapter Nineteen

A vibrating sound from her phone startled Rosie awake as she tried to find her bearings. She fumbled for her phone and quickly turned off her alarm. It was Sunday, so she wasn't even sure why it had been set, but most of this weekend had been such a blur that she'd probably done it accidentally at some point. The emergency room visit yesterday came back to hit her like a brick, and then she was suddenly aware of the strong arms wrapped around her where she was lying on her bed.

Evan had slept over. Hell, Evan had done a lot more than sleep last night. She could feel her cheeks warming as she remembered the way she'd straddled him and how he'd felt plunged deep in her core. God, that man was magic with his hands... with his everything.

There was zero chance the twins would be waking up this early on a weekend, but she still found the mom anxiety beginning to take hold as she imagined one of them walking into her room and seeing her with Evan. Her kids were old enough to figure out that something more than just friends was happening, though hopefully they couldn't piece together much more than that.

Somehow, the alarm must not have woken Evan, though, because she could still feel a slow rhythmic breathing coming from him and brushing against her cheek. Rosie twisted her body slowly, trying to be careful not to jostle him awake as she turned to face him in their embrace. She'd never noticed before how long his eyelashes were, since they were so blond, but at this distance she could see how thick they were. He had the same nose as his father, too, which was a good thing. It was a strong feature paired with his sharp jawline, and even in a state of rest, he appeared formidable. There was no doubt in her mind, though, that his coloring was from his mother. Everly Nowak was a natural blond, and Evan only had whispers of darker hues running through his straight hair. His beard had a tinge of red that only started at his sideburns, almost like drawing an exact line between the blond and the strawberry blond.

"It's weird to watch people when they're sleeping." Evan's mouth suddenly began moving, and Rosie was so startled by the sudden noise that she shoved back from him and found herself toppling to the floor.

Dazed for a moment, she tried to catch her breath. "What the h—"

"Are you okay?" Evan's face appeared over the edge of the bed, looking down at her on the floor.

"How long were you awake?" she asked, pushing up on her elbows. "You scared the hell out of me."

He grinned and reached a hand down to help her back up to her feet. She righted herself with less grace than she'd hoped for, but, at least she wasn't sprawled across the floor anymore.

Evan stood as well and straightened his clothes. "You got any coffee?"

"Uh, yeah, I should have some K-cups somewhere." She led them out of the bedroom and into the kitchen and rummaged in the drawer beneath her Keurig coffee maker. "What about holiday blend?"

"What holiday is it?" he asked.

"I think this is from last Thanksgiving," she admitted, laughing lightly as she popped it in the machine. "I'm sure it's still fine. How did you sleep?"

He leaned sideways against the countertop. "I actually slept better than I have in years. Until you started moving around, I was out like a light."

"Hmm," she hummed lightly, absentmindedly wiping the counter with a dish towel. It wasn't like she was going to read too much into that, but she couldn't help feeling excited about his admission. Honestly, she'd slept really well, too. The feeling of satisfaction was bone-deep, and not in just a sexual way. It was like finding something that just fits and wondering how she hadn't always had it in her life before. "Do you have work today?"

He shook his head. "Not on Sundays. I promised to take Tess to the farmers market when she wakes up. She is obsessed with the goat lady."

Rosie laughed and nodded in agreement at the comment about one of the vendors who was well known for her goat milk products at their local market. "You won't find better goat cheese anywhere in the state."

"That's what I hear." He took the mug from her when it was done and held it up to his nose, inhaling the deliciously pungent smell before putting it back down. "What about you? Bookstore?"

"No, Davon works the weekend shifts." She grabbed another mug from the cupboard and a tea bag from the drawer, making herself a cup of hot water in the coffee machine to drop her tea bag into. "Sundays are my catch-up days from the week. Laundry, chores, and, uh…"

She hesitated for a moment before completing her

sentence, but he lifted his brows, willing her to continue. "Well, I also work on my column on Sundays. It's a bit of a secret, but I actually write the Miss Mommy column in the *Heart Lake Herald*. It's just a fun little side gig, you know?"

Evan smiled, and she felt the tension in her chest ease at his acceptance. She hadn't told anyone outside her best friends about her role at the paper, but she wanted to open up to him more. Everything they'd shared over the last day—or weeks, really—made her feel safer with him than she felt with most people. Normally one to hold on tight to the reigns of control, she wanted to let go just a little. She wanted to be open and vulnerable, and it felt like a weight had lifted off of her in telling him her secret.

"I actually already knew that," Evan admitted, finally taking a sip of his coffee.

Rosie felt her body seizing up, responding like a record-scratch moment. Full halt. What the actual heck. *He knew?* "You . . . you knew?"

"Yeah, but I wasn't sure if you wanted me to know." Evan huffed a sheepish laugh, as if he hadn't just figuratively punched her in the stomach. "You and I have actually been corresponding for a while. I'm Clueless Dad."

She grabbed the edge of the counter to steady herself, her face feeling like it was about to go up in flames. "You're Clueless Dad? You. Are. THE. Clueless Dad?"

His expression conveyed that he was beginning to pick up on the fact that this conversation was not going in a jovial direction. He frowned, his brows knitting together as he placed the coffee mug back down on the counter. "Yeah . . . to be honest, I thought you probably had figured it out based on our conversations."

If the tile floor had opened into a spontaneous sinkhole in

that exact moment, Rosie would happily have allowed herself to be consumed by the earth, never to be seen again. It felt horrible to have been played the fool. He knew the truth about her column and strung her along? It felt like a betrayal of trust. Worse, she felt so vulnerable, like he was standing on high ground and she was sliding down a hill. God, she wanted to erase the last few weeks with a magic wand. Instead, she cleared her throat and did everything she could to avoid looking at him directly in his eyes.

"Rosie, are you okay?" he prompted again. "Was that... was I wrong?"

"I did *not* know you were Clueless Dad," she confirmed, her teeth gritted and her voice both flat and full of fury at the same time. "I didn't realize you knew who I was. This whole thing..." She groaned. "Look, I think you should leave before the twins wake up and see you here. This was... last night was a mistake."

"What?" Evan physically took a step back, his face ashen. "What do you mean?"

"I just don't have time for games or whatever, you know? I've got a full plate. The kids, the bookstore, my column. I don't have room for anything else in my life, certainly not getting played by you and your alter ego." Her arms were crossed over her chest now, and all she wanted to do was find a magic cure to make her feel less out of control right then. It felt like her entire life was spinning around her and she was just an observer along for the ride. That wasn't how she operated, and it wasn't how she stayed sane, or ran a successful business, or was a good mom. She had to stay in control. She couldn't let things throw her off track like this, and a man falling into her bed—or couch—after leading a double dating life was absolutely off the damn tracks.

"If I gave you the impression that last night was fake to me, I'm incredibly sorry," Evan replied. He stepped forward and took her hand in his. She felt stiff and glued her gaze to the countertop instead of his face. "Rosie, I'd like to see where this goes. I've been looking into options for staying in Heart Lake full-time. I want to stay for my family, but also...I want to stay for you."

"Evan..." His name got stuck in her throat and tears were threatening to slide down her face.

"I'm serious," he continued, cutting her off. He squeezed her hand tighter. "Last night wasn't nothing to me. I love being part of your family, and I love you being part of mine. The last few weeks have felt incredible—cathartic, even."

His declarations were welling in her chest like her rib cage was about to give way to an internal combustion. *He wanted to stay here and be part of her family?* She hadn't even known who he was for the last few weeks. All of this was too much, too quickly, and she had to throw dynamite at the moment. "You're not a part of my family, Evan."

He let go of her hand, clearing his throat as he shoved his hands into his pockets instead. "Well, I mean..."

"No, Evan," she continued, because it was too late to stop the self-destructive meltdown that was already barreling through her brain. "We are *not* family. I'm not even sure we are friends at this point. I don't even know who you really are. And at the end of the day, you're not the twins' father— Billy is."

The kitchen was suddenly so quiet, she could hear the hum of the refrigerator like it was coming through a megaphone. Evan's face turned stony in an almost imperceptible way, but she saw it. She saw him close up and close off, and that's exactly what she'd wanted.

But it wasn't at all.

"I'm going to go." His voice had a catch in it, a rasp that he seemed to be trying to push away as he diverted his gaze and looked toward the front door. "Thanks for the coffee."

She turned her head to follow him as she watched him leave the kitchen, walk past the bedroom they'd just spent hours in, and out the front door. A hollow thud echoed as it closed between them, and she was pretty sure she was going to be sick.

"Wow."

Rosie startled at the exclamation, glancing to the left to see her daughter standing at the hallway entrance, still in her pajamas. "Becs, hey. Sorry, I didn't know you were awake."

Becca walked farther into the kitchen and leaned against the wall. "Mom, you were just really mean to Mr. Nowak. I'm not going to pretend like I didn't just see all that."

"It's complicated," Rosie began, trying to find her words. How the heck was she supposed to explain this to a kid? "I am sorry you saw that. You're right. I wasn't being very nice just then."

"You weren't telling the truth, either," her daughter added. "Zander and I do think of the Nowaks like family. I think it would be sort of cool for Tess to be my sister. Zander does, too, even if he won't admit it. And we really like you and Mr. Nowak dating. It's obvious you're really happy when he's around."

"Dating? We're, uh, well, I wouldn't call it dating." Rosie cleared her throat and looked away from her daughter. She grabbed a dish towel and wiped the counter for the third time that morning. This might be the cleanest her kitchen counters had ever been.

"We're not babies anymore, Mom." Becca didn't let up. "We have eyes."

"Okay, maybe we were dating, or some version of that," Rosie admitted, finally facing her daughter. "But it's not going to work out. I don't want anyone getting their hopes up. They're going back to Chicago at the end of the summer, and we don't *need* anyone. We're fine. I'm fine. We don't need them."

"No, but we want them," Becca shot back. "All of us—you, too."

"Becca, please," Rosie begged. "I can't have this conversation right now. You don't understand adult relationships, okay? It's complicated. This is what's best. Just believe me. I'm your mother, and I know what I'm talking about."

Her daughter rolled her eyes with a flourish and huffed back down the hallway toward her bedroom. Seconds later, her bedroom door slammed shut loudly.

Rosie felt her stomach drop, so she wiped the counter a fourth time as she replayed the last two conversations in her mind. *I'm going to go.* Evan's last words played on repeat and she could still see the hurt in his expression. She felt sick that she'd put that feeling there, but she hadn't had another choice. Had she? She'd spent the better part of the last decade alone, and she was doing just fine. Changing that up now was a risk she wasn't willing to take. It was just a way to set her up for disappointment. Billy had done nothing but disappoint her in her life. Hell, his father sent a check, but still didn't want to meet his grandkids. He'd been a disappointment, too.

That was the entire reason for how she'd set up her life. She didn't rely on anyone. She needed no one. And she wasn't about to let Evan and his family in to ruin that now. Even if that ache in her chest made her doubt her decision.

Chapter Twenty

"Wait...why?" Tess had her hands on her hips and a glare on her face as she stared him down. "I thought we were going to stay."

"It was a fun idea." Evan cleared his throat and finished folding the pair of jeans in his hands. He placed it carefully in his suitcase. "But it isn't practical, you know? Our life is in Chicago. Your school, my job, our house. And we aren't far from here. We can come see Grandma and Grandpa anytime."

"But...but...I thought you wanted to stay? I do! Don't you care about that?" Tess was not going to let this one go, but he'd expected her defiance when he'd announced that they needed to pack to head back home this week.

It was two weeks earlier than he'd originally planned, but there was no way he could stay in this town and run into Rosie every day and not feel like his heart hadn't been ripped out and stomped on. Plus, he had been really phoning it in at work this summer, and he needed to refocus and make sure he was hitting his target numbers. He'd hired a tutor to prep Tess for the school year as well, because they'd spent most of this past summer playing around. He didn't want her to fall into bad habits. After all, look what happened when he had. He'd let his guard down and he'd been open to maybe doing things differently, living differently...and it had all gone up in flames.

If he'd been prepared and rational instead of following the whims of his heart, then he could have avoided all of this.

"Dad, stop packing!" Tess was trying to pull at his suitcase now.

Evan straightened and let go. He wasn't about to fight her for it. "I hear that you don't like this choice. I get it. But I'm the parent. I know what's best for this family, and returning home is what's best. We've got a lot to catch up on before the school year starts."

"What about Grandma and Grandpa? What about Rosie and the twins?" Tess was actively removing the clothes from his suitcase and putting them back in the drawer. "We can't just leave them, Dad!"

"We'll be back to visit your grandparents often, like we've always done," he assured her. "They are not going anywhere."

Even as he said that, a nervous thought entered his head about how he didn't really know how long he had with his parents at this point. He tried not to think about his father's health and instead focused on Tess.

Tess kept unpacking his bag. "Okay, what about Rosie? She loves you."

"What?" Surprise caught in Evan's throat and he took a step back. "What are you talking about?"

"You and Rosie? You're dating, right?" Tess asked. "So, is it love?"

Evan shook his head. "Tess, I'm not...we're not...nothing is happening between Rosie and me."

"Why not?" Tess had stopped moving long enough to cross her arms over her chest and stare him down. "You love her, too. Why are you pretending that you don't?"

"You know how much I love your mom," Evan responded, feeling flustered as he tried to come up with an explanation that would make sense to her. Hell, none of this made sense to him, either.

Tess shook her head. "This isn't about Mom. Mom is gone. Rosie is right here."

"Tess!" Evan admonished her. "Don't talk that way about your mother."

She rolled her eyes again, letting out a loud exasperated sigh. "Dad, I love Mom, but you're the one who told me she would want to see me keep living and making a life for myself. She'd say the same thing to you, too."

With that, she walked out of the room and left Evan standing there completely unsure how to move forward. He hadn't given his daughter enough credit. She had been paying attention, and she wasn't wrong. Still, she didn't know everything, and he certainly wasn't about to tell her about his breakup with Rosie yesterday morning.

Was it even a breakup? They hadn't technically been together, but he had basically professed his love for her and had it thrown back in his face. When he'd first left her house that morning, he'd been furious at the things she'd said to him, but anger was a secondary emotion, and by the time he got home, he'd reflected on it enough to realize he wasn't angry. He was hurt. Deeply, deeply hurt. He didn't think Rosie was a bad person, and he didn't hate her, but the trust they'd been building had been wiped away instantaneously at her words. He'd found himself calling his old therapist last night and asking for an emergency phone session. It had been really helpful to have somewhere to vent and share his feelings, but she had pushed for him to try and see things from Rosie's perspective—that she'd felt betrayed that he didn't admit to knowing her secret. He just wasn't ready for that yet. The hurt was still too much to overlook, and she'd set a pretty firm boundary.

She did not want to be with him. Period.

He had to respect that choice, even if he was pretty sure this entire fiasco had *self-sabotage* written all over it.

"She's a fiery one," Evan's father announced himself from the doorway.

Evan furrowed his brow. "What?"

"Tess." Antoni nodded down the hall to where Tess had departed. "I could hear her screaming from the back porch."

"Sorry," he replied, shaking his head. He opened his suitcase back up and began repacking his clothes into it. "She's going to be fine. We just had a disagreement."

"Yeah, I think we all heard that disagreement. You're leaving, huh?" His father made no motion to go anywhere, and Evan prepared himself for an imminent lecture—or silence.

"We've got a lot to get back to in Chicago," Evan replied, staying evasive as he packed. He didn't want to divulge more information, because he wasn't even sure what he'd say. How could he explain what had happened this summer? How could he explain how he felt? So far, he really couldn't, except that it all hurt. It hurt so damn much. "We'll be back to visit all the time, though, Dad."

"I know." Antoni was quiet for a moment, just watching him. "It's just...your mother and I...we were...well, never mind." Finally, he let out a deep sigh, and turned and walked away.

Evan paused for a moment, looking up from the suitcase to watch his father's retreat. They were right back to their silence, the missing communication he'd worked so hard to change between them. He had a hunch that his father wanted him to stay, but he wouldn't actually ask. The man didn't have an expressive bone in his body.

A lifelong entrepreneur and business owner, Antoni Nowak was an independent leader. He'd been the oldest son. He worked. And worked. And worked more. Providing for his family is what mattered. Period. It was one of the things Evan admired most about his father, and yet, it put a huge barrier between them, preventing them from emotionally connecting in any way. Why did that feel so familiar? His mind couldn't help but slip over to Rosie, wondering if her inability to open up and let him in wasn't somewhat similar. Even if it was, there wasn't anything he could do about that. He'd spent a lifetime trying to crack his father open, and he'd failed repeatedly. He didn't have it in him to fail again with someone else.

Maybe Rosie had done him a favor after all.

"Evan!" his mother's voice called out to him from somewhere else in the house.

He kept packing and called back to her. "Up here!"

"Evan!" she called again, and this time he tuned in to her voice and tone. It was strained, panicked.

He immediately dropped the clothes he was holding and moved into the hallway. "Mom, where are you?"

"Living room! I need your help." Her tone thinned, like she was exerting a lot of energy.

Evan headed to the living room at double-time pace, turning the corner to find his father in the middle of the floor, lying on the rug. His mother's arm was around him, trying to help him stand up. Antoni seemed a little dazed and confused, mumbling something unintelligible to his mother.

"Dad!" Evan was by his father's side immediately, helping lift him up and securing him in a seated position on the couch. "What happened?"

Everly was wringing her hands, nervously watching them both. "He went to get up from the couch and just...went down. I don't know!"

"Okay." Evan examined his father's eyes, but it was like Antoni wasn't looking at him, even though that's exactly what he was doing. "Dad, can you see me? Are you okay?"

"What? Yeah, yeah, I'm good." His father's words were a bit slurred and his head was bobbing in an unnatural way.

"Mom, call 911." Evan wasn't about to take any chances. He wanted a professional to examine his father immediately. The Parkinson's diagnosis was scary enough, and he didn't understand enough about it to know if this was normal or not. "Dad, we're going to go to the hospital and just get you checked out, okay? Tess, come down here, please!"

His daughter appeared at the bottom of the stairs a minute later. "What's going on? Is Grandpa okay?"

"I need you to call Rosie and ask her to come pick you up. You can stay over there tonight if she's available." Evan glanced over at his mother who was talking to the 911 operator. He would follow the ambulance to the hospital, since no doubt his mother would ride in the back with his father. But he wasn't about to have Tess go to the hospital if she didn't have to. He didn't know what they were going to tell him, and he couldn't risk Tess seeing something she couldn't handle. Or that he couldn't handle. "We're going to have Grandpa checked out at the hospital."

Tess pulled her cell phone out and began dialing. "Can I stay here alone until she comes?"

Given the last twenty-four hours, Rosie was the last person he wanted to interact with, but his back was against the wall. She's the only person he knew that Tess would feel comfortable with and he was pretty confident she would come and help if he needed it. He wasn't sure why he felt so sure of that after what happened between them, but he did.

"Yeah." Evan was nervous about that, but she was old enough to do so for short periods of time. "But do not go anywhere unless it's with Rosie and the twins. Bring your flash cards with you."

"My flash cards??" Tess looked confused, her brows furrowed. "Dad, are you being serious? Grandpa is sick!"

"I know, Tess." His words were short and curt, but he wasn't about to argue with her again. Everything felt like it was slipping out of his control in the last twenty-four hours, and now his father was potentially hurt or sick or God knows what. But Tess was right. Who gives a flying fig about flash cards. "Sorry, never mind. Just get some clothing together."

"They are on their way," his mother came up beside him. "She said two to three minutes at most."

"Okay, great. Dad, how are you feeling?" Evan got down on one knee in front of his father, trying to examine his eye contact.

"I'm fine." Antoni's eye contact finally seemed a bit more stable and like he was actually locating and focusing on Evan. "Really, you guys are overreacting. It was just a dizzy spell."

"I'm sure, Dad, but we need to make sure you didn't hit your head or have a stroke or something," Evan explained. He could see the flash of red and blue lights out the window and turned to his mother. "Mom, can you open the front door and tell the paramedics we're in here?"

"Sure, sure." His mother nodded, still wringing her hands and looking around nervously. "Uh, I'll get his wallet. It has our insurance cards."

"Rosie is on her way." Tess reappeared at the bottom of the stairs to announce the plans.

Evan felt a small sense of relief with that news. "Okay, great. Please turn on the porch light."

"Which one of these is the health insurance?" Everly pushed a stack of cards into his hands. "The writing is so small."

"Well, this one is a gift card to the Gas and Pass." Evan shuffled through the cards quickly. "And this is dental insurance. Why do you have a membership to Meats that Beats? What the heck is that?"

"They send you a cut of meat every month with a matching playlist," his father announced from where he was sitting on the couch. "So, you can listen to music while you eat the meat."

"Okay, he definitely needs to get checked out by professionals." Evan finally found the insurance cards as the paramedics came in and began asking Antoni questions and looking in his eyes with a flashlight. One paramedic took out a blood pressure cuff and began measuring on Antoni's upper arm.

"His blood pressure is very low," the paramedic said, concerned. "Sir, we're going to help you out to the ambulance. Can you sit in a wheelchair?"

"Sure, sure." Antoni tried to push himself up off the couch but toppled slightly over to the side.

One of the paramedics grabbed him quickly. "Sir, please wait. We're going to help you into the chair."

"I'm fine," Antoni tried to assure them, pushing their hands away.

"Dad, stop. You have to let them help you," Evan tried to reason with him, but the paramedics wouldn't let him get closer. Antoni grumbled but acquiesced to them, and Evan watched nervously as they lifted him into a wheelchair.

"Can I ride with him?" his mother asked, her hand on Antoni's shoulder. "I need to go with him. He gets confused."

The paramedics assured her that she could and she followed closely as they maneuvered him out of the house and carried him down the porch stairs. Evan was right behind, his car keys in hand, when he saw Rosie's car pull up in front of his parents' house. Her front tire hit the curb from how fast she was going, and she jumped out immediately and called over the top of the car. "Evan, are you guys okay?"

He didn't have the ability to respond to that right now, but instead just nodded and waved from a distance. Everything about the last few minutes felt chaotic and all he could focus on was getting his dad safely to the hospital.

"Tess, stay with Rosie!" he called back to his daughter who was standing on the porch looking younger than she had in years, a vulnerability in her expression that he didn't often see. Hell, he couldn't remember the last time he'd seen it. A paramedic helped Everly up into the back of the ambulance after his father and Evan headed for his car. "Mom, I'll follow you guys there."

He waited in the front seat of his car as the ambulance pulled out of the driveway and flicked its lights on. A blaring siren pierced his eardrums as he put the car in gear and followed it down their street. He knew his father was fine. Most likely, completely fine. At least, that's what he needed to tell himself.

Evan thought back to his half-packed suitcase still lying on his bed and the way his father had looked at him before walking off and then collapsing in the living room. *How could he ever leave now?*

Chapter Twenty-One

"Are you okay?" Rosie asked the young girl as she walked up the steps to Evan's parents' house.

Tess nodded but didn't respond verbally. She looked fragile in that moment, like she might completely fall apart if forced to say one word.

Rosie understood the feeling and put her arm around Tess and ushered her inside. "Come on. Let's go get some water."

She was grateful that she'd gotten Tess's call when she'd been at her father's house with the twins for dinner. Thomas and Marvel jumped at the chance to babysit the twins while she ran over here—a much shorter drive than if she'd been at her house in the woods. Despite everything that had happened yesterday morning with Evan, there hadn't been a moment's pause when it came to helping his daughter. She hadn't even had to think about it. It felt natural, it felt obvious.

It felt like family.

The pit in her stomach that she'd been trying to ignore sank harder. She busied herself with grabbing Tess a glass of water and some cookies from the pantry. Tess didn't eat a bite though, instead tracing her finger up and down the side of the water glass and making lines in the condensation.

"I don't know how long your father is going to be gone," Rosie finally broke the silence as she sat in the chair across the kitchen table. "But do you want to come over to my dad's house? The twins are there and I'm sure they'd love to play with you and keep you distracted."

Tess nodded, still not speaking.

"Okay. Well, drink a little water and then grab whatever you need, and we'll go. I'll leave your dad a note on the counter." Rosie grabbed a notepad and pen that were already lying out on the kitchen table and began scrawling a note.

"What if he dies when we're back in Chicago?" Tess's small voice echoed through the room, her eyes still focused on her glass of water.

"Honey," Rosie nearly cooed, reaching a hand out and placing it on top of hers. "Your grandfather is going to be okay."

"But if he's not? And I'm not here?" Tess looked up then, and the bottom edge of her lashes were welling with tears. "I wasn't there when my mom died. I was at school. I didn't get to say goodbye..."

She trailed off and a sob caught in her throat.

Rosie stood and circled around the table, wrapping her arms around Tess. She could feel her shoulders shaking and muffled sobs coming from where her face was pressed against Rosie's chest. They stayed like that for a few minutes until Tess's cries calmed down and she pulled away, grabbing a napkin to wipe her face.

"I was sixteen years old when my mother died," Rosie started. She wasn't sure where she was going with her story, but the ache in her chest felt like she needed to get it all out. Everything she saw on Tess's face felt so goddamn familiar, and it had been awhile since she'd let herself sit in those memories. "I was at my friend Nola's house. Her grandmother, Gigi, was taking care of both of us and Amanda while our parents were all at the hospital. My dad didn't want me to be there. I remember he thought he was helping me by not allowing me to see Mom like that, but I was pretty angry at him for a long time. I still wish I had been there."

Tess nodded slowly, as if she understood. "Dad said he was sorry I wasn't there when my mom died. He said they hadn't known that that day would be...that day. If he had, I'd have been there."

Rosie felt her heart swelling in her chest. Of course, Evan had told his daughter that. Of course, he'd wanted them to be together and hold his daughter in that moment. A rush of regret hit her like a tidal wave and she could feel her own tears threatening to fall. She blinked quickly, trying to push them back, but there was no use. Tears streamed down her face faster than she could keep up and she ducked her face into her hands.

"What's wrong?" Tess put her hand on Rosie's knee. "Are you okay?"

"Yes, yes." Rosie cleared her throat and dabbed at her eyes with the sleeve of her shirt. "I'm so sorry. I'm the adult. I shouldn't be over here crying. You're going through so much."

Tess just shrugged, her nose still bright pink from her own tears. "Everyone needs to cry sometimes. It's good not to cry alone."

And that was the full damn truth, wasn't it? Rosie felt Tess's words and wondered how someone so young could say something so wise. It's good not to cry alone. But Rosie did everything alone. Not because she had to or needed to, but because she felt like she was supposed to. She had pushed Evan away just like she had everyone else in her life who tried to step in and help her raise her children or save her bookstore. She could do it all herself. She didn't need anyone else.

But, God, she wanted someone else. She wanted someone to be there to hold her when she cried. She wanted someone to curl up with at night and kiss good morning with stale breath and raise a family together that stayed together. She wanted all of that, and Evan had offered that to her. He'd offered her his heart.

And she'd said no.

Hell, she'd said worse than no. She'd basically taken it and stomped on it and thrown it in the lake.

"Tess, your father is a smart man," Rosie finally said.

Tess smiled at that, and her sad expression turned mischievous in a quick change. "Does that mean you're going to ask him to stay here? And you guys are going to date for real?"

Rosie reached out and squeezed Tess's hand. Christ, these kids saw so much more than she realized. "I'd love to, honey. But...I think I messed things up with your dad. He's had a rough few years, you know? I don't need to make things harder on him."

It felt wrong even as she was saying it, but there was no way she could ask him to change his plans yet again. Not after everything she'd said to him yesterday. But she was going to apologize. That much she definitely owed him, but even more so, she needed to do it for herself. She needed to admit out loud that it was okay to be supported by other people, to turn to her community for love and help. It shouldn't have taken her all these years to learn that, but Evan had made the point finally loud and clear to her.

"Come on," Rosie continued. "Let's grab your stuff and head out. I'll text your dad and check to see if they got to Heart Lake Hospital yet."

Tess looked disappointed but got up and went upstairs. She returned a minute later with a small backpack and joined Rosie in her car. Ten minutes later, they were pulling up to Thomas's house and Rosie's phone notified her of an incoming text message.

He's okay. They think it was a low-blood-pressure issue. Orthostatic hypertension or something like that. Probably need some medication and monitoring but then we'll be able to discharge later. Can you keep Tess until then?

Rosie read Evan's message and felt the fear gripping around her heart ease. She was glad that it wasn't anything worse than that, though she could imagine how scared Evan must be after all he'd lost in the past. She wanted to drop Tess off with her dad and rush to the hospital to hug him, hold his hand through the entire thing... but she couldn't do that. He didn't want that after what she'd said to him.

Sure. We're here whenever, she texted back.

"Hey, Tessy girl," Marvel greeted them as she opened the front door to Thomas's house. "The twins are in the basement watching a movie. Want to go join? I'm making popcorn now!"

"Thank you!" Tess ran off in the direction that Marvel pointed her.

Rosie followed Marvel back to the kitchen and helped her open a few bags of popcorn and stick them in the microwave one at a time. She grabbed a few small bowls from under the counter, as well as some salt and movie-theater butter—her favorite addition to homemade popcorn. Technically it was just soybean oil and not really butter, but she always grabbed a bottle at the grocery store before a big movie night, and a non-soy version for Zander. Thankfully, her father stocked both as well.

"Where's Dad?" Rosie asked Marvel, realizing she hadn't

seen him since returning. When she'd left, he'd been in the recliner in the living room watching the news as usual.

"He went upstairs to take a nap," Marvel replied, grabbing a fully popped pack out of the microwave and replacing it with an uncooked pack. "He's not been sleeping too well lately. Though I imagine you haven't either." She winked at Rosie and wiggled her brows. "How are things going with the hot single dad?"

Rosie looked down, trying to ignore the warm feeling rushing into her cheeks. "Uh…not great. I think I kind of messed things up on that front. He's headed back to Chicago soon anyway. It wouldn't have worked out."

"Why the hell not?" Marvel put her hands on her hips. "You were the first person he called when he had an emergency. The entire town has seen how you look at each other. And the twins and Tess are basically long-lost siblings at this point. Have you seen them together? It's the cutest freaking little pod of tween affection you've ever seen."

That last part was certainly true. "The kids do get along really well."

"See? So, whatever dumb shit you said, just go apologize." Marvel shrugged like it was the most obvious answer in the world. "You'd need a court order to keep me away from the man I love, and hell, that's not been shown to be very effective with me in the past, either."

"Wait, what?" Rosie looked up at the woman currently dating her father. "Uh, is there a story there that I should know?"

"Better that you don't, dearie." Marvel laughed and poured the bag of popcorn out into a large bowl. "But you would be wise to listen to me. You like that boy. He likes you. The rest—it will all work itself out."

"The twins' father is back in town," Rosie reminded Marvel. "It's not as cut-and-dry as that."

"A speed bump, at best. It's not like you're going back to him or anything."

Rosie shook her head. "Definitely not."

"Did you see his latest music video? He had a literal snake crawling out of his pants. I swear to God, I don't understand music anymore. Give me The Beatles and I'm on cloud nine." Marvel shook her head. "An entire damn snake, Rosie. In his pants!"

She chuckled, partially because of Marvel's strong opinion on the matter, but also because she'd been weirded out too when she'd seen that debut a few months back. That was before he'd come back into the twins' lives, but it was certainly a very clear reminder that she wasn't the type of groupie to hang around backstage at Billy's shows anymore. In fact, it made her laugh to think that she ever was that person, once upon a time.

"He's been okay with the twins so far. They do enjoy spending time with him." Rosie thought back to the recent allergic reaction. "He definitely has a lot to learn about being a parent."

"There's plenty of time for that." Marvel waved her hand. "The twins can teach him as they go, but I bet they'd be more than open to the Nowak boy being in their life, too."

Rosie was quiet for a moment. "How would I even explain that to them? They have never seen me date—ever. I haven't since Billy. At least, not seriously enough to bring someone home. What if they get attached and then things don't work out?"

"I think they're already attached, dearie," Marvel pointed out. "And according to you, you already messed it up and we're all still here. He still called you to take care of his daughter in a moment of need. This isn't rocket science, you know."

She laughed at how blunt Marvel put everything, but there was a lot of truth to what she'd said. There was no doubt that the twins were very attached to Tess. They talked about her nonstop, and they talked about Evan, too. That ship had already sailed, even if she'd tried to sink it yesterday.

And he had called. Or Tess had. But still... he'd wanted her in a moment when things were hard. Maybe he just didn't have anyone else to call, or maybe... maybe there was still a chance for them.

Chapter Twenty-Two

"Dad, you heard the doctor!" Evan grabbed his father's arm, securing him as the old man tried to stand up from his seat in the car. "You're moving too fast. You have to get up slowly or you could pass out again."

"Yeah, yeah," Antoni acquiesced, allowing him to help him. "Those doctors always tell you to be careful. It's their job. I've been getting up and down by myself for more than sixty years."

"Antoni, please just listen to the doctors," Everly chided her husband. She was holding a plastic bag labeled Patient Belongings and a small white paper bag from the hospital pharmacy. "Let's just get you inside and set up with some of *The First 48.*"

"Ooh, I love that show," Antoni agreed, always the true-crime buff. "They filmed an episode not too far from here, you know. Out in Grand Rapids. Body was found in a lake. Not our lake though."

"Okay, Dad. Enjoy that." Murder and gruesome crimes weren't exactly the conversation Evan wanted to have right now. He helped his father settle in on the couch in the living room and checked on his mother who was organizing pill bottles in the kitchen. "Mom, do you need anything? I'm going to go grab Tess from the Deans'."

She shook her head. "No, he's fine now. Just a little

light-headed. This blood pressure medicine should help going
forward."

"Yeah," Evan agreed. "Still, don't let him stand up too
quickly."

"I'll do my best, but you know your father." Everly smiled
at him. "Go on. Go get Tessy. And don't hurry back. If you
want to spend some time with the Dean girl, we're fine over
here. I really like her, Evan. She's been really good for you
this summer, and it's nice seeing you so happy again."

"Mom, we're not..." He didn't know how to finish that
sentence. A familiar ache settled in his chest as he thought
of yesterday and the way Rosie had turned him away. Her
words still stung, but seeing her today and how quickly she'd
stepped in to help with Tess... it didn't match up. It made
her words feel hollow, and he found himself doubting their
validity. She had been lying—if not to him, then definitely
to herself. There wasn't a doubt in his mind that Rosie loved
him the same way he loved her.

He just had to get her to admit it.

Twenty minutes later, he'd finished helping his parents
settle in and was pulling his car into Thomas Dean's driveway. He'd been to this house a few times as a kid, but it had
been years. Everything looked the same though, including
being able to see through the large front window directly
into the kitchen. Rosie was standing by the table laughing,
her head tipping back slightly when she did so. The twins
and Tess were sitting all around the table, along with Marvel
and Thomas, and there was a big bowl of what looked like
spaghetti from this distance, but he couldn't be too sure.

They looked like a happy family, and he could feel a lump
beginning to form in his throat. He hadn't been able to give
Tess that in years. Not since Layla. This wasn't the same as

Layla—nothing ever would be—but God, it felt good to see his daughter laughing and loved in a warm home like this.

How could he even think about going back to Chicago? If his father's incident today hadn't been enough to change his mind, surely this was. He needed to stay in Heart Lake for Tess and his family, but he wanted to stay in Heart Lake for him...and Rosie.

Evan stepped out of the car and headed up the walkway, knocking firmly on the front door. He briefly considered just walking right in—he was pretty sure that was the expected move in this small town—but he still felt somewhat hesitant.

Rosie swung open the front door with a huge smile on her face that suddenly disappeared when she saw him. Her brow furrowed and a look of concern swept over her. "Is everything okay? How's your father?"

"He's okay. He's home." Evan pushed his hands into his pockets and looked down at his shoes for a minute. "Can I, uh, can I talk to you outside for a minute?"

She paused a moment, then glanced back to where he could hear the laughter and chatter from the kitchen. "Sure. Yeah. Let's go around back. There's a path on the side of the house to the lake."

He nodded and followed her lead as she closed the front door behind her and walked down the steps. She turned on the grass and cut across the yard, circling around the back of the house with him only a few steps behind.

"Do you want to sit out there?" Rosie pointed to a worn gazebo on the edge of the property that he remembered getting drunk under in high school a few times. There was a stack of wood and construction supplies next to it on the ground. "Sorry it's a bit messy. Tanner's rebuilding it. This thing has taken a beating over the years."

"I remember," Evan agreed as he followed her under the gazebo.

She sat on a bench that circled the entire thing and offered him the seat next to her. "Do you want to sit?"

"Yeah." He wasn't sure why he felt so nervous, but it could have something to do with the fact that he had no idea what the hell he wanted to say right now—or how to say it. "Rosie, about yesterday—"

"Evan, I am so sorry." She cut him off before he could finish his first sentence. "Yesterday was...awful. I was awful. I shouldn't have said the things I said. I hate that when I get scared, I snap first and react calmly later. I'm working on it, but...I'm so sorry you got the brunt of it yesterday."

He appreciated her insight, but still felt things were unanswered. "You were scared?"

"Absolutely terrified," she confirmed, but didn't offer further explanation.

Evan chuckled lightly, shaking his head. "Well, that makes two of us, then. Rosie, I...I still feel the same way I felt yesterday. A little worse for the wear, maybe, but it's all still there."

He could see her visibly swallow hard, her gaze focused on something slightly off to the side of him like she couldn't look directly at him. Her response came out barely above a whisper. "Everything?"

"I didn't know how lonely I was until this summer," Evan lowered his voice as he responded to her, his tone soft and gentle. "I've been plugging along, just trying to keep everything together since Layla died. But I haven't been enjoying life. And, honestly, Layla would kick my ass for that."

Rosie laughed, her eyes finally meeting his. "She sounds like someone I would have been friends with."

Evan nodded, because he could absolutely see that happening in an alternate universe. "You guys would have liked each other. Tess is the one who reminded me of this earlier today, actually. I've made a lot of mistakes there, Rosie. God, I wish I could go back and rearrange my priorities with her. I've spent the last few years focused on academics and school placements and making sure her grades are perfect. I haven't actually *seen* my daughter growing up right before my eyes."

"Kids say the wisest things out of nowhere," Rosie agreed. "Becca had a similar come-to-Jesus talk with me yesterday. We must be doing something right with them."

"Maybe," he agreed. "But I want to do better going forward. I want to give her the things Layla wanted for her—love, family, closeness. Those are the things I want, too. Rosie, I want those things with you."

She was quiet for a moment, and he saw the glistening of an escaped tear run down her cheek. "What about Chicago?" she whispered.

"I'm not going back to Chicago," he replied, making the decision in that moment. He was going to sell his house and buy something up here. Hell, he might just rent it out and still buy something up here. Whatever it was that he was going to do, he knew, gut deep, that he wasn't leaving Heart Lake. He wasn't leaving his parents, and he damn sure wasn't leaving Rosie.

She looked up at him. "You're staying here?"

Evan reached for her now, taking her hand in between his and tugging her to him gently. She let him move her, her hands twisting in the fabric on the front of his shirt as he pulled her onto his lap. "Rosie, I love you. I'm not going anywhere unless it's with you."

A quiet sob left Rosie's lips and her tears began to fall faster. She leaned in and kissed him, her lips hard against his. Her arms wrapped around his neck, pinning herself to him. It felt like days, weeks, months, and not enough seconds until they finally pulled apart.

Rosie's face was flushed, and her expression was worried. "Evan, I'm so sorry for what I said. I didn't mean any of it. I... want you to stay. I want to be part of each other's family. I love you, too. Do you believe me?"

Evan moved his hand from her back to the base of her neck, letting his fingers tangle in her hair just enough to pull her to him. His mouth found hers again and he replied between kisses. "More than anything."

"Whoo! About time!" someone shouted from behind them, and Evan startled. He glanced over Rosie's shoulder to see Marvel standing on the deck raising her hands in a cheer. She turned toward the house. "Hey, Thomas, look what's happening in your gazebo! Kids, come out here."

"Oh my God," Rosie groaned, quickly pushing off his lap and straightening her clothes. "Why is my family so freaking insane?"

Evan laughed and stood up next to her, reaching one hand out to her. She intertwined her fingers with his and he squeezed. "Come on. Let's go face the firing squad."

"Are you sure?" Rosie was grinning, too. "They're truly insane people."

"I'm absolutely positive." He lifted her hand to his lips and kissed the back of her knuckles. "I'm not going anywhere, Rosie. Not even if you try to sabotage this again."

She laughed. "Well, now you just sound like a stalker."

"If you'll have me," he teased back, before getting the sudden urge to kiss her again. He dropped her hand and instead wrapped his arms around her waist and lifted her off the ground and spun her in a circle. "Damn it, Rosie Dean. I'm going to marry you one day."

"Evan!" she squealed, patting his shoulders to try and get him to put her down. "You're insane!"

But when her lips pressed down on his and her hands held his face, he realized that this might be the sanest he's ever been. And he couldn't believe he'd waited this long to find the woman who'd been right here in his hometown the entire time.

"Welcome home, Evan Nowak," she whispered in his ear as he finally lowered her back to the ground. "Come on, let's go tell the kids what they already all guessed."

"We should have asked them to tell us earlier," Evan joked. "But, better late than never."

Hand in hand, he walked with the woman he loved up to the house, and when he saw the way Tess smiled at them as they approached, he felt an overwhelming sense of peace. It felt like Layla was there in that moment, telling him that this was what she wanted. He could feel tears springing to his eyes, but he couldn't remember the last time he'd felt this damn happy. But he suspected he would have a lot of that joyful feeling going forward as he finally came home...this time, for good.

Epilogue

"That's how I knew I was pregnant," Nola said. She was seated in the rocking chair of the nursery, a little baby attached to her nipple, feeding. Motherhood looked damn good on her best friend, and Rosie was already head over heels in love with her brand-new tiny niece. "My boobs felt like they were heavy bowling balls and hurt so freaking bad. I wouldn't let Tanner anywhere near them for the entire first trimester."

"First of all, gross." Rosie didn't like thinking about her brother's sex life. "But second, it could just be a period symptom, too, right?"

Nola shrugged. "Do you normally get that symptom, or symptoms at all?"

She didn't. Rosie had been pretty regular most of her life and blessed with usually pain-free monthly cycles. This month, however, she was two days late and her breasts felt like they were swollen. "What the hell am I going to tell Evan? Should I take a test? Do I take a test then tell Evan, or do the test with him there?"

"Rosie, chill," Nola calmed her nervous rambling. "You've got time. Whatever you decide is fine! I'm sure Evan will be thrilled no matter how he finds out."

"Do you think?" Rosie found herself chewing on the edge of her thumbnail. "We haven't talked about kids at all. Like, not even once. We already have three between the two of us and we've only been dating for eight months. Literally not even a full school year. Hell, we haven't even talked about marriage!"

"You've known each other your whole lives though," Nola pointed out. "And you guys are only a week out from closing on a house together. I'd say it's fair to assume he's all in at this point—and you are, too."

"I'm going to text Amanda and ask her to bring a test with her when she gets here," Rosie decided, since she knew Amanda would be here shortly for the Sunday family barbecue at Nola and Tanner's house. All of the families were going to be there, including her parents and Evan's parents, and, best of all, Layla's parents. They still lived in Chicago, but Rosie had been adamant that it was important to her that they were allowed as much access to Tess and their new life in Heart Lake as they wanted. Not that Evan hadn't given them that before, but he had not been as proactive about making plans as Rosie tended to be. He'd admitted that he'd let the relationship become a bit distant because of how much it hurt to be reminded of Layla, but now he said remembering her felt only positive. That meant a lot to Rosie—more than she could even explain, really. After losing her own mother as a young girl, she knew what a hole that had left in her heart, and she would do anything she could to mitigate as much of those feelings as she could for Tess.

She'd fallen head over heels in love with Evan's daughter, just like she knew she would. There was no denying that Tess, Becca, and Zander acted like they'd been together their entire lives. They bickered like siblings, played like best friends, and had even gotten in the habit recently of working together to prank Evan and Rosie. Their latest escapade had been clear plastic wrap across the toilet, which was an experience Rosie would prefer to never repeat again.

"She said she'd swing by the pharmacy on the way here," Rosie confirmed, looking up from her phone after reading Amanda's text response to her. "So, I guess one way or the other…maybe I'll have an answer today?"

Nola smiled at her. "We need more babies around here anyway."

Rosie still wasn't sure how she felt about that. She had kind of assumed that part of her life was over now that the twins were getting older, but she'd be lying if she didn't admit that there was a buzz of excitement humming through her veins right now. "Do you need anything from the kitchen? Water? Snacks?"

Nola shook her head and pointed to the caddy beside her that was basically a breastfeeding cart on wheels and completely stocked with everything from granola bars to nipple cream. "I'm good. I'll be down shortly once she's asleep."

"Okay." Rosie said goodbye and headed downstairs to the kitchen to see what she could help with.

Marvel was pulling a tray of cookies out of the oven and they looked…pink?

"What are those?" Rosie asked, eyeing the oval shaped cookies.

"Vulva cookies," Marvel responded, as if that was something she said every day. "We're celebrating Nola's graduation from pelvic-floor therapy!"

"Uh…" Rosie wasn't sure she could come up with a response to that one. "Well, okay. I'm going to check on the kids."

"They're out back playing on the dock. The men are watching them," Marvel confirmed before sticking her head back in the oven for the next batch.

Rosie made her way out onto the back porch where she could see all three kids with their fishing rods down at the end of the dock. She smiled when she saw Billy sitting there with them, though he looked like he had no clue what he was doing when it came to fishing. Becca was trying to show him how to untangle his rod, and Zander was laughing. It made her heart warm to see them getting along with their father.

Billy had become a regular part of their lives, though she wouldn't say he'd ever really stepped into the father-figure role. Instead, though, he popped into town between shows and tours to see the kids and had even bought himself a condo in the next town over so he had a regular place to stay when he visited. He was going on tour this summer, so he'd been here more than usual, and she appreciated that he was finally putting in the time. Plus, she appreciated that he'd finally started paying child support, including a lump sum that only partially made up for the years without.

"Hey, babe," Evan called out to her and she turned her attention to where he was standing at the grill with Tanner and Layla's father, Jack. Evan's father, Antoni, was seated in a chair close by, his cane propped up next to him. "Can you grab the plate of uncooked burgers in the fridge? It's time to grill them!"

She nodded, grinning, and hurried back inside to fetch the platter of perfectly formed patties.

When she returned to the grill area, Evan leaned in and kissed her. "Thanks, love."

"Can mine have extra cheese?" she asked, eyeing the pack of cheese slices to the side.

Evan laughed. "I already set aside a few for you. I know how much you love your cheese."

Rosie pushed up on her toes and planted another kiss on

him. God, she loved this man. She couldn't even remember how she'd once thought she had to be an island—taking care of herself, entirely independent, never leaning on anyone for support or kindness. Now, she luxuriated in living life *with* Evan. And that didn't just mean side by side, but rather completely intertwined. The house that they were buying together had been a labor of love for the both of them and was only a few properties down from his parents' house. Her bookstore was thriving more than ever, and Evan frequently would come do a shift if Davon was out or if she needed extra help behind the counter.

"Rosie!" Amanda called out to her as she walked around the side of the house and headed down to where they were seated in the grill area on the stone patio. "Can you come here a minute?"

She felt her heart leap into her throat seeing the small white bag in Amanda's hand that she knew carried the pregnancy test. Taking a deep breath, Rosie leaned closer to Evan and whispered in his ear. "Hey, come meet me in the bathroom in three minutes."

Evan's brow lifted and a mischievous smile crossed his face. "Okay."

She could feel the butterflies rolling around her stomach, but there was no doubting it was excitement now. She ran off to Amanda and quickly took the bag from her before running into the house.

"You could say thank you!" Amanda called after her, chuckling.

"Thank you!" Rosie said over her shoulder, then ducked into the bathroom off the main hallway. With shaky hands, she tore open the box and quickly glanced over the instructions. It seemed pretty self-explanatory, and she made quick work of shoving the stick between her thighs and peeing on the end. When she was done, she recapped it and placed it on the counter. The results window was still dark and process-ing, so she pulled up her pants and washed her hands.

As soon as she was done, there was a soft knock on the door. "Rosie?"

She pushed open the door and ushered Evan inside, quickly closing it behind him. He immediately wrapped his arms around her and pulled her in for a kiss. She got lost for a moment as he pressed her up against the wall and his tongue found hers.

God, the way this man kissed was as electric today as it had been the first time they'd found themselves tangled around each other. Her left leg was already lifting to wrap around him, and he pulled her against him so firmly that she could feel how excited he was.

"This was a fantastic idea," Evan groaned against her ear. "You look incredible in those jeans. I've been thinking about this all day."

Her heart swelled in her chest, threatening to pound against her rib cage. Her mind was completely blank, and all she could focus on was the feeling of being one with the man she loved.

Until the alarm on her phone went off.

"What's that?" Evan pulled away just enough to breath-lessly ask about the beeping coming from her pocket.

She suddenly remembered why she'd asked him in here in the first place—and it hadn't been for a quickie. "Oh, shit. Evan..." She pushed against him until he stepped back and she was back on her own two feet.

"What?" His brow furrowed and then he glanced side-ways to the sink counter. His eyes went wide. "Is that a preg-nancy test?"

She fumbled with the phone in her pocket, turning off the alarm. "Uh, yeah . . . that was actually why I asked you to meet me in here."

"You're pregnant!" Evan's face lit up in a smile and he rushed forward, grabbing her in a giant embrace and spinning around. They nearly toppled over and hit the toilet, since there wasn't much room to move around. "Oh my God, we're going to have a baby!"

Rosie laughed. "Evan! I haven't even looked at the test yet! I just peed on it, and it takes three minutes. That's what the alarm was for. I wanted you to be here when I found out . . . if it's even true. It might not be!"

"Oh, it's true," Evan replied, letting go of her and picking up the test from the counter. "That's a big old plus sign, Rosie. We're having a baby."

Now her eyes went wide and she grabbed the stick from him. Sure enough, there was a very obvious plus sign in the response window. She was pregnant. "Oh, my God! I can't believe it!"

"Are you happy?" Evan asked her, his arm wrapping around her waist as he placed a kiss on her temple.

She nodded, tears beginning to blur her vision. She hadn't expected to get this emotional, but she felt like she was going to scream, burst into tears, and cheer all at the same time. "Are you?"

"Damn ecstatic," he replied. "But, uh, listen, I was going to save this for later, but in light of this news, I can't wait a second longer."

Rosie frowned. "What?"

Evan reached into his pocket and pulled out a small velvet ring box. "The kids and I have a whole proposal thing planned later, so you're going to have to act surprised. But

I don't want one minute to go by of you carrying my baby without you knowing that I'm one hundred percent committed to this baby, to you, to the twins."

"Evan..." She could feel the lump returning to her throat, her hand on her chest.

He got down on one knee, which was quite a feat given that he was basically kneeling between a toilet and a towel rod. He held the ring up to her, opening the box to reveal a gorgeous oval diamond on a thin silver band. "Rosie Dean, will you marry me? Like, as soon as possible?"

"Yes!" She threw her arms around his neck and kissed him so hard that they both fell backward and found themselves wedged into the corner. Rosie laughed as they tried to extract themselves, and then they both stood and he placed the ring on her finger. She held up her hand, looking at the sparkling ring. "Oh, my God. Pregnant and engaged. We're having a baby..."

"Damn right." Evan kissed her temple again and then placed a hand on her stomach. "Are you the big wedding type, or a backyard kind of thing?"

"I'm a let's-go-to-the-courthouse tomorrow type," she joked, but actually, that sounded fantastic to her.

Evan laughed. "Well, okay then. I'll book us an appointment at city hall as soon as they open. Now, give me the ring back."

"What?!" She held it to her chest possessively. "Why?"

"I told you, the kids and I have this whole elaborate proposal set up later this afternoon. We'll have to redo the whole thing and pretend like it's the first time." Evan was smiling as he held the ring box open for her to return her ring. "I can't wait to ask you again."

She laughed. "What if I don't say yes?"

"No take-backs," he kidded.

Rosie placed the ring back in the box, then grabbed the pregnancy stick and tucked it into her pocket. "Should we head back out there?"

"They are probably wondering where we are by now," Evan joked. "Although, highly unlikely they've guessed what just happened."

"We're getting married," Rosie whispered the words against his lips as she pushed up on her toes and kissed him. "And we're having a baby."

He held her against him, kissing her again and again in small pecks. "We're a whole damn family now."

Read on for a sneak peek of the first
book in the charming Heart Lake series:

Dreaming of a Heart Lake Christmas

AVAILABLE NOW

"It's still leaning to the left!"

Tanner Dean rubbed a calloused hand across his forehead and brows, trying to swallow the irritation building in him, while his other hand held steady a twenty-foot-tall Christmas tree in his father's vaulted-ceiling living room. He pushed the tree more toward the right. "How's this?"

"Now it's too far to the right. The base isn't even. You'll have to take it down and cut it," Thomas Dean replied, barking orders from the stuffed recliner that had definitely seen better days. The rest of Thomas's living room and his entire house was professionally decorated—Tanner's sister, Rosie, had enlisted their cousin Amanda's help with that—and it was beautiful enough to be photographed in *Home Digest*, except for the plaid recliner with loose threads and faded patches placed in the center of the living room with perfect proximity to the fireplace to feel the warmth on cold winter nights. With the damn chair aimed squarely at the television, it was a safe bet that is where Tanner would find his father if he ever needed him.

Tanner still had memories of his mother arguing with his father over how ugly the chair was. In fact, he was pretty sure that his father had kept it all those years just to annoy her. After she'd passed away from breast cancer while Tanner was still in high school, his father had never really been the same. He was pretty sure he kept the chair now as a token of her memory. If there was one thing he'd known about his parents, it was how deeply they loved each other—and how passionately they argued with one another. He didn't remember a day when the two weren't on opposite sides of an issue, but their love and dedication to each other and their children was unwavering.

Tanner and his father weren't in complete agreement about everything either, but Tanner did appreciate how his dad had stepped up and taken care of Rosie and him after their mother had died. He cooked dinner for them every night, always welcomed their friends over with a hot pot of chili, and still made it to watch every game Tanner played while also running a successful local business. He was ornery in his old age, but there was no doubt that he was a good man and an even better father.

"Dad, it's even. I already made sure of it before I put it in the stand. Just tell me if it's straight, will you?" Tanner grabbed the saw and went to work at the base of the tree, attempting to flatten the trunk to allow for a straighter edge. Hopefully then it would stand up in a simple line and his father could return to his shows.

"No, I think the base is uneven," Thomas remarked before taking a sip of his dark beer.

Tanner sent up a silent prayer for patience before shifting the tree a bit to the left and then back to its original spot. "Now?"

He was trying his best to be understanding, but a *please* or *thank you* here or there certainly might have helped the situation. Tanner knew that his father's bad back was keeping him from being part of the holiday prep, as well as from his work at Dean & Son Custom Construction. That didn't make it any less frustrating to get unsolicited advice on how to saw a tree when Tanner himself was a professional woodworker. Dean & Son Custom Construction wasn't a one-man

show, and Tanner had come on board against his better judg-
ment at the behest of his father. It wasn't that he hated it—
in fact, he was very talented at all things construction and
woodworking. Genetics clearly carried skills down a gen-
eration. But Tanner also didn't love it. He saw the passion in
his father's eyes when he used to work, and that same feeling was missing for Tanner. Still, however, it was his father's
dream to leave the company to him. So, here they were.

"If you're going to do something, do it right," Thomas
continued to rant from the recliner.

A loud pounding came from the front door.

"What in the heck?" Thomas jolted in his chair and
turned to look at the door. "Who is that?"

Tanner stood up abruptly and unceremoniously dumped
the tree on the living room carpet to go find out the answer.

"You can't just leave it like this," his dad protested.
"You're getting pine needles all over the carpet!"

Tanner shrugged his shoulders. "I have to answer the
door. It's probably some carolers from Grace Lake Church
down the street."

Truthfully, some young kids singing Christmas songs
badly would be an enjoyable break from the tension in the
Dean household. Tanner swung open the large wooden front
door, smiling wide when he suddenly froze.

Nola Bennett was standing on the front porch with his
niece and nephew in either hand. Former queen bee of Heart
Lake High School, Nola had been his teenage crush for as
long as he could remember. She was older now as she stood
in front of him with her jaw tight and her nostrils flared—
the typical irritated expression she always had when they
were around one another. But age had done nothing to dim
her beauty. Her brown hair now had red highlights that perfectly matched the rosy tone of her flushed cheeks, and her

deep-brown eyes were as piercing as they always were. Her nose was pointed, but in a way that fit her face perfectly and gave her an edge that matched her personality. Despite their history of bickering over literally everything and the fact that there had never been so much as a single romantic moment between them, Tanner had never found anyone who interested him half as much as she did.

"Tanner Dean, you are the worst babysitter I have ever seen," Nola announced without waiting a beat.

Tanner quickly pushed aside his thoughts, because clearly this was not a social visit. "Excuse me?"

Nola dropped the children's hands and pointed a finger at Tanner. "Rosie left the twins in your care and I find them out in the street throwing snowballs at cars? Alone in the dark? I almost swerved off the road and crashed!"

"I told them to stay in the front yard." Tanner shot a disapproving look at his niece and nephew, his head cocked to the side.

"I couldn't help it, Uncle Tanner! It's so snowy!" Zander ducked his gaze, ran off the porch, and threw his body into a snow pile. Pushing up out of the cold fluff, the young boy launched a snowball directly at Tanner. It landed square on his chest, startling him.

"Gotcha!" Zander squealed.

"Oh, now you're going to pay." Tanner used his deepest voice, the one the kids thought was hilarious when he was actually trying to sound scary. It rumbled in his chest and he didn't miss the surprised look on Nola's face as she considered him. He hadn't been able to hit those deep notes in high school, but it was a different story now, and he could tell that she recognized the change. "Let me grab my gloves."

"Wait, this is not—" Nola looked between him and the kids, but Becca had run to join her brother and they were stockpiling snowballs in a hurry. "Okay, I guess we're doing this. Tanner, time to dig deep and show 'em what you got! Are you ready?"

He tossed her a pair of gloves from the closet by the front door and pulled on his own worn leather pair. "Born ready."

Nola lifted one brow, but a smirk quirked the corner of her lips. She pulled on the gloves he'd given her and grabbed at some snow on the railing to begin rolling into a ball. With one swift move, she chucked it right at the side of his head. Icy cold dripped down his stubbled cheek and neck, sliding under the collar of the thermal shirt he was wearing. He shivered as the cool liquid trailed down his muscled chest.

"Hey!" Tanner shouted, amused but pretending not to be. "You're supposed to be on my team!"

She shook her head, but her eyes were sparkling with enthusiasm. "Never. Kids, let's get Uncle Tanner!"

"Yay!" Becca and Zander both began launching snowballs at their uncle as Nola hid behind the porch post and tossed a few his way as well.

Tanner grinned and tried to take cover behind a bush, but three-to-one was a losing battle. "White flag! White flag! I admit defeat," he finally said after his shirt was entirely soaked with icy slush. He waved his arms ceremoniously at the kids, dodging a few last throws. "Time to go inside and get some hot chocolate. It's too cold out here!"

"Hot chocolate with marshmallows!" Zander screamed, instantly forgetting about the snowball fight. He and his sister raced into the house, cheering and shedding wet clothes and outerwear with each step.

"I didn't say anything about marshmallows," Tanner shouted back, but the kids were out of earshot at that point. And there was no way he wasn't going to give them an entire scoop of marshmallows each anyway. While he may not have any kids of his own, Tanner adored his niece and nephew with his whole heart and it was impossible not to spoil them as much as he could.

Nola stepped back onto the porch, batting some snow off her jacket. She shook out her thick brown hair, small snowflakes clinging to her extra-long eyelashes, the cold reddening the tip of her pert nose. With a tired sigh, she arched one of her thick brows that seemed almost too perfect. This woman in front of him felt so much like a stranger. "So, okay, that was fun, but seriously, Tanner. You've gotta watch them more carefully. They could have caused an accident."

She handed him back the gloves he'd given her, then pushed her hands into her jacket pockets for warmth. Although *jacket* was a stretch, because it was more of a windbreaker. Of course she'd come back to town in December only to forget to bring proper gear for the snow. He didn't understand her sometimes. It's not like Chicago was a beach town—plus, she grew up here.

Annoyance tightened his gut as his gaze traveled down to her inappropriate footwear. "My apologies. I wasn't expecting the queen to arrive on her sleigh from the big city. Maybe you forget how we roll out here by the water, but in Heart Lake, kids can play in their neighborhood without adults helicoptering around."

Nola lifted her chin slightly, a look of both frustration and guilt crossing her face. "I'll have you know that Rosie and I keep in touch via text, and we try to do video calls with the kids at least every other month. I may not always be around, but I am still their godmother."

That, he did know. Despite her city lifestyle and complete lack of interest in all things Heart Lake, Nola had always treated his niece and nephew with the most love and affection he'd ever seen. Second to himself, of course. She was undoubtedly an amazing godmother, and anytime he saw her at a family gathering, she was usually fawning over the twins or laughing with his sister.

Admittedly, he found himself watching her a lot longer than he'd like to at those events. They were just so few and far between, considering she'd come to town for a day and then be off to the city again for months. The last time he'd seen her had probably been at her grandmother's funeral. It was a rare occasion where they hadn't fought at all and had been quite civil, actually. He had loved Gigi just as much as everyone in town had, and there was no doubt the loss was hard on Nola. He knew too much about losing a loved one to see it as anything other than completely heart-wrenching.

"Well, why don't you come in for some hot chocolate with us, then? I'll even throw in a few marshmallows," he offered, realizing too late that he wanted her company a lot more for himself than he did for the kids.

"Next time," she said, quickly rejecting his offer with a small wave. "I have to run, but I'll catch up with Rosie and the twins later."

"When I'm not around?" he asked, lifting one brow.

"It would certainly be preferred that way," Nola shot back over her shoulder as she walked to her car.

Tanner chuckled lightly as he watched her tread through the snow in heels, nearly falling a dozen times before she finally made it to her vehicle. God, that woman irritated him so much, and yet... he'd rather watch her drive off into the cold night than return to the Great Tree Debate with his ornery, old father.

About the Author

Bestselling author Sarah Robinson is a native of the Washington, DC, area and has both her bachelor's and master's degrees in criminal and clinical psychology. She works as a counselor by day and a romance novelist by night. She owns a small zoo of furry pets and is actively involved in volunteering in her community.

You can learn more at:

BooksbySarahRobinson.com
Twitter: @Booksby_Sarah Facebook.com/
    BooksbySarahRobinson
Instagram: @BooksbySarahRobinson
Pinterest.com/BooksbySarahRobinson

**For a bonus story from another author that
you'll love, please turn the page to read** *Kiss
Me in Sweetwater Springs* **by Annie Rains.**

If Lacy Shaw could have one wish, it would be
that the past would stay in the past. And with
her high school reunion coming up, she has
no intention of reliving the worst four years of
her life. Especially when all she has to show
for the last decade is how the shy bookworm
blossomed into...the shy town librarian.
Ditching the event seems the best option until a
blistering-hot alternative roars into Lacy's life.
Perhaps riding into the reunion on the back of
Paris Montgomery's motorcycle will show her
classmates how much she really has changed...

While growing up as a foster kid, Paris
Montgomery only felt at home in Sweetwater
Springs, which is why he picked the small
town to start over after his divorce. He can't
afford to ruin this refuge with another doomed
relationship—especially one with a woman who
is his total opposite. But when the town's sweet
librarian offers to help him reconnect with his
foster dad, he finds they have more in common
than he thought. Both are about to discover that
home is where the heart is.

FOREVER

Chapter One

Lacy Shaw looked around the Sweetwater Springs Library for the culprit of the noise, a "shhh" waiting on the tip of her tongue. There were several people reading quietly at the tables along the wall. A few patrons were wandering the aisles of books.

The high-pitched giggle broke through the silence again.

Lacy stood and walked out from behind her counter, going in the direction of the sound. She wasn't a stickler for quiet, but the giggling had been going on for at least ten minutes now, and a few of the college students studying in the far corner kept getting distracted and looking up. They'd come here to focus, and Lacy wanted them to keep coming.

She stopped when she was standing at the end of one of the nonfiction aisles where two little girls were seated on the floor with a large book about animals in their lap. The *shhh* finally tumbled off her lips. The sound made her feel even more like the stuffy librarian she tried not to be.

The girls looked up, their little smiles wilting.

Lacy stepped closer to see what was so funny about animals and saw a large picture of a donkey with the heading "Asses" at the top of the page. A small giggle tumbled off Lacy's lips as well. She quickly regained control of herself and offered a stern expression. "Girls, we need to be quiet in the library. People come here to read and study."

"That's why we're here," Abigail Fields, the girl with long, white-blond curls, said. They came in often with their nanny, Mrs. Townsend, who usually fell asleep in the back corner of the room. The woman was somewhere in her eighties and probably wasn't the best choice to be taking care of two energetic little girls.

"I have to write a paper on my favorite animal," Abigail said.

Lacy made a show of looking at the page. "And it's a donkey?"

"That's not what that says," Willow, Abigail's younger sister, said. "It says..."

"Whoa!" Lacy held up a hand. "I can read, but let's not say that word out loud, okay? Why don't you two take that book to a table and look at it quietly," she suggested.

The little girls got up, the older one lugging the large book with both hands.

Lacy watched them for a moment and then turned and headed back to her counter. She walked more slowly as she stared at the back of a man waiting for her. He wore dark jeans and a fitted black T-shirt that hugged muscles she didn't even have a name for. There was probably an anatomy book here that did. She wouldn't mind locating it and taking her time labeling each muscle, one by one.

She'd seen the man before at the local café, she realized, but never in here. And every time he'd walked into the café, she'd noticed him. He, of course, had never noticed her. He was too gorgeous and cool. There was also the fact that Lacy usually sat in the back corner reading a book or people-watching from behind her coffee cup.

What is he doing here?

The man shifted as he leaned against her counter, his

messenger bag swinging softly at his lower hip. Then he glanced over his shoulder and met her gaze. He had blue crystalline eyes, inky black hair, and a heart-stopping smile that made her look away shyly—a nervous remnant of her high school years when the cool kids like him had picked on her because of the heavy back brace she wore.

The brace was gone. No one was going to laugh at her anymore, and even if they did, she was confident enough not to find the closest closet to cry in these days.

"Hey," he said. "Are you Lacy Shaw, the librarian here?"

She forced her feet to keep walking forward. "I am. And you are?"

He turned and held out a hand. "Paris." He suspended his hand in midair, waiting for her to take it. When she hesitated, his gaze flicked from her face to her hand and then back again.

She blinked, collected herself, and took his hand. "Nice to meet you. I'm Lacy Shaw."

Paris's dark brows dipped farther.

"Right," she giggled nervously. "You didn't need me to introduce myself. You just asked if that's who I was. Do you, um, need help with something? Finding a book maybe?"

"I'm actually here for the class," he said.

"The computer skills class?" She walked around the counter to stand behind her computer. "The course instructor hasn't arrived yet." She looked at the Apple Watch on her wrist. "It's still a little early though. You're not late until you're less than five minutes early. That's what my mom always says."

Lacy had been wanting to offer a computer skills class here for months. There was a roomful of laptops in the back just begging for people to use them. She'd gotten the computer skills teacher's name from one of her regular patrons here, and she'd practically begged Mr. Montgomery over the phone to take the job.

"The class runs from today to next Thursday. It's aimed toward people sixty-five and over," she told the man standing across from her, briefly meeting his eyes and then looking away. "But you're welcome to attend, of course." Although she doubted he'd fit in. He appeared to be in his early thirties, wore dark clothes, and looked like his idea of fun might be adding a tattoo to the impressive collection on his arms.

Paris cleared his throat. "Unless I'm mistaken, I *am* the instructor," he said. "Paris Montgomery at your service."

"Oh." She gave him another assessing look. She'd been expecting someone...different. Alice Hampton had been the one to recommend Paris. She was a sweet old lady who had sung the praises of the man who'd rented the room above her garage last year. Lacy never would've envisioned the likes of this man staying with Mrs. Hampton. "Oh, I'm sorry. Thank you for agreeing to offer some of your time to our senior citizens. A lot of them have expressed excitement over the class."

Paris gave a cursory glance around the room. "It's no problem. I'm self-employed, and as I told you on the phone, I had time between projects."

"You're a graphic designer, right?" she asked, remembering what Alice had told her. "You created the designs for the Sweetwater Bed and Breakfast."

"Guilty. And for a few other businesses in Sweetwater Springs."

Lacy remembered how much she'd loved the designs when she'd seen them. "I've been thinking about getting something done for the library," she found herself saying.

"Yeah? I'd be happy to talk it over with you when you're ready. I'm sure we can come up with something simple yet classy. Modern. Inviting."

"Inviting. Yes!" she agreed in a spurt of enthusiasm before quickly feeling embarrassed. But that was her whole goal for the library this year. She wanted the community to love coming in as much as she did. As a child growing up, the library had been her haven, especially during those years of being bullied. The smell of books had come to mean freedom to her. The sound of pages turning was music to her ears.

"Well, I guess I better go set up for class." Paris angled his body toward the computer room. "Five minutes early is bordering on late, right?" he asked, repeating her words and making her smile.

He was cool, gorgeous, *and* charming—a dangerous combination.

* * *

Paris still wasn't sure why he'd agreed to this proposition. It paid very little, and he doubted it would help with his graphic design business. The librarian had been so insistent on the phone that it'd been hard to say no to her. Was that the same woman who'd blushed and had a hard time making eye contact with him just now? She looked familiar, but he wasn't sure where or when they'd ever crossed paths.

He walked into the computer room in the back of the library and looked around at the laptops set up. How hard could it be to teach a group of older adults to turn on a computer, utilize the search engine, or set up an email account? It was only two weeks. He could handle that.

"You're the teacher?" a man's voice asked behind him.

Paris whirled to face him. The older man wore a ball cap and a plaid button-down shirt. In a way, he looked familiar. "Yes, sir. Are you here for the class?"

The man frowned. "Why else would I ask if you were the teacher?"

Paris ignored the attitude and gestured to the empty room. "You have your pick of seats right now, sir," Paris told him. Then he directed his attention to a few more seniors who strolled in behind the older man. Paris recognized a couple of them. Greta Merchant used a cane, but he knew she walked just fine. The cane was for show, and Paris had seen her beat it against someone's foot a couple of times. She waved and took a seat next to the frowning man.

"Paris!" Alice Hampton said, walking into the room.

He greeted her with a hug. After coming to town last winter and staying at the Sweetwater B&B for a week, he'd rented a room from Alice for a while. Now he had his own place, a little cabin that sat across the river.

All in all, he was happy these days, which is more than he could say when he lived in Florida. After his divorce, the Sunshine State had felt gloomy. He hadn't been able to shake the feeling, and then he'd remembered being a foster kid here in Sweetwater Springs, North Carolina. A charity event for bikers had given him an excuse to come back for a visit, and he'd never left. Not yet, at least.

"I told all my friends about this class," Alice said. "You're going to have a full and captive audience with us."

Nerves buzzed to life in his stomach. He didn't mind public speaking, but he hoped most were happy to be here, unlike the frowner in the corner.

More students piled in and took their seats, and then the timid librarian came to the door. She nibbled on her lower lip, her gaze skittering everywhere but to meet his directly. "Do you need anything?"

Paris shook his head. "No, we have plenty of computers. We'll just get acquainted with them and go from there."

She looked up at him now, a blush rising over her high cheekbones. She had light brown hair spilling out of a messy bun and curling softly around her jawline. She had a pretty face, made more beautiful by her rich brown eyes and rose-colored mouth. "Well, you know where I am if you do need something." She looked at the group. "Enjoy!"

"You hired a looker!" Greta Merchant hollered at Lacy. "And for that, there'll be cookies in your future, Ms. Lacy! I'll bring a plate next class!"

The blush on Lacy's cheeks deepened as her gaze jumped to meet his momentarily. "Well, I won't turn down your cookies, Ms. Greta," she said.

Paris watched her for a moment as she waved and headed back to her post.

"The ink in those tattoos going to your brain?" the frowner called to him. "It's time to get started. I don't have all day, you know."

Paris pulled his gaze from the librarian and faced the man. "Neither do I. Let's learn something new, shall we?"

An hour later, Paris had taught the class of eleven to turn on and turn off the laptops. It'd taken an excruciating amount of time to teach everyone to open a browser and use a search engine. Overall, it'd gone well, and the hour had flown by.

"Great job," Alice said to him approvingly. She patted a motherly hand on his back that made him feel warm and appreciated. That feeling quickly dissipated as the frowner headed out the door.

"I already knew most of what you taught," he said.

Who was this person, and why was he so grouchy?

"Well, then you probably didn't need this class," Paris pointed out politely. "Actually, you probably could've taught it yourself."

The frowner harrumphed. "Next time *teach* something."

Paris nodded. "Yes, sir. I'll do my best."

"Your best is the only acceptable thing," the man said before walking out.

Paris froze for a moment, reaching for the memory that the frowner had just stirred. *Your best is the only acceptable thing.* His foster dad here in Sweetwater Springs used to say that to him. That man had been nothing but encouraging. He'd taught Paris more about life in six months than anyone ever had before or since.

Paris hadn't even caught his student's name, and there was no roster for this computer skills class. People had walked in and attended without any kind of formal record.

Paris watched the frowner walk with slow, shuffled steps. He was old, and his back was rounded. A hat sat on his head, casting a shadow on his leathered face. All Paris had really seen of him was his deep, disapproving frown. It'd been nearly two decades since Paris had laid eyes on Mr. Jenson, but he remembered his former foster dad being taller. Then again, Paris had been just a child.

When Paris had returned to Sweetwater Springs last year, he'd decided to call. Mrs. Jenson had been the one to answer. She'd told him she didn't remember a boy named PJ, which is the name Paris had gone by back then. "Please, please, leave us alone! Don't call here again!" she'd pleaded on the line, much to Paris's horror. "Just leave us alone."

The memory made Paris's chest ache as he watched the

older man turn the corner of the library and disappear. He resisted the urge to follow him and see if it really was Mr. Jenson. But the Jensons had given Paris so much growing up that he was willing to do whatever he could to repay their kindness—even if it meant staying away.

* * *

Lacy was checking out books for the Fields girls and their nanny when Paris walked by. She watched him leave. If you flipped to the word *suave* in the dictionary, his picture was probably there.

"I plan to bring the girls to your summer reader group in a couple weeks," Mrs. Townsend said.

Of course she did. That would be a convenient nap time for her.

"I always love to see the girls." Lacy smiled down at the children. Their father, Granger Fields, and his family owned Merry Mountain Farms in town where Lacy always got her blue spruce for the holidays.

Lacy waved as the little girls collected their bags of books and skipped out with Mrs. Townsend following behind them.

For the rest of the afternoon, Lacy worked on ongoing programs and plans for the summer and fall. At six p.m., she turned off the lights to the building and headed into the parking lot.

She was involved with the Ladies' Day Out group, a gaggle of women who regularly got together to hang out and have fun. Tonight, they were meeting at Lacy's house to discuss a book that she'd chosen for everyone to read. They were in no way a book club, but since it was her turn to decide what they did, Lacy had turned it into one this time.

Excitement brimmed as she drove home. When she

pulled up to her small one-bedroom house on Pine Cone Lane, she noticed two of her sisters' cars already parked in the driveway. Birdie and Rose had texted her during the day to see what they could do to help. Seeing the lights on inside Lacy's home, they'd evidently ignored Lacy's claims that she didn't need anything and had used her hideaway key under the flowerpot.

"Honey, I'm home!" Lacy called as she headed through the front door.

Birdie, her older sister by one year, turned to face her. "Hey, sis. Rose and I were just cleaning up for you."

"Great." Lacy set her purse down. "Now I don't have to."

"What is this?" Rose asked, stepping up beside Birdie. Rose was one year younger than Lacy. Their mom had been very busy those first three years of marriage.

Lacy looked at the small postcard that Rose held up.

"You were supposed to RSVP if you were going to your ten-year class reunion," Rose said. "You needed to send this postcard back."

"Only if I'm going," Lacy corrected.

"Of course you're going," Birdie said. "I went to my ten-year reunion last year, and it was amazing. I wish we had one every year. I wouldn't miss it."

Unlike Lacy, her sisters had been popular in school. They hadn't had to wear a bulky back brace that made them look like a box turtle in its shell. It had drawn nothing but negative attention during those long, tormenting years.

"It's not really a time in my life that I want to remember," Lacy pointed out as she passed them and headed into the kitchen for a glass of lemonade. Or perhaps she should go ahead and pour herself something stronger. She could tell she might need it tonight.

A knock on her front door made her turn. "Who is that?" Lacy asked. "I scheduled the book discussion for seven. It's only six." Lacy set down the glass she'd pulled from the cabinet and went to follow her sisters to the door.

"About that," Birdie said a bit sheepishly. "We changed the plan at the last minute."

Lacy didn't like the sound of that. "What do you mean?"

"No one actually read the book you chose," Birdie said as Rose let the first arrivals in. "Instead, we're playing matchmaker tonight. What goes together better than summer and love?"

Lacy frowned. "If you wanted summer love, I could've chosen a romance novel to read instead."

Birdie gave her a disapproving look. Lacy doubted anyone was more disappointed about tonight's shift in festivities than her though.

Chapter Two

Paris hadn't been able to fully concentrate for the last hour and a half as he sat in front of his computer working on a job for Peak Designs Architectural Firm. His mind was in other places. Primarily the library.

The Frowner, as he'd come to think of the old man in his class, was forefront in his mind. Was it possible that the Frowner was Mr. Jenson?

It couldn't be. Mr. Jenson had been a loving, caring guy, from what Paris remembered. Granted, loving and caring were subjective, and Paris hadn't had much to go on back then.

Mrs. Jenson had been the mother that Paris had always wished he had. She'd doted on him, offering affection and unconditional love. Even though Paris had been a boy who'd landed himself in the principal's office most afternoons, Mrs. Jenson had never raised her voice. And Mr. Jenson had always come home from his job and sat down with Paris, giving him a lecture that had proved to be more like a life lesson.

Paris had never forgotten those lessons. Or that man.

He blinked the memories away and returned his attention to the design he was working on. It was good, but he only did excellent jobs. *Your best is the only acceptable thing.*

He stared at the design for another moment and then

decided to come back to it tomorrow when he wasn't so tired. Instead, he went to his Facebook page and searched Albert Jenson's name. He'd done so before, but no profiles under that name had popped up. This time, one did. The user had a profile picture of a rose instead of himself. Paris's old foster dad had loved his rose gardens. This must be him!

Paris scrolled down, reading the most recent posts. One read that Mr. Jenson had gone to the nursing home to visit his wife, Nancy.

Paris frowned at the news. The transition must have been recent because Mrs. Jenson had been home when he'd called late last year. She'd been the one to pretty much tell him to get lost.

He continued to scroll through more pictures of roses and paused at another post. This one read that Mr. Jenson had just signed up for a computer skills class at the Sweetwater Library.

So it was true. Mr. Jenson, the foster dad who'd taught him so much, was also the Frowner.

* * *

Lacy had decided to stick to just lemonade tonight since she was hosting the Ladies' Day Out group. But plans were meant to be changed, as evidenced by the fact that the book discussion she'd organized had turned into the women sitting around her living room, eyes on a laptop screen while perusing an online dating site.

"Oh, he's cute!" Alice Hampton said, sitting on the couch and leaning over Josie Kellum's shoulder as she tapped her fingers along the keys of Lacy's laptop. Not that anyone had asked to use her computer. The women had just helped themselves.

Lacy reached for the bottle of wine, poured herself a deep glass, and then headed over to see who they were looking at. "I know him," she said, standing between her sisters behind the couch. "He comes into the library all the time."

"Any interest?" Josie asked.

Lacy felt her face scrunch at the idea of anything romantic with her library patron. "Definitely not. I know what his reading interests are and frankly, they scare me. That's all I'll say on that."

She stepped away from her sisters and walked across the room to look out the window. The moon was full tonight. Her driveway was also full, with cars parked along the curb. She wasn't a social butterfly by any means, but she looked like one this evening and that made her feel strangely satisfied.

"So what are your hobbies, Lacy?" Josie asked. "Other than reading, of course."

"Well, I like to go for long walks," Lacy said, still watching out the window.

Josie tapped a few more keys. "Mmm-hmm. What's your favorite food?"

Lacy turned and looked back at the group. "Hot dogs," she said, earning her a look from the other women.

"Do you know what hot dogs are made out of?" Greta wanted to know.

"Yes, of course I do. Why do I feel like I'm being interviewed for one of your articles right now?"

"Not an article," Birdie said. "A dating profile."

"What?" Lacy nearly spilled her glass of wine as she moved to look over Josie's shoulder. "What are you doing? I don't want to be up on Fish In The Sea dot com. Stop that."

Birdie gave her a stern look. "You have a class reunion coming up, and you can't go alone."

"I'm not going period," Lacy reiterated.

"Not going to your class reunion?" Dawanda from the fudge shop asked. She was middle-aged with spiky, bright red hair. She tsked from across the room, where she sat in an old, worn recliner that Lacy had gotten from a garage sale during college.

Lacy finished off her wine and set the empty glass on the coffee table nearby. "I already told you, high school was a miserable time that I don't want to revisit."

"All the more reason you *should* go," Birdie insisted. Even though she was only a year older, Birdie acted like Lacy's mother sometimes.

"Why, so I can be traumatized all over again?" Lacy shook her head. "It took me years to get over all the pranks and ridicule. Returning to the scene of the crime could reverse all my progress."

"What progress?" Rose asked. "You never go out, and you never date."

Lacy furrowed her brow. "I go to the café all the time."

"Alone and you sit in the back," Birdie pointed out. "Your back brace is gone, but you're still hiding in the corner."

Lacy's jaw dropped. She wanted to argue but couldn't. Her sister was right.

"So we're making Lacy a dating profile," Josie continued, looking back down at the laptop's screen. "Twenty-eight years old, loves to read, and takes long walks in the park."

"I never said anything about the park," Lacy objected.

"It sounds more romantic that way." Josie didn't bother to look up. "Loves exotic fruit..."

"I said hot dogs."

This time Josie turned her head and looked at Lacy over her shoulder. "Hot dogs don't go on dating profiles...but cute, wagging dogs do." Her fingers started flying across the keyboard.

"I like cats." Lacy watched for another moment and then went to pour herself another glass of wine as the women created her profile at FishInTheSea.com.

After a few drinks, she relaxed a little and started feeding Josie more details about herself. She wasn't actually going to do this, of course. Online dating seemed so unromantic. She wanted to find Mr. Right the old-fashioned way, where fate introduced him into her life and sparks flew like a massive explosion of fireworks. Or at least like a sparkler.

* * *

An hour later, Lacy said goodbye to the group and sat on the couch. She gave the book she'd wanted to discuss a sidelong glance, and then she reached for her laptop. The dating profile stared back at her, taking her by surprise. They'd used a profile picture from when she'd been a bridesmaid at a wedding last year. Her hair was swept up and she had a dipping neckline on her dress that showed off more skin than normal. Lacy read what Josie and her sisters had written. The truth was disregarded in favor of more interesting things.

Lacy was proud of who she was, but the women were right. She wasn't acting that way by shying away from her reunion. She was acting like the girl in the back brace, quietly sitting in the far corner of the room out of fear that others might do something nasty like stick a sign on her back that read KICK ME! I WON'T FEEL IT!

"Maybe I should go to the reunion," she said out loud. "Or maybe I should delete this profile and forget all about it."

The decision hummed through her body along with the effect of one too many glasses of wine. After a moment, she shut the laptop and went to bed. She could decide her profile's fate tomorrow.

* * *

The next morning, Paris woke with the birds outside his window. After a shower and a quick bite, he grabbed his laptop to work on the deck, which served as his office these days. Before getting started on the Peak Designs logo, he scrolled through email and social media. He clicked on Mr. Jenson's profile again, only to read a post that Paris probably didn't need first thing in the morning.

> The computer skills class was a complete waste of time. Learned nothing. Either I'm a genius or the instructor is an idiot.

The muscles along the back of his neck tightened. At least he didn't need to wonder if Mr. Jenson would be back.

He read another post.

> Went to see Nancy today. I think she misses her roses more than she misses me. She wants to come home, and this old house certainly isn't home without her.

Paris felt like he'd taken a fall from his bike, landing chest-first and having the breath knocked out of him. Why wasn't Mrs. Jenson home? What was wrong with her? And why was Mr. Jenson so different from the man he remembered?

Paris pushed those questions from his mind and began work on some graphic designs. Several hours later, he'd achieved much more than he'd expected. He shoved his laptop into its bag, grabbed his keys, and rode his motorcycle to the library. As he walked inside, his gaze immediately went to the librarian. Her hair was pulled back with some kind of stick poking through it today. He studied her as she checked books into the system on her desktop.

She glanced up and offered a shy wave, which he returned as he headed toward the computer room. He would have expected Mr. Jenson not to return to class today based on his Facebook comments, but Mr. Jenson was already waiting for him when he walked in. All the other students from the previous day filed in within the next few minutes.

"Today I'm teaching you all to use Microsoft Word," he told the group.

"Why would I use Microsoft Word?" Alice Hampton asked. Her questions were presented in a curious manner rather than the questions that Mr. Jenson posed, which felt more like an attack.

"Well, let's say you want to write a report for some reason. Then you could do one here. Or if you wanted to get creative and write a novel, then this is the program you'd use."

"I've always wanted to write a book," Greta told Alice. "It's on my bucket list, and I'm running out of time."

"Are you sick?" Alice asked with concern, their conversation hijacking the class.

"No, I'm healthy as a buzzard. Just old, and I can't live forever," Greta told her.

"Love keeps you young," Edna Baker said from a few chairs down. She was the grandmother of the local police chief, Alex Baker. "Maybe you should join one of those online dating sites."

The group got excited suddenly and turned to Paris, who had leaned back against one of the counters, arms folded over his chest as he listened.

He lifted a brow. "What?"

"A dating site," Edna reiterated. "We helped Lacy Shaw join one last night in our Ladies' Day Out group."

"The librarian?" Paris asked, his interest piquing.

"Had to do it with her dragging and screaming, but we did it. I wouldn't mind making a profile of my own," Edna continued.

"Me too." Greta nodded along with a few other women.

"I'm married," Mr. Jenson said in his usual grumpy demeanor. "I have no reason to be on a dating site."

"Then leave, Albert," Greta called out.

Mr. Jenson didn't budge.

"We're here to learn about what interests us, right?" Edna asked Paris.

He shrugged. There was no official syllabus. He was just supposed to teach computer literacy for the seniors in town. "I guess so."

"Well, majority rules. We want to get on one of those dating sites. I think the one we were on last night was called Fish In The Sea dot com."

Paris unfolded his arms, debating if he was actually going to agree to this. He somehow doubted the Sweetwater Springs librarian would approve, even if she'd apparently been on the site herself.

"Fine, I'll get you started," Paris finally relented, "but tomorrow, we're learning about Microsoft Word."

"I don't want to write a report or a novel," Mr. Jenson said, his frown so deep it joined with the fold of his double chin.

"Again, don't come if you don't want to," Greta nearly shouted. "No one is forcing you."

Paris suspected that Mr. Jenson would be back regardless

of his opinions. Maybe he was lonely. Or maybe, despite his demeanor, this was his idea of a good time.

After teaching the group how to use the search bar function and get to the Fish In the Sea website, Paris walked around to make sure everyone knew how to open an account. Some started making their own profiles while others watched their neighbors' screens.

"This is Lacy's profile," Alice said when he made his way to her.

Paris leaned in to take a closer look. "That's not the librarian here."

"Oh, it is. This photo was taken when she was a bridesmaid last year. Isn't she beautiful?"

For a moment, Paris couldn't pull his gaze away from the screen. If he were on the dating site, he'd be interested in her. "Likes to hike. Loves dogs. Favorite food is a hot dog. Looking for adventure," he read. "That isn't at all what I would have pegged Lacy as enjoying."

Alice gave him a look. "Maybe there's more to her than meets the eye. Would you like to sit down and create your own profile? Then you could give her a wink or a nibble or whatever the online dating lingo is."

He blinked, pulled his gaze from the screen, and narrowed his eyes at his former landlord. "You know I'm not interested in that kind of thing." He'd told Alice all about his past when he'd rented a room from her last year. After his messy marriage, the last thing he wanted was to jump into another relationship.

"Well, what I know is, you're young, and your heart can take a few more beatings if it comes to it. Mine, on the other hand, can't, which is why I'm not creating one of these profiles."

Paris chuckled. "Hate to disappoint, but I won't be either."
Even if seeing Lacy's profile tempted him to do otherwise.

* * *

At the end of the hour, Paris was the last to leave his class,
following behind Mr. Jenson, who had yet to hold a personal conversation with him or say a civilized thing in his
direction.

He didn't recognize Paris, and why would he? Paris had
been a boy back then. His hair had been long and had often
hung in his eyes. His body had been scrawny from neglect
and he hadn't gotten his growth spurt until well into his teen
years. He hadn't even had the same last name back then.
He'd gone by PJ Drake before his parents' divorce. Then
there was a custody battle, which was the opposite of what
one might think. Instead of fighting *for* him, his parents had
fought over who *had* to take him.

"Mr. Jenson?" Paris called.

The older man turned to look at Paris with disdain.

"How was the class?"

"An utter waste of time."

Paris liked to think he had thick skin, but his former foster dad's words had sharp edges that penetrated deep. "Okay,
well what computer skills would you like to learn?"

The skin between Mr. Jenson's eyes made a deep divot
as he seemed to think. "I can't see my wife every day like
I want to because I don't drive. It's hard for an old man like
me to go so far. The nurses say they can set up Skype to talk
to her, but I don't understand it. They didn't have that sort of
thing when I was old enough to learn new tricks."

"Never too late," Paris said. "A great man once taught me
that."

That great man was standing in front of him now, whether he knew it or not. And he needed his own pep talk of sorts. "Come back tomorrow, and we'll get you set up for that."

Mr. Jenson frowned back at him. "We'll see."

* * *

Lacy was trying not to panic.

A blue circle had started spinning on her laptop screen five minutes ago. Now there were pop-up boxes that she couldn't seem to get rid of. She'd restarted her computer, but the pop-up boxes were relentless. She sucked in a breath and blew it out audibly. Then another, bordering on hyperventilation.

"You okay?" a man's voice asked.

Her gaze lifted to meet Paris's. "Oh. Yeah." She shook her head.

"You're saying yes, but you're shaking your head no." His smile was the kind that made women swoon, and for a moment, she forgot that she was in panic mode.

"My computer seems to be possessed," she told him.

This made Paris chuckle—a sound that seemed to lessen the tension inside her. "Mind if I take a look?"

She needed to say no. He was gorgeous, charming, and cool. And those three qualities made her nervous. But without her computer, she wouldn't be able to pay her bills after work. Or delete that dating profile that the Ladies' Day Out group had made for her last night. *Why didn't I delete it right away?*

"Yes, please," she finally said.

Paris headed around the counter. "Did you restart it?" he asked when he was standing right next to her. So close that she could smell the woodsy scent coming off his body. She could also feel a wave of heat radiating off him, burning the superficial layer of her skin. He was gorgeous, charming, cool, *and* he smelled divine. What woman could resist?

"I've restarted it twice already," she told him.

"Hmm." He put his bag down on the floor at his feet and stood in front of her computer. She couldn't help a closer inspection of the tattoos that covered his biceps muscles. They were colorful and artistically drawn, but she could only see parts of them. She had to resist pulling back the fabric of his shirt to admire the artwork there. What was wrong with her?

Paris turned his head to look at her. "Is it okay if I close out all the programs you currently have running?"

"Of course."

He tapped his fingers along her keys, working for several long minutes while she drifted off in her own thoughts of his muscles and tattoos and the spicy scent of his aftershave. Then he straightened and turned back to her. "There you go, good as new."

"Wow. Really? That was fast."

He shrugged a nonchalant shoulder. "I just needed to reboot and run your virus software."

"You make it sound so easy."

"To me it is. I know computers. We have a kinship."

Lacy felt the same way about books. She reached for her cup of coffee that she'd purchased this morning, even though a jolt of caffeine was probably the last thing her nerves needed right now.

Paris pointed a finger at the cup. "That's where I know you from. You're the woman at the café. You always sit in the back with a book."

Her lips parted as she set her cup down. "You've noticed me?"

"Of course. Why wouldn't I?"

She shrugged and shook her head. "We've just never spoken." And she'd assumed she was invisible in the back corner, especially to someone like him. "Well, thank you for fixing my computer."

"Just a friend helping a friend." He met her gaze and held it for a long moment. Then he bent to pick up the strap of his bag, hung it over his shoulder, and headed around to the other side of the counter. "Be careful on those dating sites," he said, stopping as he passed in front of her. "Always meet at a safe location and don't give anyone your personal information until you know you can trust them."

"Hmm?" Lacy narrowed her eyes, and then her heart soared into her throat and her gaze dropped to her fixed computer. Up on the screen, first and foremost, was Fish-InTheSea.com. She giggled nervously as her body filled with mortification. "I didn't... I'm not..." Why wouldn't her mouth work? "This isn't what it looks like."

Paris grinned. "The women in my class told me about last night. Sounds like you were forced into it."

"Completely," she said with relief.

He shrugged. "I doubt you need a website to find a date. They created a really attractive profile for you though. It should get you a lot of nibbles from the fish in the sea."

She laughed because he'd made a joke, but there was no hope of making intelligible words right now. Instead she waved and watched him leave.

"See you tomorrow, Lace," he called over his shoulder.

* * *

That evening, Paris kicked his feet up on the railing of his back deck as he sat in an outdoor chair, laptop on his thighs, watching the fireflies that seemed to be sending him secret messages with their flashing lights. The message he needed right now was "get back to work."

Paris returned to looking at his laptop's screen. He'd worked on the graphic for Peak Designs Architectural Firm all evening, and he was finally happy with it. He sent it off to the owner and then began work on a new agenda for tomorrow's class. He'd be teaching his students how to Skype, and he'd make sure Mr. Jenson knew how to do it on his own before leaving.

Paris liked the thought of reuniting Mr. and Mrs. Jenson through technology. It was the least he could do for them. Technology shouldn't replace person-to-person contact, but it was a nice substitute when two people couldn't be together. Paris suspected one of the main reasons Mr. Jenson even came to the library was because it was one of the few places within walking distance from his house.

Creating an agenda for live communication technology took all of ten minutes. Then Paris gave in to his impulse to search FishInTheSea.com. He found himself looking at Lacy's profile again, staring at the beautiful picture on the screen. Her brown hair was down and spilling over one shoulder in soft curls. She had on makeup that accentuated her eyes, cheekbones, and lips. And even though she looked so different from the person he'd met, she also looked very much the same.

"Why am I on a dating site?" he muttered, his voice blending with the night sounds. And for that matter, why was he staring at Lacy's profile? Maybe he was just as lonely as Mr. Jenson.

Chapter Three

"I love the design," Pearson Matthews told Paris on Friday afternoon as Paris zipped down the gently winding mountain road on his bike. The pavement was still wet from the rain earlier this morning. Puddles splashed the legs of his jeans as he hit them.

He had earbuds in place under his helmet so he could ride hands-free and hold a conversation without the roar of the engine interfering. "I'm glad you like it, sir."

"Love. I said love," Pearson said. "And I plan to recommend you to everyone I know. I'm part of the Chamber of Commerce, so I have business connections. I'm going to make sure you have enough work to keep you in Sweetwater Springs for years to come."

Paris felt a curious kick in his heart. He loved this town and didn't like to think about leaving...but he had never been one to stick anywhere for long either. He credited the foster system for that. "Thank you."

"No need for thanks. You did a great job, and I want others to know about it. You're an asset here."

Paris resisted saying thank you a second time. "Well, please make sure anyone you send my way tells me that you referred them. I give referral perks."

Pearson was one of the richest men in the community, so he likely didn't need any perks. "Sounds good. I'll talk to you soon."

They hung up, and Paris continued down the road, slowing at the entrance to the local library. His heart gave another curious kick at the thought of Lacy for a reason he didn't want to investigate. He parked, got off his bike, and then walked inside with his laptop bag on his shoulder.

Lacy wasn't behind the counter when he walked in. His gaze roamed the room, finding her with two little girls that he'd seen here before. She was helping them locate a book. One little girl was squirming as she stood in place, and Paris thought maybe she needed to locate a restroom first.

"Here you go. I think you girls will like this one," he heard Lacy tell them. "Abby, do you need to use the bathroom?"

The girl bobbed her head emphatically.

"You know where it is. Go ahead." Lacy pointed to the bathroom near the front entrance's double doors, and both girls took off in a sprint. Lacy watched them for a moment and then turned back to her computer. She gasped softly when she saw Paris. "You're here early. Do you need something?" she asked.

Need something? Yeah, he needed an excuse for why he'd been standing here stupidly waiting to talk to her.

"A book maybe?" Lacy stepped closer and lowered her voice.

"Yeah," he said. "I'm looking for a book."

"Okay. What exactly are you looking for?" she asked.

He scanned the surrounding shelves before his gaze landed back on her. "Actually, do you have anything on roses?"

Lacy's perfectly pink lips parted.

Paris had been trying to think of something he could do for his former foster parents, and roses had come to mind. Albert Jenson loved roses, but his wife, Nancy, adored the thorny beauties. "I was thinking about making a flower garden at the nursing home, but my thumbs are more black than green."

Lacy giggled softly. "Follow me." She led him to a wall of books in the nonfiction area and bent to inspect the titles.

Paris tried and failed not to admire her curves as she leaned forward in front of him. *Get it together, man.*

"Here you go. *The Dummie's Guide to Roses.*" She straightened and held a book out to him.

"Dummie's Guide?"

Her cheeks flushed. "Don't take offense. I didn't title it."

Paris made a point of looking at the other titles that had sandwiched the book on the shelf. "No, but you didn't choose to give me the one titled *Everything There Is to Know About Roses* or *The Rose Lover's Handbook.*" He returned to looking at her, fascinated by how easily he could make her blush. "Any luck on Fish In The Sea dot com?"

She looked away, pulling her hands to her midsection to fidget. "I've been meaning to cancel that. The ladies had good intentions when they signed me up, albeit misguided."

"Why did they choose you as their victim?"

Lacy shrugged. "I have this high school reunion coming up. They thought I'd be more likely to go if I had a date."

"You're not going to your own reunion?" Paris asked.

"I haven't decided yet," she said as she inched away and increased the distance between them.

Unable to help himself, Paris inched forward. He told himself it was because they had to whisper and he couldn't hear her otherwise.

"Have you gone to one of yours?" she asked.

"No." He shook his head. "I never stayed in one place long enough while I was growing up to be considered an official part of a class. If I had, I would." He looked at her. "You should go. I'm sure you could find a date, even without the dating site." Part of him was tempted to offer to take her himself. By nature, he was a helpful guy. He resisted offering though because there was another part of him that wanted to be her date for an entirely different reason.

He lifted *The Dummie's Guide to Roses.* "I'll just check this out and get set up for my class."

Lacy headed back behind the counter and held out her hand to him. "Library card, please."

"Library card?" he repeated.

"I need it to check you out."

He laid the book on the counter. "I, uh, I..."

"You don't have one?" she asked, grinning back at him.

"I do most of my reading on the computer. I guess it's been a while since I've checked a book out."

"No problem." She opened a drawer and pulled out a blank card. "I can make you one right now. Do you have a driver's license?"

He pulled out his wallet and laid his license on the counter. He watched as she grabbed it and got to work. Then she handed the card back to him, her fingers brushing his slightly in the handoff. Every nerve in his body responded to that one touch. If he wasn't mistaken, she seemed affected as well.

There was the real reason he hadn't offered to be her date for her class reunion. He was attracted to Lacy Shaw, and he *really* didn't want to be.

*   *   *

Lacy lifted her gaze to the computer room in the back of the library where Paris was teaching a class of unruly elders.

From afar, he actually seemed to be enjoying himself. She'd called several people before Paris, trying to persuade them to teach a class here, and everyone had been too busy with their own lives. That made her wonder why a guy like Paris was able to accept her offer. Did he have any family? Close friends? A girlfriend?

She roped in her gaze and continued checking in books from the pile beside her. Paris Montgomery's personal life was none of her business.

"Ms. Shaw! Ms. Shaw!" Abigail and Willow Fields came running toward the checkout counter.

"What's wrong, girls?" Lacy sat up straighter, noting the panic in the sisters' voices.

"Mrs. Townsend won't wake up! We thought she was sleeping, but she won't wake up!"

Lacy took off running to the other side of the room where she'd known Mrs. Townsend was sleeping. Immediately, she recognized that the older woman was hunched over the table in an unnatural way. Her skin was a pale gray color that sent chills up Lacy's spine.

Panic gripped Lacy as she looked around at the small crowd of people who'd gathered. "Does anyone know CPR?" she called. There were at least a dozen books here on the subject, but she'd never learned.

Everyone gave her a blank stare. Lacy's gaze snagged on the young sisters huddled against the wall with tears spilling over their pale cheeks. If Mrs. Townsend died in front of them, they'd be devastated.

"Let's get her on the floor," a man's voice said, coming up behind Lacy.

She glanced back, surprised to find Paris in action.

He gently grabbed hold of Mrs. Townsend and laid her on

the floor, taking control of the situation. She was never more thankful for help in her life.

"Call 911!" Lacy shouted to the crowd, relieved to see a young woman run toward the library counter where there was a phone. A moment later, the woman headed back. "They're on their way."

Lacy nodded as she returned to watching Paris perform chest compressions. He seemed to know exactly what to do. Several long minutes later, sirens filled the parking lot, and paramedics placed Mrs. Townsend onto a gurney. They revived her just enough for Mrs. Townsend to moan and look at the girls, her face seeming to contort with concern.

"It's okay. I'll take care of them, Mrs. Townsend," Lacy told her. "Just worry about taking care of yourself right now."

Lacy hoped Mrs. Townsend heard and understood. A second later, the paramedics loaded the older woman in the back of the ambulance and sped away, sirens screaming as they tore down the street.

Lacy stood on wobbly legs and tried to catch her breath. She pressed a hand against her chest, feeling like she might collapse or dissolve into tears.

"You all right?" Paris asked, pinning his ocean-blue gaze on hers.

She looked at him and shook her head. "Yes."

"You're contradicting yourself again," he said with a slight lift at one corner of his mouth. Then his hand went to her shoulder and squeezed softly. "Why don't you go sit down?"

"The girls," Lacy said, suddenly remembering her promise. She turned to where the sisters were still huddled and hurried over to where they were. "Mrs. Townsend is going to get help at the hospital. They'll take good care of her there, I promise."

Abby looked up. "What's wrong with her?"

Lacy shook her head. "I'm not sure, honey. I'm sure everything will be okay. Right now, I'm going to call your dad to come get you."

"He's at work," Willow said. "That's why we were with Mrs. Townsend."

"I know, honey. But he won't mind leaving the farm for a little bit. Follow me to the counter. I have some cookies up there."

The girls' eyes lit up, even as tears dripped from their eyelashes.

"I can call Granger while you take care of the girls," Paris offered.

How did Paris know that these sweet little children belonged to Granger Fields? As if hearing her thoughts, he explained, "I did some graphic design work on the Merry Mountain Farms website recently."

"Of course. That would be great," Lacy said, her voice sounding shaky. And she'd do her best to calm down in the meantime too.

* * *

Thirty minutes later, Granger Fields left the library with his little girls in tow, and Lacy plopped down on her stool behind the counter. The other patrons had emptied out of the library as well, and it was two minutes until closing time.

"Eventful afternoon," Paris said.

Lacy startled as he walked into view. She hadn't realized he was still here. "You were great with the CPR. You might have a second career as a paramedic."

He shook his head. "I took a class in college, but I'll stick to computers, thanks."

"And I'll stick to books. My entire body is still trembling."

Paris's dark brows stitched together. "I can take you home if you're not up for driving."

"On your bike?" she asked. "I'm afraid that wouldn't help my nerves at all."

Paris chuckled. "Not a fan of motorcycles, huh?"

"I've never been on one, and I don't plan to start this evening. It's time to close, and my plans include calling the hospital to check on Mrs. Townsend and then going home, changing into my PJs, and soothing my nerves with ice cream."

Paris leaned against her counter. "While you were with the girls, I called a friend I know who works at Sweetwater Memorial. She checked on things for me and just texted me an update." He held up his cell phone. "Mrs. Townsend is stable but being admitted so they can watch her over the next forty-eight hours."

Lacy blew out a breath. "That's really good news. For a moment there, she looked like she might die. If we hadn't gone over to her when we did, she might have just passed away in her sleep." Lacy wasn't sure she would've felt as safe in her little library ever again if that had happened.

"Life is fragile," Paris said. "Something like this definitely puts things into perspective, doesn't it?"

"It really does." Her worries and fears suddenly seemed so silly and so small.

Paris straightened from the counter and tugged his bag higher on his shoulder. "See you tomorrow," he said as he headed out of the library.

She watched him go and then set about to turning off all the lights. She grabbed her things and locked up behind her as she left, noticing Paris and his motorcycle beside her car in the parking lot.

"If I didn't know you were a nice guy, I might be a little

scared by the fact that you're waiting beside my car in an empty parking lot."

"I'm harmless." He hugged his helmet against him. "You looked a little rattled in there. I wanted to make sure you got home safely. I'll follow you."

Lacy folded her arms over her chest. "Maybe I don't want you to know where I live."

"The end of Pine Cone Lane. This is a small town, and I get around with business."

"I see. Well, you don't need to follow me home. Really, I'm fine."

"I'd feel better if I did."

Lacy held out her arms. "Suit yourself. Good night, Paris." She stepped inside her vehicle, closed the door behind her, and cranked her engine. It rolled and flopped. She turned the key again. This time it didn't even roll. "Crap." This day just kept getting better.

After a few more attempts, Paris tapped on her driver's-side window.

She opened the door. "The battery is dead. I think I left my lights on this morning." It'd been raining, and she'd had them on to navigate through the storm. She'd forgotten her umbrella, so she'd turned off her engine, gotten out of her car, and had darted toward the library. In her rush, she must've forgotten to turn off her lights.

"I'll call Jere's Shop. He can jump your battery or tow it back to your house," Paris said.

Lacy considered the plan. "I can just wait here for him and drive it back myself."

"Jere is dependable but slow. You don't need to be out here waiting for him all evening. Leave your keys in the ignition, and I'll take you home."

Lacy looked at the helmet that Paris now extended toward her, her brain searching for another option. She didn't want to be here all night. She could call one of her sisters, but they would then follow her inside, and she didn't want to deal with them after the day she'd had either.

She got out of the car and took the helmet. "Okay," she said, shaking her head no.

This made Paris laugh as he led her to his bike. "You are one big contradiction, Lacy Shaw."

* * *

Paris straddled his bike and waited for Lacy to take the seat behind him. He glanced over his shoulder as she wrung her hands nervously. She seemed to be giving herself a pep talk, and then she lunged, as if forcing herself, and straddled the seat behind him.

Paris grinned and waited for another long second. "You know, you're going to have to wrap your arms around my waist for the ride."

"Right," he heard her say in a muffled voice. Her arms embraced him, clinging more tightly as he put the motorcycle in motion. Before he was even down the road, Lacy's grasp on him was so tight that her head rested on his back. He kind of liked the feel of her body hugging his, even if it was because she was scared for her life.

He knew the way to her house, but at the last second, he decided to take a different route. Lacy didn't speak up, so he guessed her eyes were shut tightly, blocking out the streets that zipped past.

Instead of taking her home, he drove her to the park, where the hot spring was. There were hiking trails and a hot dog vendor too. On her profile, Lacy had said those were among her favorite things, and after this afternoon, she deserved a few guilty pleasures.

He pulled into the parking lot and cut the engine. Slowly, Lacy peeled her body away from him. He felt her shift as she looked around.

She removed her helmet. "Why are we at the park?"

Paris glanced back. "Surprise. I thought I'd take your mind off things before I took you home."

She stared at him, a dumbfounded expression creasing her brow. "Why the park?"

"Because you love to take long hikes. And hot dogs, so I thought we'd grab a couple afterward. I didn't wear my hiking boots, but these will work for a quick half mile down the trail. Your profile mentioned that you love the hot spring here."

Lacy blinked. "You read my dating profile?"

"Great late-night reading." He winked.

She drew her hand to her forehead and shook her head. Something told him this time the head shake wasn't a yes. "Most of the information on my profile was exaggerated by the ladies' group. Apparently, they didn't think the real Lacy Shaw was interesting enough."

"You don't like hiking?"

"I like leisurely walks."

"Dogs?" he asked.

"Cats are my preference."

Paris let his gaze roam around them briefly before looking back at her. "What *do* you like?"

"In general?" she asked.

"Let's start with food. I'm starving."

She gave him a hesitant look. "Well, the hot dog part was true, but only because I added that part after they left."

Paris grinned, finding her adorable and sexy at the same time. "I happen to love a good chili dog. And there's a stand at the far side of the park." He waited for her to get off the bike and then he climbed off as well. "Let's go eat, shall we?"

"Saving someone's life works up an appetite, I guess."

"I didn't save Mrs. Townsend's life," he said as they walked. "I just kept her alive so someone else could do that."

From the corner of his eye, he saw Lacy fidgeting.

He reached for her hand to stop the motion. "I brought you here to take your mind off that situation. Let's talk about something light."

"Like?"

"You? Why did you let the Ladies' Day Out group make you a dating profile if you don't want to be on the site?"

Lacy laughed softly as they stepped into a short line for hot dogs. "Have you met the Ladies' Day Out group? They are determined and persistent. When they want something, they don't take no for an answer."

"You're part of the LDO," he pointed out.

"Well, I don't share that same quality."

"You were persistent in getting me to agree to teach a class at the library."

"True. I guess when there's something I want, I go after it." They reached the front of the line and ordered two sodas and two hot dogs. One with chili for him and one without for her.

Lacy opened the flap of her purse, and Paris stopped her. "I brought you here. This is my treat."

"No, I couldn't—"

She started to argue, but he laid a ten-dollar bill in front of the vendor. "It's just sodas and hot dogs." He glanced over. "You can treat me next time."

Her lips parted. He was only teasing, but he saw the question in her eyes, and now it was in his mind too. Would there really be a next time? Would that be so bad?

After collecting the change, they carried their drinks and hot dogs to a nearby bench and sat down.

"I didn't think I'd like teaching, but it's actually kind of fun," Paris confessed.

"Even Mr. Jenson?" she asked before taking a huge bite of her hot dog.

"Even him. But he didn't show up today. Maybe he dropped out." Paris shrugged. "I changed the syllabus just for him. I was planning to teach the class to Skype this afternoon."

"You didn't?"

He shook his head. "I went back to the lesson on Microsoft Word just in case Mr. Jenson showed up next time."

"Maybe he didn't feel well. He's been to every other class this week, right?"

Paris shook his head. "But he's made no secret that he doesn't like my teaching. He's even blasted his opinions all over Facebook."

Lacy grimaced. "Oh my. He treats everyone that way. I wouldn't take it personally. It's just how he is."

"He wasn't always that way. He used to be really nice, if memory serves me correctly."

Lacy narrowed her eyes. "You knew him before the class?"

Paris looked down at his half-eaten hot dog. "He and Mrs. Jenson fostered me for a while, but he doesn't seem to remember me."

"You were in foster care?"

"Yep. The Jensons were my favorite family."

Her jaw dropped. "That's so interesting."

Paris angled his body toward her. "Do you know what's wrong with Mrs. Jenson?"

Lacy shrugged. "I'm not sure. All I know is she's forgetful. She gets confused a lot. I've seen her get pretty agitated with Mr. Jenson too. They used to come into the library together."

"Maybe that's why he's so bitter now," Paris said, thinking out loud. He lifted his hot dog to his mouth and took another bite.

"Perhaps Mr. Jenson just needs someone to help him."

Paris chewed and swallowed. "I'm not even sure how I could help Mr. Jenson. I've been reading up on how to make a rose garden, but that won't make his wife well again."

Lacy hummed thoughtfully. "I think Mr. Jenson just needs someone to treat him nicely, no matter how horrible he is. No matter what he says to me, I always offer him a big smile. I actually think he likes me, although he would never admit it." She giggled to herself.

Paris looked at her. "You seem to really understand people."

"I do a lot of people-watching. And I had years of being an outcast in school." She swiped at a drop of ketchup at the corner of her mouth. "When you're hiding in the back of the classroom, there's not much else to do but watch everyone else. You can learn a lot about a person when they think no one is paying attention."

"Why would you hide?" he asked, growing increasingly interested in Lacy Shaw.

She met his gaze, and he glimpsed something dark in her

eyes for a moment. "Childhood scoliosis. I had to wear a back brace to straighten out my spine."

His gaze dropped to her back. It was long and smooth now.

"I don't wear it anymore," she told him. "My back is fixed. High school is when you want to be sporting the latest fashion though, not a heavy brace."

"I'm sure you were just as beautiful."

She looked away shyly, tucking a strand of brown hair behind her ear with one hand. "Anyway, I guess that's why I know human nature. Even the so-called nice kids were afraid to be associated with me. There were a handful of people who didn't care. I'm still close with them."

"Sounds like your childhood was less than desirable. Kind of like mine," he said. "That's something we have in common."

She looked up. "Who'd have thought? The librarian and the bad boy biker."

"Bad boy?" he repeated, finding this description humorous.

Her cheeks blossomed red just like the roses he'd studied in the library book. She didn't look away, and he couldn't, even if he wanted to. Despite himself, he felt the pull between them, the sexual tension winding around its gear, cranking tighter and tighter. "Perhaps we have a lot more in common."

"Like what?" she asked softly.

"Well, we both like hot dogs."

She smiled softly.

"And I want to kiss you right now. Not sure if you want to kiss me too but…" What was he doing? It was as if something else had taken control of his mind and mouth. He was saying exactly the opposite of what he intended.

Lacy's lips parted, her pupils dilated, and unless he was reading her wrong, she wanted to kiss him too.

Leaning forward, he dropped his mouth and brushed his lips to hers. A little sigh tumbled out of her, and after a moment, she kissed him back.

Chapter Four

Sparks, tingles, the whole nine yards.

That was what this kiss with Paris was. He was an amazing kisser. He had a firm hand on her thigh and the other gently curled around the back of her neck. This was the Cadillac of kisses, not that Lacy had much experience recently. It'd been a while since she'd kissed anyone. The last guy she'd briefly dated had run the library in the town of River Oaks. They'd shared a love of books, but not much else.

Paris pulled back slightly. "I'm sorry," he said. "I didn't mean to do that."

She blinked him into focus, a dreamlike feeling hanging over her.

"All I wanted to do tonight was take your mind off the afternoon."

"The afternoon?" she repeated.

"Mrs. Townsend?"

"Oh." She straightened a touch. Was that why he'd kissed her? Was he only taking her mind off the trauma of what happened at the library? "I definitely forgot about that for a moment."

"Good." Paris looked around the park. Then he stood and offered her his hand. "Want to take a walk to the hot spring before we leave?"

She allowed him to pull her to standing. "Okay."

She followed him because he'd driven her here. Because he'd kissed her. Because she wasn't sure what to think, but one thing she knew for sure was that she liked being around Paris. He was easy to talk to, and he made her feel good about herself.

"Penny for your thoughts?" he asked a couple of minutes later, walking alongside her.

She could hear the subtle sound of water as they drew closer to the hot spring. "Oh, I was just thinking what a nice night it is."

Paris looked around. "I don't think there's a single season in this town that I don't like. The air is easier to breathe here for some reason." She watched him suck in a deep breath and shivered with her body's response.

"I've always wanted to get in a hot spring," Lacy admitted, turning her attention to the water that was now in view.

"You've never been in?" Paris asked.

Lacy shook her head. "No. That was another fabrication for the profile. I've read that a spring is supposed to help with so many things. Joint and muscle pain. Energy levels. Detoxification."

"Do you need those benefits?" he asked.

Lacy looked up at him. "Not really." All she really needed was to lean into him and press her lips to his once more.

Paris sighed as they walked. "So what should I do?"

A dozen thoughts rushed Lacy's mind. "Hmm?"

"I want to help Mr. Jenson somehow, like you suggested."

"Oh." She looked away as she swallowed. "Well, he didn't show up at today's class. Maybe you could stop by and see him. Tomorrow is Saturday, so there's no class anyway. You could check on him and make sure he's okay."

Paris stared at her. "I have to admit, that old man kind of scares me."

Lacy giggled softly. "Me too." She gasped as an idea rushed into her mind. She didn't give herself time to think before sharing it with Paris. "But I'll go with you. It's my day off."

He cocked his head. "You'd spend your day off helping me?"

"Yes, but there's a condition."

He raised a questioning brow. "What's that?"

"I'll go with you if you'll be my date to my class reunion." Seeing Mrs. Townsend at death's door this afternoon had shaken her up more than she'd realized. "I don't want to hide anymore. I want to go, have a blast, and show everyone who tried to break me that they didn't succeed." And for some reason, Paris made her feel more confident.

Paris grinned at her. "Are you asking me out, Lacy Shaw?"

She swallowed. "Yes. Kind of. I'm offering you a deal."

He shoved his hands in his pockets. "I guess Mr. Jenson might be less likely to slam the door on my face tomorrow if I have a beautiful woman by my side. You said he likes you, so..."

Her insides fluttered to life. "My old bullies might be less likely to pick on me if I have a hot graphic designer as my escort."

This made him laugh. Then Paris stuck out his hand. "Want to shake on it?"

She would prefer to kiss on it, but that first kiss had come with an apology from him. This deal wasn't romantic in nature. It was simply two people helping one another out.

* * *

Even though Paris worked for himself, he still loved a Saturday, especially this one. He and Lacy were spending the day together, and he hadn't looked forward to something like this in a while. He got out of bed with the energy of a man who'd already had his coffee and headed down the hall to brew a pot. Then he dressed in a pair of light-colored jeans and a favorite T-shirt for a local band he loved.

As he sipped his coffee, he thought about last evening and the kiss that probably had a lot to do with his mood this morning. He hadn't planned on kissing Lacy, but the feeling had engulfed him. And her signals were all a go, so he'd leaned in and gone for it.

Magic.

There'd be no kissing today though. He didn't like starting things he couldn't finish, and he wasn't in the market for a relationship. He'd traveled that path, and his marriage had been anything but the happy ending he'd envisioned. He couldn't do anything right for his ex, no matter how hard he'd tried. As soon as he'd realized she was having an affair, he'd left. He didn't stick around where he wasn't wanted.

Paris stood and grabbed his keys. Then he headed out the door to go get Lacy. He'd take his truck today so that he didn't need to torture himself with the feel of her arms around his waist.

A short drive later, he pulled into her driveway on Pine Cone Lane, walked up the steps, and knocked. She opened the door, and for a moment, he forgot to breathe. She wore her hair down, allowing it to spill softly over her shoulders just like in her profile picture. "You look, uh...well, you look nice," he finally said.

She lifted a hand and smoothed her hair on one side. "Thanks. At the library, it's easier to keep my hair pulled back," she explained. "But since I'm off today, I thought I'd let loose."

It was more than her hair. A touch of makeup accented her brown eyes, and she was wearing a soft pink top that brought out the colors in her skin. If he was a painter, he'd be running for his easel. If he was a writer, he'd grab a pen and paper, ignited by inspiration.

But he was just a guy who dabbled on computers. A guy who'd already decided he wasn't going to act on his attraction to the woman standing in front of him.

"I'm ready if you are," she said, stepping onto the porch and closing the front door behind her. She looked out into the driveway. "Oh, you drove something with four wheels today. I was ready for the bike, but I admit I'm kind of relieved."

"The bike grew on you a little bit?"

She shrugged one shoulder. "I could get used to it. My mother would probably kill you if she knew you put me on a motorcycle last night."

"I was rescuing you from being stranded in a dark parking lot," he pointed out.

"The lesser of two evils."

Paris jumped ahead to open her door, winning a curious look from her as well as a new blush on her cheeks—this one not due to makeup.

"Thanks."

He closed the door behind her and then jogged around to the driver's side. Once he was seated behind the steering wheel, he looked over. "Looks like Jere got your car back okay." He gestured toward her Honda Accord parked in front of a single-car garage.

"He left it and texted me afterward. No charge. He said he owed you." Lacy's brows subtly lifted.

"See, it pays to hang around me." Paris started the engine. "I was thinking we could stop in and check on Mrs. Townsend first."

Lacy pointed a finger at him. "I love that idea, even though I'm on to you, Paris Montgomery. You're really just procrastinating because you're scared of Mr. Jenson."

He grimaced as he drove toward the Sweetwater hospital. "That's probably true."

They chatted easily as he drove, discussing all of Lacy's plans for the library this summer. She talked excitedly about her work, which he found all kinds of attractive. Then he pulled into the hospital parking lot, and they both got out.

"We shouldn't go see Mrs. Townsend empty-handed," Lacy said as they walked toward the main entrance.

"We can swing by the gift shop before we go up," he suggested.

"Good idea. She likes magazines, so I'll get her a couple. I hope Abby and Willow are okay. It had to be confusing for them, watching their nanny being taken away in an ambulance."

"The girls only have one parent?" he asked.

"Their mother isn't around," Lacy told him.

Paris slid his gaze over. He wasn't sure he wanted to know, but he asked anyway. "What happened to their mom?" He'd heard a lot of stories from his foster siblings growing up. There were so many reasons for a parent to slip out of the picture. His story was rather boring in comparison to some. His parents didn't like abiding by the law, which left him needing supplementary care at times. Then they'd decided that another thing they didn't like was taking care of him.

"Their mother left right after Willow was born. There was speculation that maybe she had postpartum depression."

Paris swallowed as they veered into the gift shop. "It's good that they have Granger. He seems like a good dad."

"I think so too. And what kid wouldn't want to grow up on a Christmas tree farm? I mean, that's so cool." Lacy beelined toward the magazine rack in the back of the shop, picking out three. They also grabbed some chocolates at the register.

Bag of presents in hand, they left the shop and took the elevator up to the third floor to Mrs. Townsend's room. Lacy knocked, and they waited for Mrs. Townsend's voice to answer back, telling them to "come in."

"Oh, Lacy! You didn't have to spend your Saturday coming to see me," Mrs. Townsend said as they entered her room. "And you brought a friend."

"Mrs. Townsend, this is Paris Montgomery. He did CPR on you in the library yesterday."

Mrs. Townsend's eyes widened. "I didn't even know I needed CPR. How embarrassing. But thank you," she told Paris. "I guess you were instrumental in saving my life."

"It was no big deal," he said.

"To the woman who's still alive today it is." Mrs. Townsend looked at Lacy again, her gaze dropping to the bag in her hand. "What do you have?"

"Oh, yes." Lacy pulled the magazines out and offered them to Mrs. Townsend, along with the chocolates.

Mrs. Townsend looked delighted by the gifts. "Oh my goodness. Thank you so much."

"Are you doing okay?" Lacy asked.

Mrs. Townsend waved a hand. "The doctors here have been taking good care of me. They tell me I can go home tomorrow."

Lacy smiled. "That's good news."

"Yes, it is. And I'll be caring for the girls again on Monday. A little flutter in the heart won't keep me from doing what I love."

Lacy's gaze slid to meet Paris's as worry creased her brow. He resisted reaching for her hand in a calming gesture. His intentions would be innocent, but they could also confuse things. He and Lacy were only out today as friends. Nothing more.

They stayed and chatted a while longer and then left, riding down the elevator in silence. Paris and Lacy walked side by side back to his truck. He opened the passenger-side door for her again and then got into the driver's seat.

"I'm glad Mrs. Townsend is okay," Lacy said as they pulled back onto the main road and drove toward Blueberry Creek Road, where Albert Jenson lived.

"Me too," Paris told her.

"But what happens next time?"

"Hopefully there won't be a next time."

"And if there is, hopefully you'll be around," Lacy said. Something about her tone made him wonder if she wanted to keep him around for herself too.

A few minutes later, he turned onto Mr. Jenson's street and traveled alongside Blueberry Creek. His heart quickened as he pulled into Mr. Jenson's driveway.

"I can't believe he walks from here to the library," Lacy said as he cut the engine. "That has to be at least a mile."

"He's always loved to walk." Paris let his gaze roam over the house. It was smaller than he remembered and in need of new paint. The rosebushes that the Jensons loved so much were unruly and unkempt. He was in his seventies now though. The man Paris knew as a child had been middle-aged and full of energy. Things changed. He looked over. "All right. Let's get this over with. If he yells at us, we'll know he's okay. The buddy system, right?"

"Right."

Except with each passing second spent with Lacy, the harder it was for him to think of her as just a buddy.

* * *

Lacy had never been to Mr. Jenson's home before. She'd known that the Jensons kept foster children once upon a time, but it surprised her that one of them was Paris.

"Strange, but this place feels like home to me," Paris said as he stood at the front door.

"How long did you live here with the Jensons?"

"About six months, which was longer than I lived with most."

"Makes sense why you'd think of this place fondly then." She wanted to ask more about his parents, but it wasn't the time. "Are you going to ring the doorbell?" she asked instead.

"Oh. I guess that would help." Paris pushed the button for the doorbell with his index finger and let his hands clasp back together in front of him.

"If I didn't know better, I'd think Mr. Cool was nervous," she commented.

"Mr. Cool?" He glanced over. "Any relation to Mr. Clean?"

This made her giggle until the front door opened and Mr. Jenson frowned back at them.

Lacy straightened. From the corner of her eye, she saw Paris stand more upright as well.

"Mr. Jenson," Paris said. "Good morning, sir."

"What are you doing here?" the old man barked through the screen door.

"Just checking on you. You missed a class that I put together just for you."

"I hear you were trying to kill people at the library yesterday," Mr. Jenson said, his frown steadfast. "Good thing I stayed home."

"Mrs. Townsend is fine," Paris informed him. "We just checked on her at Sweetwater Memorial."

"And now you're checking on me?" Mr. Jenson shook his head, casting a suspicious glare. "Why?"

Paris held up his hands. "Like I said, I missed you in yesterday's class."

Mr. Jenson looked surprised for a moment, and maybe even a little happy with this information. Then his grumpy demeanor returned. "I decided it wasn't worth my time."

Lacy noticed Paris tense beside her. "Actually, the class is free and taught by a professional," she said, jumping in to help. "We're lucky to have Mr. Montgomery teaching at Sweetwater Library."

Mr. Jenson gave her a long, hard look. She was prepared for him to take a jab at her too, but instead he shrugged his frail shoulders. "It's a long walk, and my legs hurt yesterday, okay? You happy? I'm not a spring chicken anymore, but I'm fine, and I'll be back on Monday. If for no other reason than to keep you two off my front porch." Mr. Jenson looked between them, and then he harrumphed and promptly slammed the door in their faces.

Lacy turned to look at Paris. "Are you sure you're remembering him correctly? I can't imagine that man was ever very nice."

"Did you see him smile at me before he slammed that door though? I think he's softening up."

Lacy laughed, reaching her arm out and grabbing Paris

momentarily to brace her body as it shook with amusement. Once she'd realized what she'd done, she removed her hand and cleared her throat. "Okay, our well-check visits are complete. Mrs. Townsend and Mr. Jenson are both alive and kicking."

"I guess it's time for me to keep my end of the deal now," Paris said, leading her back to his truck.

Lacy narrowed her eyes. "But my reunion isn't until next Saturday."

"Yes, but I'm guessing you need to go shopping for something new to wear, right? And I can't wear jeans and an old T-shirt." He opened the passenger door for her.

"You can wear whatever you want," she told him as she stepped inside. Then she turned to look at him as he stood in her doorway.

"I want to look my best when I'm standing beside you. And I hear that Sophie's Boutique is the place to go if you want to dress to impress." He closed the door behind her and walked around to get in the driver's seat.

"Are you seriously offering to go dress shopping with me right now?" she asked once he was seated. "Because guys usually hate that kind of thing."

Paris grinned as he cranked the truck. "Sitting back and watching you come in and out of a dressing room, modeling beautiful clothes, sounds like a fun way to spend an afternoon to me." He winked before backing out of the driveway.

For a moment, Lacy was at a complete loss for words. "I mean, I'm sure you have other things to do with your Saturday afternoon."

He glanced over. "None as fun as hanging out with you."

She melted into the passenger seat. No one in her life had made her feel quite as interesting as Paris had managed to do last night and today. Just the opposite, the Ladies' Day Out group, while well-meaning, had made her feel boring by elaborating on the truth.

Paris made her feel other things as well. Things that were too soon to even contemplate.

Chapter Five

Every time Lacy walked out of the dressing room, Paris felt his heart kick a little harder. The dresses in Sophie's Boutique were gorgeous, but they paled in comparison to Lacy.

"You're staring at me," she said after twirling in a lavender knee-length dress with small navy blue polka dots. "Do you like this one or not?" She looked down. "I kind of love it. It's fun, and that's what I want for my reunion." She was grinning when she looked back up at him. "I want to dance and eat all the foods that will make this dress just a little too tight the next morning." A laugh tumbled off her lips.

Paris swallowed, looking for words, but they all got stuck in his throat. His feelings for Lacy were snowballing with every passing second—and it scared him more than Mr. Jenson did.

"Well?" she said again.

"That's the one for sure." He tore his gaze from her, pushing away all the thoughts of things he wanted to do to her in that dress. He wanted to spin her around on the dance floor, hold her close, and kiss her without apology next time.

Next time?

"Oh, wow! You look so beautiful!" Sophie Daniels, the boutique's owner, walked over and admired Lacy in the dress. "Is that the one?"

Lacy was practically glowing. "I think so, yeah."

Sophie turned to look at Paris. He'd met Sophie before, and she'd flirted mildly with him. He hadn't returned the flirting though because, beautiful as she was, he wasn't interested.

But he couldn't deny his interest in Lacy.

"Now it's your turn," Lacy said.

Sophie gestured to the other side of the store. "I have a rack of men's clothing in the back. Let's get you something that will complement what Lacy is wearing but not steal her show."

"As if I could steal the attention away from her," he said while standing.

Sophie's mouth dropped open. With a knowing look in her eyes, she tipped her head, signaling for him to follow her while Lacy returned to the dressing room to change.

"You seem like a nice guy, Paris, and Lacy deserves someone who will treat her well," Sophie said to him over her shoulder as she led the way.

"It's not like that between us." He swiped a hand through his hair. "I mean, Lacy is terrific, but the two of us don't make sense."

Sophie started sifting through the men's clothes on the rack. "Why not? You're both single and attractive. She avoids the spotlight, and you kind of grab people's attention wherever you go."

"I do?" he asked.

Sophie stopped looking through the clothes to give him another knowing look. "Opposites attract is a real thing, and it makes perfect sense." She pulled out a dark purple button-down shirt that would match Lacy's dress. "Do you have black pants?"

"I have black jeans," he told her.

She seemed to think about this. "Yes, black jeans will work. You just need to dress up a little bit. You're a jeans and T-shirt kind of guy, so let's keep the jeans." She nodded as if making the decision. "You, but different."

"Me, but different," he agreed, taking the shirt from her. That's how he felt with Lacy. He was still him but more grounded. And Lacy was still reserved but also coming out of her shell, and he loved watching it happen. "Do you have any bathing suits?" he asked on a whim. "One for me and one for Lacy?"

Sophie's eyes lit up, a smile lifting at the corners of her mouth. "Of course I do."

"I'll take one for each of us then. And this shirt for the reunion," Paris said.

Sophie gave him a conspiratorial wink. "I'll take care of it."

* * *

Lacy felt like Julia Roberts in *Pretty Woman*. She loved the dress she'd picked out, and she'd enjoyed the way Paris had stared at her as she'd modeled each one before it.

They left the boutique and walked back to Paris's truck. He opened her door, and she got in, tucking her bag in the floorboard at her feet. "That was so much fun. Thank you."

He stood in the open doorway of his truck, watching her. His gaze was so intense, and for a moment, her heart sped up. Was he going to kiss her again?

"I want to take you somewhere else," he said.

She furrowed her brow. They'd already spent nearly the entire day together, not that she minded. "Where?"

He placed a second bag in her lap and winked before shutting the door behind her and walking around the truck.

Lacy peeked inside the bag and gasped as he opened his own door and got behind the wheel. "This is a bathing suit."

"You said you always wanted to go to the hot spring. You and I are on one big adventure today, so I thought it'd be fitting to end our expedition by doing something on your bucket list."

"I don't actually have a bucket list," she noted, looking down at the bathing suit again, "but if I did, this would be on it. I can't believe you got me a bathing suit." Underneath her bright pink suit in the bag was a pair of men's board shorts. "Are we really going to do this?"

Paris looked over. "Only if you agree. Will you go on a date with me to the hot spring?"

A date? Had he meant that the way it'd sounded? Because a date implied that they were more than friends, and that's the way she felt about him right now.

*   *   *

The night was alive with sounds of nature. In the past hour, the sun had gone down behind the mountains, and stars had begun to shimmer above as darkness fell.

Lacy came out of the changing room with her bathing suit on and a towel wrapped around her waist. Paris was waiting on a bench for her, bare chested and in a pair of swim shorts.

Her mouth went dry. This wasn't her. She didn't visit hot springs with gorgeous men. Her idea of fun on a Saturday night was curling up on her front porch swing with a good book. This was a nice change of pace though, and with Paris beside her, she didn't mind trying something new.

"Ready?" he asked, standing and walking toward her. He reached for her hand and took it. The touch zinged from her heart to her toes, bouncing back up through her body like a ball in a pinball machine.

The sound of water grew louder as they approached the hot spring. They were the only ones here so far this evening, which she found odd and exciting.

Paris stood at the steps and looked at Lacy. "You're going to have to drop that towel," he said, his gaze trailing from her face and down her body toward her hips.

"Right." She swallowed and let go of his hand. She was about to remove her towel, but he reached out for her and did the honors. There was something so intimate about the gesture that her knees weakened. The towel fell in his hand, leaving her standing there in just her suit. She felt exposed and so alive.

He met her gaze for a long moment and then folded the towel and left it on a bench. Turning back to her, he reached for her hand again. "Careful," he said quietly, leading her down the steps and into the water.

She moaned softly as the hot water lapped against her skin. "This is heavenly," she finally said once she'd taken a seat inside. He was still holding her hand, and that was heavenly as well. They leaned back against the spring's wall, and both of them looked up at the stars.

"Anywhere I've been in my life," Paris whispered after a moment, "I've always been under these same stars. I've always wished I was somewhere different when I looked up, but tonight, there's nowhere else I'd rather be." He looked over, his face dangerously close to hers.

She swallowed. "Are you going to kiss me again?"

His blue eyes narrowed. "Do you want me to kiss you again?"

"Ever since that first kiss."

His eyes dropped to her mouth. Her lips parted for him. Then he leaned just a fraction, and his lips brushed against hers. He stayed there, offering small kisses that evolved into something deeper and bigger. One of his hands slid up her thigh, anchoring midway. The touch completely undid her, and if they weren't in a public setting, she might have wiggled until his hand slid higher.

"Are you going to apologize again?" she asked once he'd pulled away.

He shook his head. "I'm not sorry."

"Me neither," she whispered. Then she leaned in and kissed him this time. Who was she these days? This wasn't like her at all.

They didn't stop kissing until voices approached the hot spring. Lacy pulled back from Paris. Another couple appeared and headed toward the spring. They stepped in and sat across from Lacy and Paris.

"We have to behave now," Paris whispered in Lacy's ear.

"Easier said than done." She grinned at him.

"And I'm not leaving until this little problem I have has gone down."

"What problem?" she asked, looking down through the clear bubbles. Then she realized what he was referring to, and her body grew impossibly hotter.

They returned to looking at the stars and talking in whispers, sharing even more details about themselves. Lacy could've stayed and talked all night, but the hot spring closed at ten p.m. When she finally stepped out of the water, the cool air was a harsh contrast.

After toweling off and changing in the dressing room, Lacy met Paris outside and got into his truck. He drove slowly as he took her home, their conversation touching various subjects. And the more she learned about Paris, the more she wanted to know.

Finally, he pulled into her driveway and looked at her.

"I'm not sure you should walk me to my door," Lacy said. "I'd probably end up asking you if you wanted to come inside." She nibbled softly on her lower lip. "And, well, that's probably not the best idea."

"I understand." He reached for her hand. "Thank you for the best day that I can remember."

She leaned toward him. "And the best night."

She gave him a brief kiss because there was still the risk that she might invite him inside. She was doing things that were surprising even herself. "The library is closed tomorrow. I can make lunch if you want to come over."

He hesitated.

"I mean, you don't have to, if you have something else to do."

He grinned. "I have work to do tomorrow, but a man has to eat, right? Lunch sounds nice. I'll be here."

"Perfect." She pushed the truck door open before her hormones took over and she climbed over to his side of the truck instead. "Good night, Paris."

"Good night, Lace."

Chapter Six

Lacy wasn't thinking straight last night. Otherwise, she would've remembered that a few members of the Ladies' Day Out group were coming over for lunch after church. No doubt they wanted to nag her about one thing or another. Today's topics were most likely the dating site and her reunion.

Then again, that was all the more reason for Paris to join them for lunch. His presence would kill two birds with one stone. She didn't need a dating site. And she and Paris were going to have an amazing time at her reunion next weekend.

She heard his motorcycle rumble into her driveway first. She waited for him to ring the doorbell, and then she went to answer. Butterflies fluttered low in her belly at the sight of him.

"Come in." She led him inside the two-bedroom house that she'd purchased a couple of years ago. "It's not much, but it's home."

"Well, sounds cliché, but I've learned that home really is where the heart is," he said.

She turned to look at him, standing close enough that she could reach out and touch him again. Maybe pull him toward her, go up on her tiptoes, and press her lips to his. "By cliché, you mean cheesy?"

Paris pretended to push a stake through his heart. "When

you get comfortable with someone, your feisty side is unleashed. I like it." He leaned in just a fraction, and Lacy decided to take a step forward, giving him the not-so-subtle green light for another kiss. He was right. She was feisty when she was with him, and she liked this side of her too.

The sound of another motor pulling into her driveway got her attention. She turned toward her door.

"Are you expecting someone else?" Paris asked, following her gaze.

"Yes, sorry. I didn't remember when I invited you last night, but I have company coming over today."

"Who?" Paris asked.

"My mom."

He nodded. "Okay."

"And my two sisters, Birdie and Rose," Lacy added. "*And* my aunt Pam."

Paris started to look panicked. "Anyone else?"

"Yeah. Um, Dawanda from the fudge shop. They're all part of the Ladies' Day Out group. I got a text earlier in the week telling me they were bringing lunch."

"Well, I'll get out of your guys' hair," he said, backpedaling toward the door.

She grabbed his hand, holding it until he met her gaze. "Wait. You don't need to leave. I want you here."

Paris grimaced. "Family mealtime has never really been my strong point."

Lacy continued to hold his hand. She wanted to show the women outside that she could find a guy on her own. She didn't need FishInTheSea.com. She also wanted to show them this new side of herself that seemed to take hold when she was with Paris. "They're harmless, I promise. Please stay."

Paris shifted on his feet, and she was pretty sure he was going to turn down the invitation. "You didn't take no for an answer when you wanted me to teach the computer class at the library," he finally said. "I'm guessing the same would be true now, huh?"

She grinned. "That's right."

"You're a hard woman to resist."

"Then stop trying," she said, going to answer the door.

* * *

The spread on Lacy's table was fit for a Thanksgiving dinner by Paris's standards. Not that he had much experience with holidays and family gatherings. He'd had many a holiday meal with a fast-food bag containing a burger, fries, and a small toy.

"I would've brought Denny if I'd known that men were allowed at lunch today," Mrs. Shaw said, speaking of her husband. She seemed friendly enough, but Paris also didn't miss the scrutinizing looks she was giving him when she thought he wasn't looking. He was dressed in dark colors and had tattoos on both arms. He also had a motorcycle parked in the driveway. He probably wasn't the kind of guy Mrs. Shaw would have imagined her sweet librarian daughter with.

"Good thing you didn't bring Dad," Lacy's sister Birdie said. "He would've grilled Paris mercilessly."

"Paris and I aren't dating," Lacy reiterated for the tenth time since she'd welcomed the women into her home. She slid her gaze to look at Paris, and he saw the question in her eyes. *Are we?* When the ladies had come through the front door, they'd all immediately began calling him Lacy's secret boyfriend.

"Sounds like I'd be in trouble if you and I did get together," Paris said. "Your dad sounds strict."

Lacy laughed softly. "Notice that my sisters and I are all still single. There's a reason for that."

Lacy's other sister, Rose, snorted. "Dad crashed my high school prom when I didn't come home by curfew. Who has a curfew on prom night?" Rose slid her fork into a pile of macaroni and cheese. "I thought I'd never forgive Dad for that. I liked that guy too."

"What was his name again?" Mrs. Shaw asked.

Rose looked up, her eyes squinting as she seemed to think. "I can't remember. Brent maybe. Bryce? Could've been Bryan."

"You couldn't have liked him too much if you can't remember his name," Mrs. Shaw pointed out.

Everyone at the table laughed.

"Don't you worry, Rose," Dawanda said, seated beside Mrs. Shaw. "I've read your cappuccino, and you have someone very special coming your way. I saw it in the foam."

"Well, I'll be sure to keep him away from my dad until the wedding," Rose said sarcastically, making everyone chuckle again.

Whereas some read tea leaves, Dawanda read images formed in the foam of a cappuccino. She'd done a reading for Paris last Christmas. Oddly enough, Dawanda had told him he was the only one whose fortune she couldn't read. Dawanda had assured him it wasn't that he was going to fall off a cliff or anything. His future was just up in the air. He had shut his heart off to dreaming of a life anywhere or with anyone.

He didn't exactly believe in fortune-telling, but she was spot-on with that. Some people just weren't cut out for forever homes and families. He guessed he was one of them.

"Dad's first question any time he meets any of our dates is 'What are your intentions with my girl?'" Rose said, impersonating a man's deep voice.

"He actually said that while sharpening his pocketknife for a date I brought home in college," Birdie said. "I didn't mind because I didn't like the guy too much, but what if I had?"

"Then you would've been out of luck," Lacy said on a laugh.

The conversation continued, and then Mrs. Shaw looked across the table at Paris. "So, Paris," she said, her eyes narrowing, "tell us about yourself. Did you grow up around here?"

Paris looked up from his lunch. "I spent a little time in Sweetwater Springs growing up. Some in Wild Blossom Bluffs. My parents moved around a lot."

"Oh? For their jobs? Military maybe?" she asked.

Paris shifted. Ex-felons weren't allowed to join the military. "Not exactly. I was in foster care here for a while."

"Foster care?" Mrs. Shaw's lips rounded in a little O. "That must've been hard for a young child."

Paris focused his attention back on his food. "I guess I didn't really know any different. Most of the places I landed were nice enough." And there'd been somewhere he'd wished he could stay. Six months with the Jenson family was the longest amount of time he'd ever gotten to stay. It was just enough time to bond with his foster parents and to feel the loss of them to his core when he was placed back with his real parents.

He picked up his fork and stabbed at a piece of chicken.

"And what brought you back to Sweetwater Springs? If I recall, you moved here last year, right?" Dawanda asked.

"You came into my shop while you were staying at the Sweetwater Bed and Breakfast."

Paris swallowed past the sudden tightness in his throat. He didn't really want to answer that question either. He looked around the table, his gaze finally landing on Lacy. "Well, I guess I decided to come back here after my divorce."

Lacy's lips parted.

Had he forgotten to mention that little detail to her? When he was with Lacy, he forgot all about those lonely years in Florida. All he could think about was the moment he was in, and the ones that would follow.

"That sounds rough as well," Mrs. Shaw said.

Paris shrugged, feeling weighed down by the truth. "Well, those things are in the rearview mirror now." He tried to offer a lighter tone of voice, but all the women looked crestfallen. Mrs. Shaw had already seemed wary of him, but now she appeared even more so.

"And since my husband isn't here to ask"—Mrs. Shaw folded her hands in front of her on the table—"what are your intentions with my daughter?"

"Mom!" Lacy set her fork down. "Paris and I aren't even dating." She looked over at him. "I mean, we went on a date last night. Two if you count that night at the park."

"Last night?" Birdie asked.

All the women's eyes widened.

"It wasn't like that." Lacy looked flustered. "We didn't spend the night together."

Mrs. Shaw's jaw dropped open, and Lacy's face turned a deep crimson.

Guilt curled in Paris's stomach. Lacy was trying her best to prove herself to everyone around her. Now her family and Dawanda were gawking at her like she'd lost her mind. It was crazy to think that she and Paris would be dating. Sophie Daniels had told him at the boutique that opposites attract, but he and Lacy had led very different lives.

"Sounds like you're dating to me. Are you going to go out again?" Rose asked.

"Well, Paris offered to go with me to my reunion," Lacy said.

Mrs. Shaw's smile returned. "Oh, I'm so glad you decided to go! That's wonderful, dear. I want all those bullies to see that you are strong and beautiful, smart and funny, interesting—"

"Mom," Lacy said, cutting her off, "you might be a little partial."

"But she's right," Paris said, unable to help himself.

Lacy turned to look at him, and something pinched in his chest. He'd tried to keep things strictly friendly with her, but he'd failed miserably. What was he going to do now? He didn't want a relationship, but if they continued to spend time together, she would.

"So, Paris, how did you get our Lacy to agree to go to this reunion of hers?" Mrs. Shaw asked. "She was so dead set on not attending."

"Actually, Lace made that decision on her own," he said.

"Lace?" Both Birdie and Rose asked in unison.

The nickname had just rolled off his tongue, but it fit. Lace was delicate and beautiful, accentuated by holes that one might think made it more fragile. It was strong, just like the woman sitting next to him. She was stronger than she even knew.

"Well, I'm glad she's changed her mind. High school was such a rough time for our Lacy," Mrs. Shaw said. "I want her to go and have a good time and show those bullies who treated her so badly that they didn't break her."

Paris glanced over at Lacy. He wanted her old classmates to see the same thing.

Mrs. Shaw pointed a finger at Paris, gaining his attention. "But if you take her, it won't be on the back of that motorcycle in the driveway. Lacy doesn't ride those things."

"Actually, Mom, I rode on the back of it with Paris two days ago."

Mrs. Shaw looked horrified.

"Maybe he'll let me drive it next time," Lacy added, making all the women at the table look surprised.

"Lacy rode on the back of your bike?" Birdie asked Paris. "This is not our sister. What have you done with the real Lacy Shaw?"

He looked over at the woman in question. The real Lacy was sitting right beside him. He saw her, even if no one else did. And the last thing he wanted to do was walk away from her, which was why he needed to do just that.

* * *

An hour later, Lacy closed her front door as her guests left and leaned against it, exhaling softly.

"Your mom and sisters are great," Paris said, standing a couple of feet away from her. "Your aunt too."

She lifted her gaze to his. "You almost sound serious about that."

"Well, I'm not going to lie. They were a little overwhelming."

"A little?" Lacy grinned. "And they were subdued today. They're usually worse."

Paris shoved his hands in his pockets. "They love you. Can't fault them for that."

The way he was looking at her made her breath catch. Was he going to kiss her again?

"I guess not."

"They want what's best for you," he continued. Then he looked away. "And, uh, I'm not sure that's me, Lace."

She straightened at the sudden shift in his tone of voice. "What?"

He ran a hand over his hair. "When we were eating just now, I realized that being your date might not be doing you any favors. Or me."

"Wait, you're not going to the reunion with me anymore?" she asked.

He shook his head. "I just think it'd be better if you went with someone else."

"I don't have anyone else," she protested, her heart beating fast. "The reunion is in less than a week. I have my dress, and you have a matching shirt. And you're the one I want to go with. I don't even care about the reunion. I just want to be with you."

He looked down for a moment. "You heard me talking to your family. I've lived a different life than you. I'm an ex-foster kid. My parents are felons." He shrugged. "I couldn't even make a marriage work."

"Those things are in the past, Paris. I don't care about any of that."

He met her gaze again. "But I do. Call me selfish, but I don't want to want you. I don't want to want things that I know I'll never have. It's not in the cappuccino for me, Lacy." His expression was pained. "I really want you to believe me when I say it's not you, it's me."

Her eyes and throat burned, and she wondered if she felt worse for herself or for him. He obviously had issues, but who didn't? One thing she'd learned since high school was that no one's life was perfect. Her flaws were just obvious back then because of the back brace.

She'd also learned that you couldn't make someone feel differently than they did. The only feelings you could control were your own. The old Lacy never stood up for herself. She let people trample on her and her feelings. But she'd changed. She was the new Lacy now.

She lifted her eyes to meet Paris's and swallowed past the growing lump in her throat. "If that's the way you feel, then I think you should go."

Chapter Seven

On Monday afternoon, Paris looked out over the roomful of students. Everyone had their eyes on their screens and were learning to Skype. But his attention was on the librarian on the other side of the building.

When he'd driven to the library, he'd lectured himself on why he needed to back away from Lacy Shaw. Sunday's lunch had made that crystal clear in his mind. She was smart and beautiful, the kind of woman who valued family. Paris had no idea what it even meant to have a family. He couldn't be the kind of guy she needed.

Luckily, Lacy hadn't even been at the counter when he'd walked in and continued toward the computer room. She was probably hell-bent on avoiding him. For the best.

"Does everyone think they can go home and Skype now?" Paris asked the class.

"I can, but no one I know will know how to Skype with me," Greta said.

Janice Murphy nodded beside her.

"Well, you could all exchange information and Skype with each other," Paris suggested.

"Can we Skype with you?" Alice asked.

Warmness spread through his chest. "Anytime, Alice."

"Can I Skype you if my wife doesn't want to talk to me?" Mr. Jenson asked. "To practice so I'm ready when she does?"

Paris felt a little sad for the older man. When Paris had been a boy in their home, they'd been the happiest of couples. "Of course. If I'm home and free, I'll always make time to Skype with any one of you," he told the group, meaning it. They'd had only a few classes, but he loved the eclectic bunch in this room.

When class was over, he walked over to Mr. Jenson. "I can give you a ride home if you want."

Mr. Jenson gave him an assessing stare. "If you think I'm climbing on the back of that bike of yours, you're crazy."

Paris chuckled. "I drove my truck today. It'll save you a walk. I have the afternoon free too. I can take you by the nursing home facility to see Mrs. Jenson if you want. I'm sure she'd be happy to see you."

Mr. Jenson continued to stare at him. "Why would you do that? I know I'm not that fun to be around."

Paris clapped a gentle hand on Mr. Jenson's back. "That's not true. I kind of like being around you." He always had. "And I could use some company today. Agreeing would actually be doing me a favor."

"I don't do favors," the older man said. "But my legs are kind of hurting, thanks to the chairs in there. So walking home would be a pain."

Paris felt relieved as Mr. Jenson relented. "What about visiting Mrs. Jenson? I'll stay in the truck while you go in, and take as long as you like." Paris patted his laptop bag. "I have my computer, so I can work while I wait."

Mr. Jenson begrudgingly agreed and even smiled a little bit. "Thank you."

Paris led Mr. Jenson into his truck and started the short drive toward Sweetwater Nursing Facility.

"She sometimes tells me to leave as soon as I get there," Mr. Jenson said as they drove.

"Why is that?"

Mr. Jenson shrugged. "She says she doesn't want me to see her that way."

Paris still wasn't quite sure what was wrong with Mrs. Jenson. "What way?"

"Oh, you know. Her emotions are as unstable as her walking these days. That's why she's not home with me. She's not the same Nancy I fell in love with, but she's still the woman I love. I'll always love her, no matter how things change."

"That's what love is, isn't it?" Paris asked.

Mr. Jenson turned to look out the passenger-side window as they rode. "We never had any kids of our own. We fostered a few, and that was as close as we ever got to having a family."

Paris swallowed painfully.

"There was one boy who was different. We would've kept him. We bonded and loved him as our own."

Paris glanced over. Was Mr. Jenson talking about him? Probably not, but Paris couldn't help hoping that he was. "What happened?"

"We wanted to raise him as part of our family, but it didn't work out that way. He went back to his real parents, which I suppose is always best. I lost him, and now, most days, I've lost my wife too. That's what love is. Painful."

Paris parked and looked over. "Well, maybe today will be different. Whatever happens, I'll be in the truck waiting for you."

Mr. Jenson looked over and chuckled, but Paris could tell by the gleam in his eyes that he appreciated the sentiment. He stepped out of the truck and dipped his head to look at Paris in the driver's seat. "Some consolation prize."

* * *

Two nights later, Lacy sat in her living room with a handful of the Ladies' Day Out members. They'd been waiting for her in the driveway when she'd gotten home from the library and were here for an intervention of sorts.

"Sandwiches?" Greta asked, her face twisting with displeasure.

"Well, when you don't tell someone that you're coming, you get PB&J." Lacy plopped onto the couch beside Birdie, who had no doubt called everyone here.

"You took your online profile down," Birdie said, reaching for her own sandwich.

"Of course I did. I'm not interested in dating right now."

"You sure looked interested in Paris Montgomery," Dawanda said, sitting across from them. "And you two looked so good together. What happened?"

All the women turned to face Lacy.

She shrugged. "My family happened. No offense. You all behaved—mostly," she told her mom and sisters. "We just decided it'd be best to part ways sooner rather than later."

Birdie placed her sandwich down. "I thought you were the smart one in the family."

Rose raised her hand. "No, that was always me." A wide grin spread on her face. "Just kidding. It's you, Lacy."

Birdie frowned. "I was there last weekend. I saw how you two were together. There's relationship potential there," she said.

Lacy sighed. "Maybe, but he doesn't want another relationship. He's been hurt and..." She shrugged. "I guess he just doesn't think it's worth trying again." That was her old insecurities though so she stopped them all in their tracks.

"Actually, something good came out of me going out with him a few times."

"Oh?" Birdie asked. "What's that?"

"I'm not afraid to go to my reunion, even if I have to go on my own."

"Maybe you'll meet someone there. Maybe you'll find 'the one,'" Rose said.

"Maybe." But Lacy was pretty sure she wouldn't find the *one* she wanted. He'd already been found and lost.

"I'll go with you if you need me to," Josie offered. She wasn't sitting on the couch with Lacy's laptop this time. Instead, she held a glass of wine tonight, looking relaxed in the recliner across the room.

"I wonder what people would think about that," Birdie said.

Lacy shrugged. "You know what, I've decided that I don't care what the people who don't know me think. I care about what I think. And what you all think, of course."

"And Paris?" Dawanda asked.

Lacy shook her head, but she meant yes. Paris was right. Her gestures often contradicted what she really meant. "Paris thinks that we should just be friends, and I have to respect that."

Even if she didn't like it.

Chapter Eight

Paris was spending his Saturday night in Mr. Jenson's rosebushes—not at Lacy's class reunion as he'd planned. He'd clipped the bushes back, pruning the dead ends so that they'd come back stronger.

Over the last couple of days, he'd kept himself super busy with work and taking Mr. Jenson to and from the nursing facility. He'd read up on how to care for rosebushes, but that hadn't been necessary because Mr. Jenson stayed on the porch barking out instructions like a drill sergeant. Paris didn't mind. He loved the old man.

"Don't clip too much off!" Mr. Jenson warned. "Just what's needed."

"Got it." Paris squeezed the clippers again and again, until the muscles of his hand were cramping.

Despite his best efforts, he hadn't kept himself busy enough to keep from thinking about Lacy. She'd waved and said hi to him when he'd gone in and out of the library, but that was all. It wasn't enough.

He missed her. A lot. Hopefully she was still going to her reunion tonight. He hoped she danced. And maybe there'd be a nice guy there who would dance with her.

Guilt and jealousy curled around Paris's ribs like the roses on the lattice. He still wanted to be that guy who held her close tonight and watched her shine.

"Done yet?" Mr. Jenson asked gruffly.

Paris wiped his brow and straightened. "All done."

Mr. Jenson nodded approvingly. "It looks good, son."

Mr. Jenson didn't mean anything by calling him son, but it still tugged on Paris's heartstrings. "Thanks. I'll come by next week and take you to see Mrs. Jenson."

"Just don't expect me to get on that bike of yours," the older man said for the hundredth time.

"Wouldn't dream of it." As Paris started to walk away, Mr. Jenson called out to him.

"PJ?"

Paris froze. He hadn't heard that name in a long time, but it still stopped him in his tracks. He turned back to face Mr. Jenson. "You know?"

Mr. Jenson chuckled. "I'm old, not blind. I've known since that first computer class."

"But you didn't say anything." Paris took a few steps, walking back toward Mr. Jenson on the porch. "Why?"

"I could ask you the same. You didn't say anything either."

Paris held his hands out to his sides. "I called last year. Mrs. Jenson answered and told me to never call again."

Mr. Jenson shook his head as he listened. "I didn't know that, but it sounds about right. She tells me the same thing when I call her. Don't take it personally."

Paris pulled in a deep breath and everything he'd thought about the situation shifted and became something very different. They hadn't turned him away. Mr. Jenson hadn't even known he'd tried to reconnect.

Mr. Jenson shoved his hands in the pockets of his pants. "I loved PJ. It was hard to lose him…You." Mr. Jenson cleared his throat and looked off into the distance. "It's been hard to lose Nancy, memory by memory, too. I guess some part of me didn't say anything when I realized who you were because I was just plain tired of losing. Sometimes it's easier not to feel anything. Then it doesn't hurt so much when it's gone." He looked back at Paris. "But I can't seem to lose you even if I wanted to, so maybe I'll just stop trying."

Paris's eyes burned. He blinked and looked down at his feet for a moment and then back up at the old man. He was pretty sure Mr. Jenson didn't want to be hugged, but Paris was going to anyway. He climbed the steps and wrapped his arms around his foster dad for a brief time. Then he pulled away. "Like I said, I'll be back next week, and I'll take you to go see Mrs. Jenson."

"See. Can't push you away. Might as well take you inside with me when I go see Nancy next time. She'll probably tell you to go away and never come back."

"I won't listen," Paris promised.

"Good." Mr. Jenson looked relieved somehow. His body posture was more relaxed. "Well, you best get on with your night. I'm sure you have things to do. Maybe go see that pretty librarian."

Paris's heart rate picked up. He was supposed to be at Lacy's side tonight, but while she was bravely facing her fears, he'd let his keep him away. His parents were supposed to love him and stand by him, but they hadn't. His ex-wife had abandoned him too. He guessed he'd gotten tired of losing just like Mr. Jenson. It was easier to push people away before they pushed him.

But the Jensons had never turned their back on him. They'd wanted him and he wished things had gone differently. Regardless of what happened in the past, it wasn't too late to reconnect and have what could've been now.

As he headed back to his bike, Paris pulled his cell phone out of his pocket and checked the time. Hopefully, it wasn't too late for him and Lacy either.

* * *

Lacy looked at her reflection in the long mirror in her bedroom. She loved the dress she'd found at Sophie's Boutique. She had a matching pair of shoes that complemented it perfectly. Her hair was also done up, and she'd put on just a little bit of makeup.

She flashed a confident smile. "I can do this."

She took another deep breath and then hurried to get her purse and keys. The reunion would be starting soon, and she needed to leave before she changed her mind. The nerves were temporary, but the memories from tonight would last. And despite her worries, she was sure they'd be good memories.

She grabbed her things and drove to Sweetwater Springs High School where the class reunion was taking place. When she was parked, she sat for a moment, watching her former classmates head inside. They all had someone on their arm. No one was going in alone. Except her.

She imagined walking inside and everyone stopping to stare at her. The mean girls from her past pointing and laughing and whispering among each other. That was the worst-case scenario and probably wasn't going to happen. But if it did, she'd get through it. She wasn't a shy kid anymore. She was strong and confident, and yeah, she'd rather have Paris holding her hand, but she didn't need him to. "I can do this," she said again.

She pushed her car door open, locked it up, and headed inside. She opened the door to the gymnasium, accosted by the music and sounds of laughter. It wasn't directed at her. No one was even looking at her. She exhaled softly, scanning the room for familiar faces. When she saw Claire Donovan, the coordinator of the event, standing with Halona Locklear and Brenna McConnell, she headed in that direction. They were always nice to her.

"Lacy!" Brenna exclaimed when she saw her walking over. "It's so good to see you." She gave her a big hug, and Lacy relaxed a little more. "Even though we all see each other on a regular basis," she said once they'd pulled apart.

Lacy hugged the other women as well.

"So you came alone too?" Lacy asked Halona.

"Afraid so. My mom is watching Theo for a few hours. I told her I really didn't need to come, but she insisted."

Brenna nodded as she listened to the conversation. "Sounds familiar. Everyone told me that you can't skip your high school reunion."

"This is a small town. It's not like we don't know where everyone ended up," Halona said. "Most everyone anyway."

"Don't look now," Summer Rodriquez said, also joining the conversation, "but Carmen Daly is veering this way."

Lacy's heart sank. Carmen was the leader of her little pack of mean girls. How many times had Lacy cried in the girls' bathroom over something Carmen had said or done to make her life miserable?

Lacy subtly stood a little straighter. Her brace was gone, and whatever Carmen dished out, she intended to return.

"Hi, ladies," Carmen said, looking between them. She was just as beautiful as ever. Lacy knew Carmen didn't live in Sweetwater Springs anymore. From what Lacy had heard, Carmen had married a doctor and lived a few hours east from here. Her vibrant smile grew sheepish as she looked at Lacy. "Hi, Lacy."

Every muscle in Lacy's body tensed. "Hi, Carmen."

Then Carmen surprised her by stepping forward to give her a hug. For a moment, Lacy wondered if she was sticking a sign on her back like she'd done so long ago. KICK ME. I WON'T FEEL IT.

Carmen pulled back and looked Lacy in the eye while her friends watched. "Lacy, I've thought about you so many times over the years. I'm so glad you're here tonight."

Lacy swallowed. "Oh?"

"I want to tell you that I'm sorry. For everything. I'm ashamed of the person I was and how I acted toward you. So many times I've thought about messaging you on Facebook or emailing you, but this is something that really needs to be done in person." Carmen's eyes grew shiny. "Lacy, I'm so sorry. I mean it."

Lacy's mouth dropped open. Of all the things she'd imagined about tonight, this wasn't one of them. She turned to look at Summer, Brenna, and Halona, whose lips were also parted in shock, and then she looked back at Carmen.

"I've tried to be a better person, but the way I behaved in high school has haunted me for the last ten years."

Lacy reached for Carmen's hand and gave it a squeeze. "Thank you. Looks like we've both changed."

"We grew up." Carmen shrugged. "Can you ever forgive me?"

"Definitely."

Carmen seemed to relax. "Maybe we can be friends on Facebook," she said. "And in real life. Maybe a coffee date next time I come home."

"I'd like that." Lacy's eyes burned as she hugged Carmen

again and watched her walk over to her husband. Then Lacy turned her back to her friends. "Is there a sign on my back?"

"Nope," Brenna said. "I think that was sincere."

Lacy faced them again. "Me too. It was worth coming here tonight just for that." Someone tapped her shoulder and she spun again, this time coming face-to-face with Paris.

"Sorry to interrupt," he said, looking just as sheepish as Carmen had a few minutes earlier.

She noticed that he was dressed in the shirt he purchased from Sophie's Boutique. "Paris, what are you doing here?"

"Hoping to get a dance with you?" He looked at the dance floor, where a few couples were swaying.

"I...I don't know," she said.

Summer put a hand on her back and gave her a gentle push. "No more sitting on the sidelines, Lacy. When a boy asks you to dance, you say yes."

Lacy took a few hesitant steps, following Paris. Then they stopped and turned to face each other, the music wrapping around them. "Paris"—she shook her head—"you didn't have to come. As you can see, I didn't chicken out. I'm here and actually having a great time. I don't need you to hold my hand."

He reached for her hand anyway, pulling her body toward his. The touch made her grow warm all over. "You never needed me. But I'm hoping you still want me."

Lacy swallowed. *Yeah*, she definitely still wanted him. She looked at his arms looped around her waist. They fit together so nicely. Then she looked back up at him. "I lied when I said that we could still be friends, Paris. I can't. I want things when I'm with you. Things I shouldn't want, but I can't help it."

"Such as?" he asked.

Lacy took a breath. She might as well be honest and scare him off for good. "I want a relationship. I want to fall in love. I want it all. And I just think it would be too hard—"

Paris dropped his mouth to hers and stopped her words with a soft kiss.

"What are you doing?" she asked when he pulled back away.

"I want things when I'm with you too," he said, leaning in closer so she could hear him over the music. "I want to kiss you. Hold your hand. Be the guy you want a relationship with. To be in love with."

Lacy's lips parted. Since they were being honest... "You already are that guy. I mean, not the love part. We haven't known each other very long, so it's too soon for that. That would be crazy."

"Maybe, but I understand exactly what you mean," he said.

She narrowed her eyes. "Then why are you smiling? You said you didn't want those things."

"Correction. I said I didn't *want* to want those things." He tightened his hold on her as they danced. "But it appears it's already too late, and you're worth the risk."

"So you're my date to this reunion tonight," Lacy said. "Then what?"

"Then tomorrow or the next day, I was thinking I'd go to your family's house for dinner and win over your dad."

Lacy grimaced. "That won't be easy. He'll want to know what your intentions are with his daughter."

Paris grinned. "My intention is to put you on the back of my bike and ride off into the sunset. What do you think he'll say to that?"

She grinned. "I think he'll hate that response. But if you're asking what I think..."

"Tell me," Paris whispered, continuing to sway with her, face-to-face, body-to-body.

"I love it." Then Lacy lifted up on her toes and kissed him for the entire world to see, even though in the moment, no one else existed except him and her.

About the Author

Annie Rains is a *USA Today* bestselling contemporary romance author who writes small-town love stories set in fictional places in her home state of North Carolina. When Annie isn't writing, she's living out her own happily ever after with her husband and three children.

Learn more at:

http://www.annierains.com/
Twitter @AnnieRainsBooks
http://facebook.com/annierainsbooks

*Looking for more second chances and small towns?
Check out Forever's heartwarming contemporary
romances!*

THE TRUE LOVE BOOKSHOP
by Annie Rains

For Tess Lane, owning Lakeside Books is a dream come true, but it's the weekly book club she hosts for the women in town that Tess enjoys the most. The gatherings have been her lifeline over the past three years, since she became a widow. But when secrets surrounding her husband's death are revealed, can Tess find it in her heart to forgive the mistakes of the past...and maybe even open herself up to love again?

THE MAGNOLIA SISTERS
by Alys Murray

Harper Anderson has one priority: caring for her family's farm. So when an arrogant tech mogul insists the farm host his sister's wedding, she turns him *and* his money down flat—an event like that would wreck their crops! But then Luke makes an offer she can't refuse: He'll work *for free* if Harper just considers his deal. Neither is prepared for chemistry to bloom between them as they labor side by side...but can Harper trust this city boy to put down country roots?

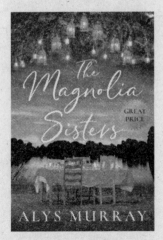

HER AMISH PATCHWORK FAMILY
by Winnie Griggs

Martha Eicher, formerly a school-teacher in Hope's Haven, has always put her family first. But now everyone's happily married, and Martha isn't sure where she fits in...until she hears that Asher Lantz needs a nanny. As a single father to his niece and nephews, Asher struggles to be enough for his new family. Although a misunderstanding ended their childhood friendship, he's grateful for Martha's help. Slowly both begin to realize Martha is exactly what his family needs. Could together be where they belong?

FALLING IN LOVE ON SWEETWATER LANE
by Belle Calhoune

Nick Keegan knows all about unexpected, life-altering detours. He lost his wife in the blink of an eye, and he's spent the years since being the best single dad he can be. He's also learned to not take anything for granted, so when sparks start to fly with Harlow, the new veterinarian, Nick is all in. He senses Harlow feels it too, but she insists romance isn't on her agenda. He'll have to pull out all the stops to show her that love is worth changing the best-laid plans.

RETURN TO HUMMINGBIRD WAY
by Reese Ryan

Ambitious real estate agent Sinclair Buchanan is thrilled her childhood best friend is marrying her first love. But the former beauty queen and party planner extraordinaire hadn't anticipated being asked to work with her high-school hate crush, Garrett Davenport, to plan the wedding. Five years ago, they spent one *incredible* night together—a mistake she won't make again. But when her plans for partnership in her firm require her to work with Rett to renovate his grandmother's seaside cottage, it becomes much harder to ignore their complicated history.

THE HOUSE ON MULBERRY STREET
by Jeannie Chin

Between helping at her family's inn and teaching painting, Elizabeth Wu has put her dream of being an artist on the back burner. But her plan to launch an arts festival will boost the local Blue Cedar Falls arts scene and give her a showcase for her own work. If only she can get the town council on board. At least she can rely on her dependable best friend, Graham, to support her. Except lately, he hasn't been acting like his old self, and she has no idea why...

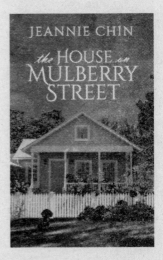

Discover bonus content and more on
read-forever.com

STARTING OVER ON SUNSHINE CORNER
by Phoebe Mills

Single mom Rebecca Hayes isn't getting her hopes up after she has one unforgettable night with Jackson, a very close—and very attractive—friend. She knows Jackson's unattached bachelor lifestyle too well. But in his heart, Jackson Lowe longs to build a family with Rebecca—his secret crush and the real reason he never settled down. So when Rebecca discovers she's pregnant with his baby, he knows he's got a lot of work to do before he can prove he's ready to be the man she needs.

A TABLE FOR TWO
(MM reissue) by Sheryl Lister

Serenity Wheeler's Supper Club is all about great friends, incredible food, and a whole lot of dishing—not hooking up. So when Serenity invites her friend's brother to one of her dinners, it's just good manners. But the ultra-fine, hazel-eyed Gabriel Cunningham has a gift for saying all the wrong things, causing heated exchanges and even hotter chemistry between them. But Serenity can't let herself fall for Gabriel. Cooking with love is one thing, but trusting it is quite another...